Praise for *New York Times* and *USA TODAY* bestselling author

ROBYN CARR

"This book is an utter delight."
—*RT Book Reviews* on *Moonlight Road*

"Strong conflict, humor and well-written characters are Carr's calling cards, and they're all present here.... You won't want to put this one down."
—*RT Book Reviews* on *Angel's Peak*

"This story has everything: a courageous, outspoken heroine, a to-die-for hero and a plot that will touch readers' hearts on several different levels. Truly excellent."
—*RT Book Reviews* on *Forbidden Falls*

"An intensely satisfying read. By turns humorous and gut-wrenchingly emotional, it won't soon be forgotten."
—*RT Book Reviews* on *Paradise Valley*

"Carr has hit her stride with this captivating series."
—*Library Journal* on the Virgin River series

"The Virgin River books are so compelling— I connected instantly with the characters and just wanted more and more and more."
—#1 *New York Times* bestselling author Debbie Macomber

ROBYN CARR

HIDDEN SUMMIT

MIRA®

Recycling programs for this product may not exist in your area.

ISBN-13: 978-0-7783-1300-7

HIDDEN SUMMIT

Copyright © 2012 by Robyn Carr

For questions and comments about the quality of this book please contact us at Customer_eCare@Harlequin.ca.

www.Harlequin.com

Printed in U.S.A.

HIDDEN SUMMIT

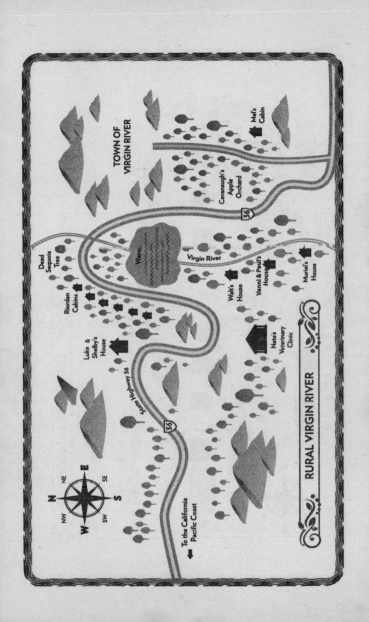

TOWN OF VIRGIN RIVER

One

Brie Valenzuela finished her large latte and looked into the empty cup. She'd been waiting in this coffee shop for over an hour, trying to look engrossed in her newspaper, but as the time ticked by, she only grew more concerned. The man she was meeting was a witness to a murder and needed a place to hide out. She'd be hooking him up with a place to stay and a job in Virgin River as a favor to one of her colleagues from the Sacramento District Attorney's office, and when a witness was late in meeting his contact, there was reason to be concerned.

Brie wanted to make a phone call to Sacramento but didn't want to alarm anyone. Instead, she asked the barista for another latte.

This witness, now known as Conner Danson, had seen a very well-known, high-profile Sacramento businessman shoot another man. Danson had been taking trash out behind his hardware store when it had happened and had seen everything. He'd called the police and become the sole witness to the crime. Thanks to his prompt report, they'd found evidence of blood in the man's car, though it had been cleaned, but no weapon. DNA tests had proved the blood belonged to the victim. But, shortly after an arrest had been made, Danson's hardware store had burned to the ground, and a threat had been left on his home phone voice mail: *You stayed out of the heat this time, but you won't slip by us again.*

Clearly the suspect, Regis Mathis, a very distinguished pillar of the community, was "connected."

Brie had served as an Assistant District Attorney with Max, officially Ray Maxwell, some years ago. Max was now the D.A. He'd suspected some trouble with other witnesses' anonymity and wasn't sure whether the leak was in his office or the Federal Marshal's unit. A cautious man, he'd set up his own program. He wasn't about to take any chances on losing the only witness to a high-profile murder. Virgin River was an excellent option.

It was another twenty minutes before the door opened and a man entered, but her first thought was that he couldn't possibly be her witness. First of all, he was too young to own a prosperous hardware store that catered to custom builders—this guy was no more than thirty-five. And he was, for lack of a more refined description, *hot.* At about six-two, he was built like a warhorse, his muscles popping into prominence beneath the white T-shirt under his opened leather jacket. Wide shoulders, narrow hips, low-slung jeans, long legs. Although he wore a very unhappy expression at the moment, his face was perfectly symmetrical—square jaw, straight nose, thick brows and deep, dark blue eyes. He sported a very handsome, sculptured and tightly trimmed mustache and goatee.

He lifted his chin in her direction. She stood and he walked toward her. She opened her arms. "Give me a hug, Conner. Like we're old friends. I'm Brie Valenzuela."

He complied a little reluctantly, nearly swallowing her small frame in his embrace. "Nice to meet you," he said quietly.

"Sit down. I'll get you a coffee. What's your pleasure?"

"Just plain old coffee. Black."

"Got it." She went to the counter, ordered, collected the coffee and returned. "So," she said. "We're about the same age. We could pass for friends from college."

"I didn't really go to college," he said. "One semester."

"That works. How old are you?"

"Thirty-five."

"Aren't you kind of young to own a successful business?"

"Used to own," he said, his expression darkening. "It was my father's. He died a dozen years ago but I was raised in that store. I took over."

"I see," she said. "So, we're friends from college. You're up here looking for something a little different after the builder you worked for in Colorado Springs shut down—there's a complete script of your history in this envelope, though I'm sure Max went over all of it with you."

He gave a nod. "And gave me my new ID. I picked up the truck this morning in Vacaville."

"I reserved you a small cabin. Very small, but comfortable. It's going to be temporary, and that's fine to say to people. And a friend of mine, Paul Haggerty, is a builder. He'll give you a job—he can keep you on through summer if necessary. It's his busy building season. That gives you six months, but you won't need that much time. I hope."

"Who knows about me?" he asked her.

"My husband, Mike, and I. And you want Mike to know. He's not just a small-town cop, he's a very experienced LAPD detective. Otherwise, you're completely anonymous. Look, I'm sorry you have to go through this, but on behalf of the state, thank you for agreeing to testify."

"Lady, don't thank me. I am out of choices," he said. "And don't stand anywhere near me in a thunderstorm because I am a magnet for lightning at this point. My life has gone straight to hell in the past year."

Brie frowned. "Don't call me lady," she said. "My name is Brie and I'm helping you. Show some gratitude. You're not the only person alive to have some bad luck. I've had my share. Now, I have a new cell phone for you. Here's the number. We gave your sister a new cell phone, as well. The area code for both phones is Colorado Springs and the D.A.'s office is picking up the tab. You won't get reception in the mountains, forests or town of Virgin River, but while you're out on construction jobs in clear areas or around here, in Fortuna, you'll have reception. And," she said, sliding him the large envelope, "directions to the Riordan cabins and to Paul Haggerty's office. Also, directions to a little bar and grill in Virgin River—good food. Do not get drunk and spill your guts or you'll probably just be moving again. If you live that long."

"I don't get drunk."

"More's the mercy," she muttered. "If you need anything, call me at this number. Do not call the D.A. He'll contact you through me. This is serious, Conner. You don't have any options. Whether you agree to testify or not, the man you witnessed committing murder obviously has the means to have you taken out. The authorities have always suspected he's that kind of man, even though he appears on the surface to be quite upstanding."

"Understand something," he said to Brie. "If it weren't for my sister and nephews, I might just go up against him because A, I'm *that* kind of man, and B, I'm a little past caring."

"Katie could be collateral damage, just being related. Remember, when you speak with your sister, no clues about where you are. Don't discuss the time zone or weather or landmarks, like redwood groves. There's no point in taking chances. Let's get through this whole. Hmm?"

He lifted his coffee cup in a silent toast. "Yeah."

"Get settled into your cabin. Go see Paul and get

your job. When you're comfortable, I'll have you to dinner. Maybe talking with Mike will settle your nerves a little."

"If you had any idea what the past year has been like…"

She put her hand over his in what might appear as a gesture of friendship to the casual observer, but her voice was firm. "I'm sure it's been hell. Can I just remind you that this is a favor for an old friend? I'm sticking my neck out for the D.A. because he's a good man and I owe him. We have a mission here. You're a friend from college, so go the extra mile and try to be pleasant. I don't need my brother and my close friends wondering why the hell I'd find you a place to live and a job because you're such an *ass!* So—"

"Brother?" he asked.

"Yes. I was an A.D.A. in Sacramento, but now I'm freelance up here and I have a husband and a little girl. I came up here to hide out while I was getting ready to testify against a rapist. I stayed after the trial."

He swallowed audibly. "Rapist, huh? Who'd he rape?"

"Me," she said. "First he beat the conviction—I was the prosecutor. Then he raped and tried to kill me. So, you can assume I understand some of what you're going through…"

He was quiet for a long moment. He had been the primary support for his sister and nephews for a few years now. He couldn't help but wonder how he'd feel if Katie had gone through something like that. It turned his stomach. Finally he swallowed thickly and asked, "Did you get him?"

"Life sentence, no parole."

"Good for you."

"This goatee," she asked, running her fingers over her own upper lip and chin. "Is it new?"

"A slight change was suggested," he said.

"I see. Well, I understand you're going to need some time to adjust. Give me a call if you get antsy, but for right now—try to enjoy the area. It's incredibly beautiful. A man could do worse."

"Sure," he said. "And, I'm sorry you had to go through what you had to go through, you know?"

"It was awful. And behind me now, as this will soon be behind you. You can get a fresh start. Um, Conner? You're not a bad-looking guy, but this wouldn't be a good time to hook up, if you get my drift."

"Not a problem," he said. "Not looking to hook up."

"Good. I guess," she said, standing. "Hug me like an old friend."

He opened his arms. "Thanks," he said roughly.

Conner followed the directions to Virgin River. Conner Danson had formerly been Danson Conner, owner of Conner's Hardware, so the name change had been merely a reversal, which was a little easier to get used to than an entirely new one. Danson was an old family name—some ancient great-grandfather. His parents, sister, nephews and ex-wife had always called him Danny. But at work he had been called Conner or sometimes Con or even Connie by quite a few. It wasn't difficult to remember to respond to the new name. He was tall, had brown hair, blue eyes, a small scar over his right eye, one slightly crooked tooth and a dimple on his left cheek.

The past five years had been a challenge and the past year, a nightmare.

Conner and his sister, Katie, had inherited their father's business—Conner's Custom Carpentry and Hardware. Construction work and running a hardware store was no walk in the park, it was very physical. His muscles had been hard-earned. They'd outsourced custom kitchen and bathroom jobs to builders and sold commercial hardware, cabinetry, fixtures, accessories and lumber used by contractors. Conner had managed it full-time with about ten employees and Katie had done the books, mostly from home so she could take care of her twin boys. Their merchandise had been high-end; the business had done well.

When Conner had been thirty, Katie's army husband had been killed in action in Afghanistan—she had been twenty-seven, pregnant and ready to give birth. At that point, Conner had had to take over their support. They couldn't sell the family business—their source of income would have dissipated in no time. And Katie couldn't contribute enough time to the family business to draw an adequate salary for herself and her sons. So—Conner had worked a little more than full-time, Katie had worked part-time and Conner had picked up the slack so Katie and the boys could live in their own home, independent.

Those days had been long, the work demanding. Many days had ended with Conner feeling as if he'd been married to a store, and while he loved his family, he hadn't had a life. Still, hard work never bothered him, and he'd remained good-natured and quick-witted. His customers and employees had enjoyed his laugh, his positive attitude. But he had needed something more.

And then he'd found the perfect woman—Samantha. Beautiful, funny and sexy Sam with the long, black hair and hypnotizing smile. And God, going to bed with her had just wound his clock! She was a whiz of an interior decorator who had helped Katie slap her little three bedroom into a showplace in nothing flat. She'd wanted him constantly. Loved sex.

Little had he known.

One year of marriage later and he'd found out she was cheating—and not with *a* guy, but with every guy she met.

"She's sick," Katie had said. "It's not even like she's unfaithful, she's a sex addict."

"I don't believe in sex addicts," Conner had said.

"She needs help," Katie had said.

"I wish her luck with that," he had replied.

Of course they divorced. He ended up paying for an expensive treatment program, but escaped alimony. He hadn't recovered from that before things got worse.

All he'd been doing was taking trash out to the Dumpster in the alley behind the store. A man in a black town car had gotten out, walked around to the passenger side, opened the door and put a bullet in the head of his passenger. Conner had crouched behind the Dumpster while the man, whom he'd unfortunately gotten a very good look at, had pulled out the victim's body and used Conner's Dumpster as the coffin. Then he'd calmly gotten back in his fancy car and driven out of the dark alley.

This was the point at which Conner would have done a few things differently, because he had seen the man and the license plate and the dead body. It would have probably been a lot easier all around if he'd pretended he hadn't seen a thing, but calling the police was an automatic response for him. Unfortunately, Conner's name had appeared on the warrant—it was how the police had been able to get it signed by a judge. Within a couple of days someone had burned the hardware store to the ground.

The ground.

At that point, even the decision not to testify would have come too late. Mr. Regis Mathis was a very important man in Sacramento. He endowed Catholic charities and supported high-profile politicians. Of course, he'd been investigated a few times by the feds for tax evasion and had a reputation for professional gambling—very successful legal gambling—but he was also a successful developer who sold golf course condo lots. He had never been indicted.

His victim, who had been found with his hands and ankles bound by duct tape, a strip across his mouth as well, had been his opposite—Dickie Randolph had been a low-class thug who'd owned a number of questionable establishments like massage parlors, strip clubs and adult clubs, all with the reputation of illegal drug use, prostitution and sex play. The two men had had nothing in common but there'd been hints of association—silent partner association that would be difficult to impossible to prove.

Immediately following the phone threat, Conner and the D.A., Max, had packed Katie and the boys off to Burlington, Vermont. Max knew of a friend of a friend's small rental house there and the same friend had hooked them up with a pediatric dentist who'd been looking for an accountant. Katie would be comfortable, independent and far, far away.

As much as Conner had wanted to accommodate his hostess, Brie Valenzuela, it had been hard to be cheery. He'd been in the wrong place at the wrong time—right on his own property—and now he'd lost too much. He missed Katie and the boys. He was going to work construction for a while before he had to testify and then get permanently relocated before Mathis could exact his revenge.

The guy who'd been upbeat in spite of everything was no more.

But as he made his way to the cabins on the river, sunlight broke through the clouds, sending a shaft of gold through the majestic redwoods. The early-March weather was wet and cold, but the beam of sunlight was promising. The green was so dense and bright with the sparkling wet of a recent rain, he was taken aback by the natural beauty of the place. Maybe, he thought... Maybe this isn't the worst place to be exiled. Time would tell.

He pulled up to the house and cabins—it was a serene little complex, lush and green, a river rushing by. A man came out of the house at the sound of Conner's truck. By the time he was getting out of the truck, the man had his hand out. "You must be Conner."

"Yes, sir," he said.

He laughed. "You start sirring me and I'll forget I'm civilian now. I'm Luke Riordan. My wife, Shelby, and I take care of these cabins. Number four is unlocked, but the key hangs on a hook by the door. We don't do meals, but we have a phone you can use if you need to. There's satellite internet hookup in case you brought a laptop. And there's a kitchenette and coffeepot, but your best bet for tonight is Jack's Bar, just ten minutes farther up 36 in Virgin River. The food is amazing and the company isn't bad."

"Thanks, I'll check that out. Are the rest of your cabins full?"

"Nah, hardly anyone right now. We're between hunting seasons, and the fishing is just starting to pick up. Deer hunting starts in the fall and then there's water fowl through January. Salmon is great from late summer to December and then slows way down. Summer people start showing up in a couple of months, so from June through January we're busy. I try to do repairs and upgrades these winter months."

"Pretty wet around here," Conner observed.

"The rain will let up in April. If we get a dry day, you're welcome to use my grill anytime. It's right in the storage shed. Also in the shed—rods and reels. Help yourself."

Conner almost smiled. "Full-service lodge."

"Not even close, my friend. We take care of the linens after you check out, but since you might be here awhile, you'll have to make use of that little washer and dryer in the cabin. We have a man, Art, who will do some cleaning in there if you feel like a little help. You know—bathroom, floor, shower, that sort of thing. There's a sign you can hang on the door if you want cleaning. He's challenged—he has Down syndrome—but he's smart and very competent. Good guy."

"Thanks, but I've been cleaning for myself for quite a while. I'll be fine."

"Let me help you unload a few things," Luke offered.

"I guess I'll move in and go have a beer and some dinner."

"Sounds like a good plan. You gonna be able to find your way back here?"

"I think so. Left turn at the dead sequoia?"

Luke laughed. "That'll get you home."

Home. It was a memory. But Conner said, "Thanks."

Luke helped him move a couple of duffels and boxes into the cabin, shook his hand and went back to his house, his family. Alone once more, Conner unpacked some clothes into the one and only chest of drawers in the room. He plugged in his laptop to recharge it—he and Katie had changed all their accounts, user names and passwords. Although Brie hadn't said anything, the D.A. had told him they could keep in touch by internet but recommended they not use their names or previously used ID's, and they should resist the urge to Skype, just on the off chance their internet access was compromised.

What remained of the hardware store had been razed, and all that was left was the lot, but it was in a prime location. Conner had insurance money for rebuilding; it had been put in an investment account under his new identity and would be there for him when this nightmare ended. With his share of the sale of the lot and insurance on the building and stock, he could start over. But not in Sacramento, where he'd spent his entire life except for two years in the army.

He got to that little Virgin River bar just before six and damn near smiled in appreciation. Conner was a custom builder at the heart of things and this establishment was put together real nice. The bar itself was a fine piece of furniture. Someone here favored beeswax as a buffer and shiner, and he could almost smell it. The place was cozy, hospitable and clean as a whistle. He found himself a spot at the end of the bar where he could observe.

"Hey, pardner, what can I get you?" the bartender asked.

"I'll take a light beer and how about a menu?"

"No problem on the beer, but I'm afraid we don't have a menu. Our cook fixes up whatever he's in the mood for. You lucked out there if you like fish—the trout are jumping and Preacher, that's the cook, has been spending some time out at the river. He has a stuffed trout that will just bring you to your knees."

"Sounds good to me," Conner said.

He was immediately served up a beer, and the bartender said, "I'm Jack. This is my place. You passing through?"

"I hope so," he said, lifting the beer to his lips.

Jack smiled. "Don't be in such a hurry. This place is about to get real pretty, soon as the rain lets up. And when you see what the melting snowpack does to that river, you'll just fall in love. No wonder our fish get so big."

And then Jack was gone, wandering down the bar to take care of other patrons, serving a few plates, picking up a few. The atmosphere was real friendly; everyone seemed acquainted, and there was a small part of Conner that wondered, *Can I make a life here? For a while?* Imagine checking into a hotel and having the manager offer housekeeping if you were in the mood, no extra charge. Imagine a bar and grill that served up only what the cook felt like.

Jack returned a little later to ask, "How you doing on that beer? Dinner's ready whenever you are."

"Sure," Conner said. "I'm ready. I'm good on the beer."

While Jack was back getting his dinner, a young woman came into the bar. She pushed down the collar of her jacket and shook out her dark blond hair—lots of loose curls reached her shoulders. She was a little on the thin side but pretty. The thing that got to him, she looked so clean. Or pure, like some Sunday-school teacher or something. Girl-next-door decent. Her complexion was peachy, her eyes dark, her lips full and pink. There was every reason why that sort of thing would appeal to Conner, after his experience with his ex-wife.

But then, Samantha had come across as squeaky clean, too, even classy. There hadn't been a hint of cheap in her. Appearances meant nothing.

Even so, Conner had been a long time without a woman, and it was wearing on him. All he wanted was to get his life back, take care of his sister and nephews, never be vulnerable to a woman again. He wasn't the least worried about dying a lonely old man; he, Katie and the boys were very close. Even if Katie found a perfect second husband, he'd always be Uncle Danny.... Well, Uncle Conner now. And that was good enough for him.

Jack put the fish in front of him but quickly headed for the other end of the bar where the Sunday-school teacher waited. Before long a man came into the bar, put an arm around the Sunday-school teacher's shoulders and gave her a kiss on the temple.

Well, that was that. Temptation eliminated, as far as Conner was concerned.

Two

Leslie Petruso pulled up to the little bar in town, parked and went inside. She immediately felt a little better, a little safer. She liked the look of the place, as though it welcomed her to a simpler life. That's all she wanted, really—something that was less complicated. She didn't have to wait long at the bar before a big, good-looking bartender was there, grinning. "What can I get you, miss?"

"How about a glass of Merlot? I'm meeting someone, but I see he's not here yet."

She was instantly served the wine. "Anyone I know?" the bartender asked.

"Maybe. Paul Haggerty?"

He smiled. "One of my best friends. We served in Iraq together a long time ago. I'm Jack," he said, putting out his hand.

"Leslie. How do you do?"

"Paul's a friend of yours?"

"I hope so," she said. "He was once my boss in

Grants Pass. One of several bosses, I should say. I was the office manager for Haggerty Construction."

"Pleasure to meet you!" Jack said. "Here for a visit?"

"Actually, if Paul hasn't changed his mind, I'm here to work as his secretary. Office manager. Whatever he needs."

"Well now," Jack said. "'Bout time he did that! His company just keeps growing. He's got himself a real fine reputation around here."

"They're the best, the Haggertys."

"And speak of the devil," Jack said, lifting his chin in the direction of the door.

She turned and smiled to see Paul. He was a sight for sore eyes. It had been a long time. His visits to Grants Pass for business had tapered off as his arm of the company in Virgin River grew larger and more demanding. He and his wife and kids still visited his family, but Leslie hadn't been a part of that side of things.

He dragged off his hat in that boyish way of his and grinned at her. He put an arm around her shoulders, leaned down to give her a kiss on the temple and said, "God, it's good to see you! How are you?"

And damn it all, her lips began to quiver slightly, and she had to press them together to keep from crying. Her eyes misted over.

"Aw, come on, honey," he said, squeezing her a little harder. "Jack, how about a beer?"

"You got it," Jack said, escaping.

"Take it easy now," Paul said. "We're going to have a drink, then I'll take you to the rental to drop off your luggage and car and then I'm taking you home to dinner. Vanni made a roast—an event at our house, you know. I'll drive you home after—to your new home."

"You don't have to go to all that trouble, Paul. I can drive."

"Getting around these mountains after dark can be dicey when they're new to you. You can start doing all that without any help from your friends tomorrow. Your furniture arrived, and since there wasn't that much, Vanni just instructed the movers to unpack the boxes and put things away. There are clean sheets on the bed and clean towels in the bathroom. You can organize it your own way when you feel like it."

"I wish she hadn't gone to so much trouble," Leslie said.

"Don't worry about it. She's so grateful you're here. She's been handling a lot of my paperwork, what I can't keep up with, and she's really too busy for even that right now."

"*She's* grateful? Oh, Paul, I'm not sure what I would have done if you hadn't stepped up with a job when your dad asked you!"

"I hope you don't regret it when you see my office. We're going to have to move a few things around, but right now I'm in a construction trailer."

"Thank you, Paul," she said. She took a sip. Then in a tremulous voice she added, "I just had to get out of there."

He gave her a moment before he asked, "That bad, huh?"

She gave a hollow little laugh and shook her head. "You have no idea how badly I wanted to hold my head high and let it all roll off. I tried pretending I didn't care, but I'm just not as strong as I'd like to be."

He put a finger under her chin and smiled into her sad eyes. "Leslie, you don't give yourself enough credit. First of all, you're not the one who looks bad—it's Greg who looks like an idiot and jerk. And second, you're an amazing woman who has the respect of the company and the whole community."

"That's nice of you to say," she replied. "But our divorce and his remarriage really took its toll. I see them everywhere! Did you know that she's now pregnant with the baby he told me he didn't want to have? Have with *me,* I guess."

Paul leaned his forehead against hers. "Les, I'm sorry."

She pulled back and lifted her chin. "I have to find a way to rebuild my self-esteem. I sure couldn't do it in Grants Pass where Greg seems to think we can remain friends."

"We'll work on that. You'll feel better about yourself in no time. Leslie, this isn't about your failure. It's about his."

"Intellectually I know that," she said. "But you have to understand, I have a lot more to overcome than you realize. I mean, I wasn't even asked to the prom."

Paul had laughed at that comment about the prom, as if she was kidding. She had worked with the Haggerty men for ten years, and they all thought she had a great sense of humor. And she knew they were absolutely on her side. Paul's dad, Stan, the founder and president of Haggerty Construction, had been determined never to work with Greg again, but his sons had all stood up to him and pointed out that refusing to do business with a successful developer was shortsighted in business. And also some sort of discrimination. "Yeah," Stan had stormed. "I discriminate against stupid assholes!"

Leslie had adored him for that!

She had been twenty-three when she married Greg Adams. He was a young developer who was becoming successful and well-known, though he was only just thirty. He was in all the fraternal and networking groups from Rotary to the Chamber of Commerce; he'd been president of each at one time or another. He'd had aspirations to run for city council, maybe mayor eventually. He was also incredibly handsome and very sexy, and she had always had a hard time believing he chose her. And even though she'd worked full-time for Haggerty Construction, she'd also joined the Junior League, library volunteers—anything she thought might help Greg's plans. Of course, Greg had encouraged her to do so.

Then, after eight years of marriage, she'd caught Greg in an affair with a twenty-seven year old attorney. He had been thirty-eight. He'd come clean immediately and confessed he was sorry she had been hurt, but he was moving on. His life had changed in ways he had never anticipated. He'd moved out of their lovely three-bedroom home the day after she'd confronted him, filing for divorce while she was still in shock.

She'd gotten the house and the mortgage, which she couldn't carry alone. He'd gotten fifty percent of the equity. She'd gotten no alimony because it seemed this successful developer had no money.

"Hah!" Stan Haggerty had roared. "That's bullshit! He has plenty of money, unless he's hidden it!"

Apparently he had, because after the divorce and sale of the home and division of the proceeds, he'd managed to buy a very large custom home in a better neighborhood, a new car and take his new lady on a lavish vacation to Aruba. A year after the divorce, he'd had a flashy wedding and invited half the town, including Leslie and her parents. They'd passed, sending regrets. A year and four months after the divorce, the new Mrs. Adams was showing.

Through all of this, Greg had phoned or stopped by regularly; it was very important to him that she know he would always love her and respect her. He wanted them to remember the good years they had together and remain the best of friends. If she hadn't been so broken down with humiliation, demoralization and envy she might've found the strength to gouge his eyes out with a dull spoon.

When he'd broken it to her that Allison was pregnant and that he hoped she would be happy for them, she'd found her bottom. She'd taken all she could take. That's when she'd gone to Stan and said she was terribly sorry, but she was giving notice.

"Where will you go?" Stan had asked.

"I don't know," she had answered. "I just have to get away from here. I know people are on my side, that they think I was wronged, but that doesn't keep them from looking at me with pity and wondering what role I played in driving my husband away. This is Greg's town. And admit it, even on my side, they admire Greg for trying so hard to split on good terms. I see Greg and Allison everywhere. He kisses her neck and pats her little belly. I'll give you a month's notice, give my apartment manager a month's notice, and I'll start looking for a job in another city. Please say you'll give me a decent recommendation."

He'd done better than that. He'd asked Paul if he needed someone. "That'll give you a lot more time to think, to recover, to get on your feet. You might even decide to come back to Grants Pass. And you'll always have a job with Haggerty Construction. In fact, I don't know how we'll make it without you."

Conner agreed with Jack about the stuffed trout. And while Conner ate, he watched the people in the bar. Jack had a running dialogue with a number of them; they joked around a lot and poked fun at each other like old friends. Jack was obviously all-purpose in his bar—he delivered dinner to a couple of little old ladies, to a family of four, to a couple of guys at the other end of the bar. He picked up empty plates. He served drinks. He leaned over a table and gave a tip on a cribbage move.

He helped the same little old ladies out of the bar and down the steps.

All things considered, if he had to be someplace, maybe this wouldn't be such a bad one. It had a lot of charm. The pace seemed slow and friendly. He was due some of that.

The couple down the bar were kind of intense, Conner decided. Their heads were close together as they talked, and if he wasn't mistaken, the Sunday-school teacher was close to tears a couple of times. Were they a couple? His hands on her were friendly, affectionate. Maybe they hit a rocky patch or something. Whatever it was, the man was consoling her while they had a drink. After about twenty minutes of that, the man plunked some bills on the bar and, with his hand at the small of her back, escorted her out.

Conner felt that grinding ache of resentment. Because of his ex, because of witnessing a crime and being driven into hiding, he wasn't going to experience that. He wasn't going to feel the satisfaction of escorting a pretty Sunday-school teacher out the door and off to some quiet and private place.

His heart was as heavy as it was hungry.

"Anything else for you, buddy?" Jack asked him.

"No, thanks. You were right about the trout— outstanding. Let's settle up."

Jack slapped a ticket on the bar, Conner dug out some money and headed out.

Back on the road, Conner passed the turnoff to the cabins and drove down the mountain until he could see service bars on his new cell phone. Finally he saw the potential for a phone call. At the first opportunity, he pulled over and called the number he had already memorized. She answered sleepily. "Aw, Katie, I woke you...."

She laughed. Katie didn't need an alias—she wasn't the witness. "We're not supposed to talk about time zones, weather, landmarks, names or anything."

"You could be asleep at any time," he said, though he knew that wasn't true. She went to bed early. She snuggled in about the same time her little boys did to keep from being too lonely. "That other thing, names, I might have trouble with that."

"Are you okay?" she asked him.

"I'm good. I'm ready to get this over with, get things back to normal."

"Things might never be normal again, have you thought about that?"

"What else is there to think about? Things won't be the way they were, maybe, but they could be normal. We'll be somewhere new, maybe, but before the boys forget what I look like, we'll be done with this and rebuilding. Tell me about you, Andy and Mitch. Everyone okay?"

"Names," she reminded him with a laugh. "Better than I expected. I have a good job with a cute, single dentist. Who knows?" He could hear a smile in her voice. "Maybe things will work out and you'll join me here."

"Who knows," he repeated with a laugh.

"Do you have a job yet?"

"Tomorrow. One is all lined up for me."

"Will you let me know if you like it?"

"Of course. Yes. Listen, I don't know how much I can say, but if I don't answer when you call, it's because of bad cell reception. I have…" He almost said *internet connection* and stopped himself. "But I'll definitely be in touch. One way or another."

"Okay, just let me know. Anyway, if I need help, you're not the one I'm going to call. They gave me other, faster options. Please don't worry. We're being well taken care of."

"I won't worry…."

"Will you do me a favor? Will you try to make friends? You finally don't have to work sixteen hours a day to keep me and the boys afloat, too, so just try to take advantage of that. Think of this as a vacation."

"Sure," he said. He wanted to argue—*vacation? I'm hiding from a murderer connected to mobsters and hit men. I've been separated from my family and left with nothing but a big question about where we're going to start over. Great vacation.*

"I don't know exactly where you are, but wherever you are there must be stuff local people do. Check it out. Go out for a couple of beers—you never do that sort of thing. And have a date…."

"Date? I don't think so…."

"You deserve to grab a little bit of fun, if not downright happiness. I mean, come on—this is temporary."

"Fun? We'll see. No happiness," he said. "The last time I felt happy, I was punished by the entire universe."

She just laughed. "Have it your way. Be as miserable as possible."

He sighed. "I'll try to enjoy this little bit of time, okay? Because when it's finally over, I'm going to rebuild. Honey, are you and the boys really okay? Happy? They aren't scared, are they?"

"We miss you. They have a hard time understanding why we can't be with you. But you know what? They have a nice school, and we haven't been here long but they've already started soccer and had a couple of friends over for pizza and a movie. My boss is easygoing and flexible—I get the feeling I'm extra help and he's getting me real cheap, maybe not actually paying my salary, if you know what I mean." She yawned. "We'll get through this with nobody hurt."

He'd always been the one to be there for T-ball or swimming lessons or soccer. It killed him to be this unavailable. "You're always the positive one," he said. He rubbed the sting out of his eyes. If they got through this, which they would, they would all be entirely new characters in this big drama—new identities, new locations. But they would be together again. "I think I admire you more than anyone I know."

"Aw, that's so sweet. And I don't deserve it."

But she did. She'd had some real rough breaks, yet she didn't treat all that as baggage. If she suffered, she suffered and got it over with and resumed her sunny outlook on life.

"Let's not use up our minutes," she said. "We're fine, you're fine. I want to talk to you again after you have a job…and remember—you promised you're going to try to find something to enjoy."

"I will," he said. "I am." And he found himself wondering if it was reasonable to hope he could meet a woman who'd settle for a no-strings thing just to take the edge off? And he further wondered how that made him very different from Samantha.

Paul told Leslie that he hadn't planned to get into the landlord business, but with real estate in a mess and interest rates low, he'd picked up a couple of small foreclosures in town. He planned to sell them when there was a sufficient economic recovery to make money. In the meantime, he rented one of the spruced-up ones to Leslie. It was probably all of a thousand square feet and adorable. And she believed he kept the rent suspiciously low.

"I'll send someone over in the next couple of weeks to clean up the yard, put down some sod on a couple of bare patches and plant some flowers along the walk," Paul told her. "When it dries out a little bit, I'm planning to pour a new drive and put up a decent covered carport with some storage. This March rain will give way to sunshine before you know it. And when you see spring here, you'll have trouble catching your breath, it's that beautiful."

The small two bedroom did have an inviting feel on this quiet and welcoming little street. The houses that lined each side were all simple, unpretentious little structures, some in better repair than others, but it had the feel of a neighborhood in need of one more good neighbor, and that was all she asked.

"Let me plant the flowers," she said. "It'll help me settle in. I've always wanted to keep a little garden, but between work and then apartment living…"

"You do anything you want, Les," he said. "Treat it like it's yours."

"I'll take you up on the sod and driveway, if you feel like it. That would be nice—a place other than the street to park."

"Consider it done," he said.

If Leslie had worried that Paul's wife would pity her, running away from her job in Grants Pass to escape her humiliating divorce, she would've been wasting her time. The reason for her being in Virgin River never even came up over dinner. Rather, Vanni really was grateful that Paul was finally getting some full-time help from someone who had worked for him before and knew the business. And the fact that she was an old friend of the Haggerty family as well, made it even better.

When Leslie settled into bed in her little rented house that night, she felt more relaxed than she had in what seemed like years. And she knew exactly why—it was the distance between her and her past. Tomorrow, when she was out and about town, or when she reported to her new job, when she shopped for groceries or treated herself to a glass of wine at Jack's, she would not run into Greg or Allison or any of their former friends. She might as well be on another continent.

In the morning when she woke, she went out onto her front porch in her robe, a cup of coffee cradled in her hands. The tops of the trees were still lost in the early-morning mist that blanketed the little town, but she could hear voices—neighbors shouting hello, cars just starting up, children laughing and yelling, probably on their way to school or to the bus stop. It was still very early. By the time she was showered and dressed in jeans and a sweatshirt over a white collared blouse, the sun was struggling to break through.

Paul had told her not to dress up, that the trailer where he kept his office was pretty rugged. She'd usually worn business attire, either skirts or slacks, to the Haggerty Construction office. In the course of a typical day she'd run into salesmen, customers, decorators, investors and developers. Paul told her the only people she was likely to run into besides himself in that trailer were crew.

She took a cup of coffee along for the ride as she followed his directions. And there it was, the trailer, sitting on a large lot that held two houses in progress. It was actually a single-wide mobile home; she assumed the bedrooms would be offices and that there would be a kitchen and bathroom.

There was one truck parked at the trailer, and it wasn't Paul's. She glanced at her watch. Seven forty-five. In the construction world, that was late. Not for the office staff, of course, but the crew usually got started as soon as they had light. Here she'd been trying to impress him by being early, and there didn't seem to be anyone here to impress.

Inside she found a man seated at what would pass for a kitchen table—a big slab of plywood balanced on sawhorses. He had a cup of coffee and appeared to be leafing through plans, but stood as she entered. "Hi," he said. "I'm Dan Brady, one of Paul's foremen. He went to meet a crew at another job and asked me to hang out until you got here. Make yourself at home. His office is down the hall," he said, pointing. "He must be putting you in the room next to that because there's a desk in there. It's old and kind of dirty and you might have to clean it up and maybe put a shim under one leg of it, but it hasn't been spoken for. Must be yours." He put out his hand.

She felt herself smile. The whole place was a wreck, messy and mud-tracked. There was a thirty-cup coffeemaker on the kitchen counter, covered with fingerprints. That would explain the tracking of mud. "I'm Leslie Petruso. Let me guess, the guys grab a cup of coffee in here." And then she took his hand in greeting.

"Especially when it's cold. When it's nice out, they're more likely to take a break sitting on the back of their trucks or something. It looks a little worse than usual, what with the rain. I hope you're not completely disgusted."

She laughed. "I've been working for a construction company for ten years now, so every now and then I did have to visit a job site. Nice to meet you, Dan."

He indicated her cup with a jut of his chin. "Can I warm that up for you?"

"Thanks," she said, handing it to him. "So, did Paul say what he'd like me to do?"

Dan gave the cup back, refreshed. "He said you'd know what to do. He carries his laptop around in the truck with him, but there's a paper schedule on his desk. I'm waiting for a crew to work on interiors on these two houses and Paul will get here when he gets here. Will you be all right if I get to work?"

"You bet. Don't worry about me."

He smiled at her. "Welcome aboard, Leslie. We'll all be happy if Paul has a little help organizing the paperwork."

"Gets a little behind on that, does he?" she asked on a laugh.

"He's a builder," Dan said with a grin. "It's hard to keep him in the office. I'll be in the house on the left, if you need me."

"Not to worry. I'm going to poke around Paul's desk and see if I can make sense of anything."

"Go for it," Dan said with a salute.

Leslie took her time looking around after Dan left. She didn't concentrate on Paul's desk or even on his office—there was plenty of time for that. She opened every cupboard and closet in the trailer before she attempted Paul's desk. And it happened spontaneously— she wiped out the sink, which led to scrubbing the countertop, which led to first sweeping, then mopping the kitchen floor. She filled the sink with soapy water, and, with rag or mop in hand, she moved through the place with a vengeance.

By the time Paul showed up at around ten, the muddy tracks and finger smears had disappeared. Even the stainless-steel thirty-cup coffeemaker was shining. And the coffee in it was fresh. "Whoa," he said.

She straightened her spine and blew a curl of hair off her forehead. "Prepare your crews for intensive training—they're going to learn to keep things clean around here."

"Oh, they know how," he said. "When we turn over a house, you could eat off the floor...."

"Yeah? Really?" she asked. "Because if you ate off that bathroom floor, you'd be dead in ten seconds. I'm not cleaning it. It's vile. The next man who comes in here with a need for it is getting the job. And then they're going to keep it clean because I can't even think about putting my—" she cleared her throat in lieu of a key word and added "—on it."

The door opened and a man looked in with blue eyes that almost knocked her out. "Oh. Excuse me. I should've knocked...."

Paul laughed and kind of rocked back on his heels. "Not a problem, come on in. The new secretary was instructing me in keeping a clean shop."

"New?" he asked.

Paul didn't respond to the question but stuck out a hand. "Paul Haggerty. How can I help you?"

"Conner Danson," he said, accepting the handshake. "A friend of mine said you might have some work...."

"Would that be Brie?" he asked.

"That's her. Old friend of mine. My last boss shut down...."

"She said something about that. And you're friends from college?"

Conner smiled. "I took a few classes after high school, but I'm not a college man. I quit, joined the army for a couple of years, then apprenticed with a carpenter. Custom kitchens and bathrooms."

Paul gestured to an album Conner held under one arm. "I bet you have some sample photos I can look at."

"You bet," he said, handing over the album.

Paul opened it and began leafing through the photos, Leslie looking over his shoulder. She kept glancing up at Conner—short brown hair, tanned face, thick eyelashes, goatee...very handsome. She'd like another look at his eyes; the blue was almost shocking.

"Wow," she said of the pictures. "Very nice work. And you say your boss shut down?"

"Not a great time for custom builders right now."

"This work is so pretty," she said. "Did you give any thought to going out on your own?"

"Lots of carpenters and refinishers out of work right now," he said with a shrug. "I contacted everyone I knew and Brie said..." He didn't finish but let it hang in the air.

"I have one good interiors man, my foreman. He's a good leader and can usually handpick crew to work with him, but I bet he'd be happy to have some talent like this to partner up with." Paul closed the album and handed it back. "I have enough contracts for custom buildings and remodels to employ you for as long as six months, but I can't guarantee any more than that."

"I'll start with that," Conner said.

"Thing is, this is the kind of stuff I like to do," Paul said. "But if I spend too much time on the detail work the big picture gets shortchanged."

"I'd be happy to watch your details," Conner said. "Besides, I don't know if I'll take to this place for the long-term. I'm a city boy. More or less."

"From?"

Conner answered according to his new bio. "Colorado Springs. If you don't mind me asking, how is it you have enough work to take on one more hire in a little place like this?"

"A combination of things," Paul said. "This place was a little light on general contractors when I first got here—not a lot of competition. And, because of the kind of place it is, beautiful and with a distinct shortage of industry, the only people who move here come because they can. Take my father-in-law, retired general— he found this place because it was perfect for hunting and keeping his horses. His lady friend is a semiretired actress—also loves hunting and has dogs and horses. Then there's Jack of Jack's Bar—not so rich and important, but a hardworking man, a retired marine who saved a couple of bucks and wanted to build his wife a nice house to raise their family.... You get the idea. People are here on purpose. And they tend to build or remodel the homes they'll have forever, homes they'll leave their children…. I love making homes for generations. My dad taught me that."

"And you're here because…?" Conner asked.

"That's easy. My wife. Before she was my wife she was my best friend's wife, and I gave my word if anything happened to him in Iraq I'd take care of her and their baby. The worst happened and I kept my word, but it was no sacrifice. I've always loved Vanni. She's expecting our third now. We just found out."

"Wow, congratulations," Conner said, dropping his gaze to the floor. He couldn't make eye contact with either of them. What he'd seen in the bar the night before sure didn't pay a tribute to the wife Paul had "always loved." He suspected his new boss was fooling around with the secretary. He'd seen them together at the bar.

"Now, I'm gonna need some information. Or—make that Leslie here is going to need some information so we can set up some benefits, take care of your payroll, the basics. And while you fill out her forms, I'm going to clean the bathroom."

"I really didn't mean you had to do it," Leslie said rather sheepishly.

"Hey, the buck stops here," Paul said. "I should've made sure it was kept clean. Vanni wouldn't even come out here—she made me take the paperwork home. I'll clean it and I'll make sure it stays clean." He grinned and put an arm around her shoulders. "The employment applications and forms are in the lower left drawer."

"I'll take care of it," she said. And she smiled warmly at Paul, then Conner. And when she caught Conner's eyes with hers, there was a zing. A spark.

Three

After filling out some paperwork, Conner walked across a muddy lot to a house that was nearly finished and introduced himself to Dan Brady.

"Oh, hey," Dan said, stretching out a hand. "Paul mentioned something about a cabinet guy heading our way!"

"I hope that's me," he said, thinking, *I used to be Dan, Uncle Danny.* But he was Conner now—a change that would probably be permanent. "I'm supposed to work with you. What are we doing here?"

Dan spread out his plans on a piece of wood set atop the base for a kitchen island. "Granite countertops, walnut cabinets with glass insets, matching bathroom counters with granite carved sinks and identical cabinets—no glass insets in the bathroom."

Conner gave a nod. "This is pretty high-end for me. I've done it, but it's been a while. I hope you don't mind if I ask for advice here and there?"

"I'll mind if you don't. I'd rather help you do it right

for the homeowner than have to go back and redo. Let's get it right the first time. Any questions, spit 'em out."

"Thanks. I appreciate that."

"I appreciate it more," Dan said. "We're on time and on budget because we build *smart*."

"I'll try to keep up with you," Conner said.

Conner hadn't been on a building crew in a long time, but he'd been involved in building in every other way. He'd built all his own displays, given classes to homeowners who'd been attempting their own renovations, instructed carpenters who'd been after something new and upscale. But of course the business of retailing had been too consuming to allow extra time for building, except for the things he'd built for his nephews—their backyard play set, shelves, cabinets, race car bed frames.

How he missed them! But having his hands on the wood was reassuring and felt good. Measuring, cutting, planing, nailing, sanding…it was therapeutic. While he couldn't really let his mind wander too much if he was going to do a good job, it was easy to take a little think time while he worked with his hands. This had always been his magic bullet—carpentry. Every so often he'd glance over at Dan to check his progress and mastery. The man's artistry shone through in no time.

"How long you been doing this, bud?" Conner asked.

"Oh, forever. My dad was a builder. We built the house we lived in, one room at a time. Really tough father, but outstanding builder. He was my first boss."

"I lost my dad twelve years ago," Conner found himself saying. And then he thought about how easy it was to just talk about himself, his authentic self. He wondered if he'd always been that way without realizing it. But of course he had—he'd never had anything to hide before. Would a clever person be able to piece together a million details and discover him? But still he added, "He was tough, too. Good but tough. How long have you worked for Haggerty?"

"Few years," Dan said. "He's solid. Good man." Dan stood tall and said, "But don't get the idea that just because he's nice, he's soft or easy. With him you earn your pay. And if you don't, you're gone fast. I repeat, fast."

Conner straightened. "You warning me for a reason?"

"Not that I can see, but a friendly word here and there never hurts. What brings you to the mountains?"

Conner gave him the standard line. Maybe it would even begin to feel natural.

"Brie? You knew Brie?"

"We were lots younger...."

"Did you know her brother, Jack?" Dan asked.

"We just had a couple of classes together. When I found myself out of work, I got in touch with everyone I'd ever met. I didn't know anyone else in her family."

Dan grinned. "You'll like Jack. But never let him know it. In fact, the best way to get on his good side is to give him a little shit. Accuse him of something. Say he's overcharging you." Then Dan chuckled and got back to work.

"Jack who owns the little bar in town?" Conner asked.

"The same," Dan said. Later, when they were done for the day, Dan said, "Hey, my fiancée's out for the evening, and I'll be having dinner at Jack's. I'll stand you a beer if you're not busy."

He used to be busy all the time, so busy there was no time for that occasional beer with friends unless he grabbed one out of Katie's fridge while he visited with her. Back when he had a wife, he'd struggled to get out of the store and home to her, but that seemed so long ago. And he'd often returned to the store for a few hours after dinner, a thing that plagued him now. Had he not given enough in that relationship? Left his wife wanting, left her believing she was some kind of addict? And after Samantha was gone, there was work and Katie and the boys. He couldn't remember when he'd last had pals.

"I could spare some time," he said to Dan. "I was planning to get dinner there myself."

"Good, then. I'll meet you there in fifteen minutes."

Back in that little bar there were now at least twenty people, all of whom seemed to know each other. Conner was a little uncomfortable about that.

Jack lifted his hand and yelled, "Hey," as Dan and Conner entered and took seats at the bar. Jack lost no time in making introductions. Whenever someone came to the bar to order a beer, he said, "This here is Conner, new to these mountains, working for Paul now." Conner met the cook and his wife, a young man named Denny who helped out behind the bar, Denny's girl, Becca, who would soon be the elementary-school teacher, "Once there is an elementary school," Jack said. "We're working on that part." He met Jack's wife, Mel, the local minister and the local doctor. Pretty soon Paul Haggerty wandered in. He was grinning when he asked Dan, "How'd this guy work out for you?"

"He did great," Dan said. "Tough loss for Colorado Springs."

"Colorado Springs?" Jack's wife piped up. It felt like she shouted it across the bar. She left her children sitting at a table with their dinner and walked toward Conner. "My sister lives there! What part of Colorado Springs?"

He struggled for a second, then made something up. "Are you familiar with Breckenridge Park?"

"No," she said. "My sister is on the northeast side of the city."

"Breckenridge is southwest," he said. "Kind of lonely out there... Not a lot of development..."

"But it's so beautiful there. I almost moved there," she said.

"But she married me," Jack put in from behind the bar.

"But I married him," Mel said with a smile. "And not only is Jack one of the best things that ever happened to me, so is this town. I hope you like it here."

"Don't push him, Mel," Jack said. "He's only been here a couple of days and it's been kinda muddy."

"I came here in March myself," Mel said. "I wasn't

impressed. I slid off a road and had to be towed out, then the porch collapsed on the cabin where I was staying, I was soaked to the bone and this lughead kept saying, 'Be patient—it's so beautiful here.'" Her blue eyes twinkled. She put a hand on Conner's arm. "Really, it is. Maybe not today, but we do have amazing days... and nights...."

"The thing that got to Mel," Jack said to Conner, "she'd been in L.A. for ten years and when she came here, she'd never seen so many stars. Just look up on a clear night. We get used to it, even take it for granted, but it's spectacular. But then...I bet Colorado Springs and the surrounding area gives you some wonderful views and skies."

It brought to Conner's mind the area east of Sacramento, in the Sierras, where the air was clean and the vistas breathtaking. He'd managed to get his nephews up on skis already. "Sure," he said, fighting homesickness. He wanted his family back, his store, all the customers who had become friends. "It's a good place, Colorado Springs," he said. "I wouldn't have left if there'd been work...."

Paul Haggerty hung out for a while, and he was as bad as Jack, introducing Conner to everyone who happened along. It wasn't long before Mike Valenzuela stopped by and introduced himself, expressing his pleasure in meeting one of Brie's old friends from college.

"Old friend from college?" Jack said in a booming voice. "You didn't mention you knew my sister!"

"I had one whole semester of college," Conner said.

"We had two classes together, that's it. When the company I worked for folded, I got in touch with everyone I knew, though Brie was a real long shot. She said she thought there was work here for someone like me. But it's not like we've been in touch the last seventeen years...."

"Not even Christmas cards," a female voice said from behind him. He turned to see Brie with a toddler on her hip. She let her down, and the little girl instantly ran to the table where Mel's kids were having dinner. "But I'll never forget Conner. He asked me out three times."

"She said no three times," he added.

Mike draped an arm around her shoulders and gave her a squeeze. "I don't blame you, man," Mike said. "I hope you're over her. I'm possessive."

"I can see that," Conner said. "No worries."

"No kidding. A friend from college," Jack said.

"I had a lot of friends, Jack. And you were pretty far away at that time," Brie reminded him. "In fact, so was Mike. I met my husband when he came to Sacramento to see Jack. They were both still in the Marine Corps. But Mike and I didn't get together until much later."

There were a few more introductions. He had a good dinner of red beans with kielbasa and rice and a second beer. And when it was almost time to escape, he saw his chance to sneak a word with Brie.

"Hey," he said a bit nervously and very quietly. "I think I just met the whole town."

"Not even close," she answered. "These are mostly the regulars and good friends."

"It doesn't feel that anonymous...."

"It is and it isn't. The town is pretty anonymous as long as you don't reach out using your real identity. See, these folks are used to meeting people like you—folks who come for a vacation or for work or to visit friends and family. And they're not the kind of people who get on Facebook or Twitter. Just stick to your story and relax. You're here for a job, you're passing through, and since you won't be putting down roots..."

"No one will email or call their cousin who lives next door to the man I'm testifying against?" he asked in a low voice.

She shook her head. "The D.A.'s detectives did an extensive background on the defendant. There's always a chance of something burrowed under the surface, but the other great thing about this little town—strangers stand out like a sore thumb. Just like you can't slip in and out of here without being noticed, neither can anyone else, like anyone who might be looking for you. We're buried in the mountains, Conner. That's why Max picked it for you."

"Makes me a little nervous. I want to get to the trial so I can end this...."

"I know," she said. "Believe me, I know."

And then she came in—Leslie. It was as if the door opened and let spring inside—she was that pretty, that fresh. He wished it could be otherwise because this was going to be problematic, but he felt the instant attraction. Like a swelling in the chest, a lift in the heart, a beam in the eyes. If he were a single guy without complications and if she weren't involved somewhere else, she would have been exactly the kind of woman he'd want to sit down and get to know.

"Well, it's been a long day," he said to Brie. "See you around."

Conner knew he was as welcome as anyone in that construction trailer for a cup of coffee or maybe a little conversation, but he resisted. He packed a lunch and filled his own thermos of coffee back at his little cabin. The bathrooms were functional in the houses he was working on with Dan, and the weather was warming up and drying out.

It was Leslie he avoided for the first two weeks he worked for Paul Haggerty. Every time he saw her he found her even prettier than the day before. Her dark eyes, so unusual on her fair face with light hair, twinkled when she smiled, and her laugh was as sweet as a melody. When he was around her, though seldom, he enjoyed her bright mood. Yet he had a dark streak of disapproval—the "Sunday-school teacher" was messing with a married man. Not something that gave him a warm flush of desire for her. But he couldn't deny it—he was attracted.

Still, there were things he couldn't help but like about her. Her sense of humor, for one thing. She made all the guys laugh, even when she was barking orders at them. Even Conner, who hadn't been a real happy-go-lucky kind of guy lately, found himself smiling. Despite her feminine appearance, she ran a tight ship. She insisted people wipe their feet, clean their coffee mugs, and although she was one woman among many men, God help the one who left the toilet seat up!

After a couple of weeks he was starting to feel the strain of his solitary life. Trying to go low-profile caused him to act aloof and unconnected. Sometimes he went to Jack's for a beer and dinner after work, but more often he drove down the mountain to Fortuna. He'd get groceries and something easy from a deli for dinner in his cabin. Occasionally he'd try a different restaurant or stop at a diner or coffee shop. And he'd always sit in his truck in the parking lot where his cell reception was good and have a conversation with Katie before she and the boys went to bed. He had to call them early—Katie was on eastern time.

That always sent a pang of sadness through him, that she liked to sleep to avoid long, lonely evenings. His beautiful sister should be among friends, should have a boyfriend. That he was lonely didn't really matter. He couldn't stand to think of Katie that way.

After talking to Katie on Saturday afternoon, he decided on a cup of coffee and a slice of pie. There was Starbucks, but he liked that place where he'd met Brie—a gaudy, girlie, turquoise place filled with fragile-looking furniture he was afraid to sit on. He always chose to sit up at the counter on a sturdy stool. Once there, he ordered his coffee and pie.

And she came in. Leslie. She didn't notice him. She was wearing some kind of leotard thing under her coat, and her hair looked kind of all over the place. And she did what she did best, laughed with the man behind the coffee bar who served her. They laughed as if they were best friends. Then she took her tall iced tea and her small muffin and went over to one of those delicate-looking miniature couches and settled in to check the messages on her cell phone. She must do as so many mountain residents did—check messages and return calls when and where there was reception.

Conner raised one finger as he would in a bar, and the guy came over. "Can I have that coffee and pie to go?" he said.

"Sure," the young blond guy said. "Everything all right?"

"Perfect. I've got a roasted chicken in the truck and I'm going to take it home and nuke it for dinner, then chase it with the key lime." He tried out a smile.

"Sounds lovely." And the man turned to get a paper cup and plastic carton of key lime pie.

"Conner?"

Damn. She was standing right beside him. He looked into her eyes, caught that delicious smile and thought, *Crap.* It zinged him. Gave him a little shock of awareness in all his male parts. "Hi," he said.

"What a surprise. I never expected to run into someone from Virgin River here. There's a yoga studio around the corner. I love yoga. I come at least twice a week."

So that explained the leotard. "I don't know anything about yoga," he admitted.

She laughed, genuinely amused. "I'd be kind of surprised if you did. Grab your coffee and join me."

"I probably better not."

"Oh?" she asked. "You have plans?"

He was struck speechless. How did you answer that? There'd been a time Conner, as Danny, had been pretty smooth with women. He'd known how to charm them or how to at least get a phone number, but it had been a long time since he'd had a woman other than his sister in his life. This lying about everything wasn't easy for him—he was used to shooting straight from the hip. With Leslie it was even more complicated—he found her attractive, and she was doing the boss. "I just don't want to get in the middle of anything."

"In the middle...?" She frowned. "What in the world are you talking about?"

"You know," he said, giving a shrug. "Your...relationship."

"What relationship? I'm single."

His brow furrowed. "Right," he said.

She continued to frown; her eyes had narrowed. "What relationship?" she demanded.

"Well...I... Looked like maybe you and the boss..." That was as much as he got out. "It's none of my business." And he thought, *I'll be dead in a month, as terrible as I am at lying, at covering up.*

She was still frowning. The blond guy behind the coffee bar put Conner's coffee and pie on the counter. "Grab your coffee and come with me," she said. And allowing for no discussion or refusal, she turned and walked away, expecting him to follow.

"Crap," he muttered. Then he let out a breath and did as she said. She sat down on a little bitty couch with spindly legs, and opposite was a chair with equally skinny, curvy legs. He looked down at her, pie in one hand and coffee in the other. "I don't know, Leslie. I don't think I should sit on that."

"It's stronger than it looks. Sit," she commanded. And he did so. "Paul is an old friend," she said. "I worked for his family in Oregon for ten years. I was trying to relocate but didn't have a new job, and he offered me one here. There is nothing the least bit inappropriate between us."

"Okay. Like I said, none of my business anyway," he said, standing to escape.

"Sit."

He did as she told him.

"Why would you assume something like that about me?"

"I…" He made a face. "The first night I was in town, I was at that little bar and you and Paul… Well, I didn't know who either of you were, but he had his arm around you. Kissed you. It looked like maybe you were crying or something. You had a drink and left together. Like a couple."

She was quiet for a moment, her lips pursed. "What nerve," she said.

"Hey, you don't owe me an explanation. It's nothing to me."

"Listen to me. Carefully. I was married while I worked for Haggerty Construction in Grants Pass. My husband and I divorced and he moved on very quickly. Actually, he moved on *before* we were divorced. He remarried right away, got his new wife pregnant. He's going to be a father. And me? Why of course I get to be friends with the charming couple. He would probably even like me to be the baby's godmother. I would have gone to hell to get out of there. This job was a lifesaver. Paul was a lifesaver. I might've been emotional about that."

Conner was quiet for a long moment, and then, inexplicably, he smiled. "Seriously?"

"Which part?" she asked, taking a sip of her tea.

"He wanted you to be friends with his new wife?"

"Yes. And be so happy for them."

"Wow," he said, still smiling. "What balls."

She cleared her throat. "Yeah. Well. He was so fucking civil even my parents thought I should just get over it. Sorry—I don't usually use that word."

"Sounds kind of apropos where the ex is concerned."

"You have *no* idea. I couldn't get away from them in that town. Paul was very sweet to help me out. I can't remember crying or getting kissed in Jack's Bar, but—"

"It looked kind of...cozy. Like maybe he was the boyfriend and the two of you were having some kind of...misunderstanding. And you have such a close— I guess I don't have much of an imagination, I could only think of one possibility."

"It's a very rude and unflattering assumption to make

about a woman. The last thing I would ever do is get involved with a married man."

"Hey, I apologize. I'm really sorry about what you're going through, but it makes a lot more sense that I'd think you were a couple than that the boss is comforting you because your ex..." He chuckled and rubbed a hand over his goatee. "Wants to be friends, does he? Wow. And I take it you don't feel like being friends?"

She glared at him. Her eyes were mere slits. "I feel like killing him, but the hell of it is, I'd probably grieve him. And pay for his funeral. I used to love him. And now I completely hate him, but not enough."

"Shew," Conner said. "I get that."

"You do?"

"I'm divorced. I didn't like it too much, either," he said. "And we're never going to be friends." And Leslie's anger at the very idea that she would mess with a married man—this was going to make fighting the attraction a lot tougher.

"I'm thirty-two," she said. "People tell me how young I am, but I've had a little trouble with passing thirty, ending an eight-year marriage, feeling like I'm starting my life over at this age. I didn't mind starting my life at twenty-two, but at thirty-two? Not so happy about it. And I highly resent the circumstances. To be frank, I'm not real happy that you pegged me as a cheater. Didn't anyone ever teach you not to jump to conclusions?"

"Didn't I apologize?" he asked. "I might be a little

cynical. I'm thirty-five and I'm not real happy about starting over, either. Job gone, divorced, relocated, et cetera."

"With how many of the guys at work did you share your speculation about Paul and me?" she asked.

"No one. I don't gossip," he said, his heavy brows drawing together in a frown. "Look, I don't blame you for being offended, but could you lighten up? I didn't mean to—"

They both turned to look as someone cleared his throat. The blond barista behind the counter was glaring at them. "I like to close by six," he said. "Do you suppose you could take the argument to Starbucks?"

As Leslie and Conner left the coffee shop, he asked, "All right, are we straight now? You accept my apology?"

"Probably. But I admit, it bothers me. It makes me wonder how many other people assume there's more to my relationship with Paul Haggerty than a very long-term, very proper friendship."

"Listen, I'm a little cynical," Conner said. "Sometimes it's not easy."

"Get over it," she said, opening her car door.

"I'll work on that. And I'll be behind you on the way back up the mountain. Not too close, but close enough to make sure you get back to town all right."

"I don't need an escort," she said.

"I'm sure you're extremely capable, but I happen to live there." And he closed her door after she was seated. "Jesus," he muttered. "Hardheaded enough?"

* * *

Leslie drove back to Virgin River with Conner's lights behind her at a respectable distance.

For Leslie, it had been over eighteen months since she'd even entertained the notion of a man in her life. She'd been grieving and damning Greg Adams, the happy-go-lucky ex, all that time. She'd been void of desire. In fact she had made up her mind that it would be a very long time before she'd let a man get close, if ever, because only a fool wouldn't be afraid to trust a man again. It would risk a broken heart. The very idea that someone thought she'd settle for a married man bit deep.

The kind of guy in her very distant future had not resembled Paul Haggerty in any way; Paul was more like a brother to her. Now Conner Danson... That was another story. If he wasn't such an ass, he would be ir-resistible.

This surprised her. Conner was nothing like the kind of man who had attracted her before. He was nothing like Greg, which should have probably recommended him, except for that ass thing. There was also the fact that Leslie was determined to paste her confidence back together with*out* the assistance of a man.

Greg had been, still was, movie-star pretty with dark hair, beautiful hazel eyes flecked with gold, a trim build with strong shoulders and arms and a smile that made girls tremble. He was fussy about what he wore and drove, and his two primary goals in life were to be rich and prominent. Leslie suspected his new lawyer wife had tipped him on how to rat-hole some money because he still *looked* pretty well-off despite escaping alimony, and while they'd been married, he'd always brought home enough money to afford all the things he wanted.

During their eight-year marriage, she'd gotten used to women flirting with him, yet she'd never doubted his fidelity, never. Greg had been amused by flirtation; clearly he enjoyed it, but it never seemed as though he'd act on it. A very attractive waitress once wrote her phone number on the check, even though they were dining together. He had looked at it, laughed, crumpled it and said, "As if."

Conner was a whole different kind of guy. *Pretty* hardly described him—Conner was taller, broader, stronger. He didn't have those classic good looks but rather willful brown hair that he kept short, a square jaw, crystal-blue eyes that peered suspiciously from behind thick lashes. He had a cute dimple in his left cheek and a nice smile, though not a frequent one, and he could effect a powerful scowl. The mustache and goatee gave him a mysterious air; he stroked it as if he wasn't quite used to it. He was much more rugged than Greg, but then he was a construction worker and he looked like one—jeans and steel-toed boots and a ton of testosterone. She'd seen him wearing the tool belt and even though she'd been around a million tool belts, he'd worn his especially well. He looked, frankly, as if he could tear the door off a car if he needed to.

Leslie had worked around construction workers for the past ten years, and, while they came in all shapes and sizes, there was something about Conner that gave her shivers. She couldn't put her finger on it. It might be the way he couldn't seem to lie or cover up; what passed through his brain shot out of his mouth. He thought she was doing the boss and couldn't just act as if he didn't notice? She'd been watching him around the job; she couldn't help it. He would be almost somber until something amused him, and then his face lit up—same reaction, his feelings kind of bubbled to the surface. He couldn't seem to hide his stunned amusement that a guy would divorce, remarry, knock up his new wife and expect the ex-wife to be okay with it all. *What balls.* Very straightforward. *Uncomplicated.* Yes, that was it—he seemed uncomplicated. After Greg, that was so inviting.

Oh, man, the last thing she needed was to get attracted to some construction worker who was temporary at best.

Then her eyes widened. Maybe the best thing in the world *would be* a temporary construction worker. No expectations. No disappointments. No one to get in the way of her mission to rebuild her confidence and self-esteem.

Conner followed Leslie at a distance so as not to blind her with the headlights of his truck in her rearview mirror. And he thought—boy, was she pissed. That was probably a good thing because he should really get over it, the attraction. He'd been warned by Brie, no relationships during this hiatus.

But the more sense he talked into himself, the more he wanted to get closer to that tough, hardheaded broad. The more he wanted her, in every physical way. Stupid idea. His life was just too *complicated*.

Four

Despite his caution, Conner caught a few minutes with Leslie every day that next week. And she grew more agreeable around him until finally she smiled at him and that caution melted like butter in the hot sun. He was back in her good graces.

With that awareness, he agreed quickly when, at the end of the week, Dan said, "Come on, let's head for the office. Les made cookies. Bring your lunch."

"Sounds good," he said.

When they got inside, Dan put his plastic lunch bucket on the table and immediately headed down the hall to the office Leslie used. She followed him back out to the kitchen.

"Hi, Conner," she said.

"Leslie," he said with a nod.

She pulled a canvas tote out of the refrigerator and began to empty the contents onto the table—a half sandwich, an apple, a yogurt, a container of green tea. "How's it going over there?" she asked, tilting her head in the direction of the two houses they'd been working on.

"We're finishing up bathrooms this week," Dan said. "We might take a couple of days next week, but that shouldn't hold up work on the exterior. Paul mentioned a remodel in Redway that he wants to tackle next. What did he say to you?" Dan asked.

"He said we're moving the trailer pretty soon. He's got a sixty-five-hundred-square foot custom home northeast of Virgin River ready to pour."

Conner knew what that meant. It would be a long time before he'd be working on the interior of that custom job. Probably months. He might even be back in Sacramento to testify before it came time to do the custom house on the same property as the trailer. He wouldn't be running into Leslie unless he drove to wherever that trailer was located to pick up his check. Even that wasn't necessary. Paul would readily bring paychecks to Jack's.

"Things have really improved since you've been here, Les," Dan said, nodding at the big plate of cookies covered with Saran on the plywood table.

"I know," she agreed. "Cookies and moderate cleanliness."

"And paperwork on time, like estimates and contracts. I'm so damn glad Paul finally got around to hiring full-time office help."

"It's nice to work with Paul again. Even for a little while."

"A little while?" Dan asked.

She ripped open her yogurt. "I don't mean to make it sound like I'm leaving tomorrow. It's just that my parents are in their late sixties and one of these days... Maybe I should say one of these *years* they're going to need me. Right now they're in great health, never slow down for a second, and Grants Pass isn't very far away so we can visit each other frequently. But they're sixty-eight, I'm their only child, I assume I'll have to return to Oregon."

"What's your best guess?" Conner blurted out. "Months or years?"

"I promised Paul six months, maybe more," she said. "Unless there's an emergency back home, of course. And...excepting emergencies...I'm not going to leave him high and dry. Vanessa would kill me."

Conner flashed his dimple in a smile, but he looked down at his sandwich. That gave him something to work with. Yes, sir.

Six months. He was a patient man. Most of the time.

"Didn't I hear you're planning a wedding?" she asked Dan.

"Not exactly. What we're planning is a marriage. Cheryl and I have been together a couple of years, this past year dedicated to finishing our house together with a little help from friends. We're in now, though still finishing things, and should be done by June. Then Cheryl wants a nice, quiet, private ceremony while we're on our way up to the San Juan Islands for some serious fishing." He laughed. "Gotta love a woman like Cheryl.

She's not only pretty and practical, she's more fun than I deserve."

"What about your families?" Leslie asked. "Won't they want some kind of wedding?"

"That's just it—our families are gone now and it's just us. I think our friends will help us celebrate the new house with a housewarming, but we want to go off alone for the rest."

Families gone...that turned over in Conner's head a bit. His family was gone temporarily, but he'd get them back. At least until Katie met someone who would take over as husband and the boys' father, and then it would be time for her to make a new life. And while they were very close, it wasn't as though Conner told her everything that was happening in his life. Back in the day, if he dated, he didn't run the details by his sister. He was more likely to mention it after the fact. Even with his wife, Katie hadn't met Samantha until they were talking about marriage.

But somehow the idea that he might never tell Katie about Leslie ate at him. Bothered him. Leslie was the kind of girl you showed off to your family.

"You're very quiet," Leslie pointed out to him.

He chewed and swallowed. "Good cookies," he said. Then he gave enough of a smile to cover his discomfort. When he looked at her, his cheeks felt warm. He hoped he wasn't blushing like a boy.

He went back to work with Dan and conversation focused only on the work they were doing. Below the chatter, Conner thought about his next move—he was helpless in fighting the idea. Finally he decided—he was going to ask Leslie when she had that yoga class again because he might drop by that coffee shop at about the same time. They could sit on those girlie chairs and talk, without Dan or any other crew coming around. Maybe they could talk without her hating him. That would be a start.

He looked at his watch. It was four. They'd be knocking off soon, and he didn't want to miss her if she quit and went home. "I'm going to walk over to the office," he told Dan. "I have a question for Leslie."

"Take your time," Dan said.

But as Conner walked out of the construction, he saw a car pull up. It was a shiny black late-model Cadillac with Oregon plates, which pulled up to the trailer and parked next to Leslie's SUV. A good-looking man in a wool coat and shiny shoes got out. He looked around, saw Conner in the front doorway, took in his surroundings and entered the trailer.

Conner had a very good idea who that might be. He wouldn't barge in on them, but he wasn't going far. He leaned against the porch post of the house in progress, near enough to rescue her if needed.

A half hour later, Dan joined him outside with his lunch pail. "You didn't get far."

"A guy went into the office," Conner said. "He's got Oregon plates," he added, indicating the car. Not a construction worker's car, that was for sure. "He might be here to see Leslie, so I'm waiting until he leaves."

"He could be here to see Paul," Dan said. "He could be a buyer or potential buyer."

"Then he'd have an appointment and Paul would be here."

Dan grinned. "You're not just another pretty face, are you, Conner? Want me to wait with you?"

Way to go low-profile, Conner chided himself. "No, thanks. I can take him."

Dan just laughed. "Then close up when you're done, will you?"

"Absolutely."

Leslie was nearly finished with the payroll books on the computer when she heard the door to the trailer open. She was used to crews coming and going, to Paul popping in now and then. But then she heard, "Leslie?"

She dropped her head on the desk. God. No.

"Leslie?"

She took a deep breath, pushed back her chair and stood up. She moved to the doorway of her office and looked down the long hall. There he was. Shit! "Greg, what are you doing here?" she said more patiently than she felt.

"Well, what do you think I'm doing here? You ran out on me with no forwarding address. You changed your cell number!"

She walked down the hall toward him, shaking her head. "Greg, we've been divorced over a year. You're remarried. Your new wife is pregnant. I didn't run out on you—I *moved.* I no longer have a relationship with you."

"Now see, that's just crazy! Of course we have a relationship, a very important one, just a different one than we had a couple of years ago."

It was exactly this kind of talk that had pushed her over the edge. And while it used to just break her heart, she'd had enough. "Are you insane?" she demanded. "Are you seriously nuts? Because it's different all right—I don't like you anymore, don't you get that? I don't want to be in touch with you. I don't want us to be friends. You wanted a new life, a different life. Go home! Wallow in it."

Now he was doing the head-shaking. "Leslie, what's happened to you? We're going to have to work on that. We're much too civilized to have hard feelings like this between us after all the good years we've had. We're going to get past the misunderstandings and forge a new, stronger friendship. I care about you. You're very important to me. *Very* important!"

She stared at him in disbelief that had become common for her when faced with Greg. "This is why I moved. Because you need medication. Listen to me carefully," she said, stepping toward him. "You cheated on me. You left me. You somehow conned me out of my half of our community property, you remarried and your new wife is pregnant with the baby you didn't want to have with me. If everyone in my life cared about me that much I would be the most pathetic creature on the face of the earth."

"The way you look at things," he muttered disparagingly.

"How did you find me?"

"I asked everyone we knew. Your parents wouldn't tell me, your old boss wouldn't tell me—"

"And did they tell you *why* they wouldn't tell you? I asked them not to. It's because of conversations like this one that I moved! So, who told?"

"One of the crew for Haggerty's said he heard you went to work for Paul in Virgin River."

"And you drove down here?" she asked, astonished. "Why didn't you just call the site?"

"I want you to look me in the eye, Leslie, and tell me we can't ever be on good terms. Because it kills me to think you hate me."

She took another step toward him. "We can be on good terms, Greg," she said with more confidence than she'd had even a few weeks ago. "As long as I never have to talk to you or see your face again. Now go home and leave me alone."

"I want to make this right, because I—"

"I know. Because you care about me. You're too late to make it right. You made your choice and I made mine and I'm done."

"I wish there was some way I could make you understand. Everything changed in an instant. I became a different man with different needs, with different expectations. It was a transition, Leslie. It wasn't something I thought about or planned. It was as if—"

In a second he was going to say, *I'd never been in*

love like this before. He'd said it to her before, and she could still feel the ache. "Go. *Leave!*"

"Now, Leslie, listen to reason...."

She marched over to the kitchen sink, pulled the fire extinguisher off the wall, freed the hose and aimed it at him.

"Okay, now you're acting unbalanced," he said.

"If you don't get in your car and head for Grants Pass immediately, I'm going to mess up your pretty cashmere coat. And your perfect *hair!*"

"Now look—"

She fired at his shiny John Lobbs.

"Hey!" he yelled, jumping back.

"Seriously, on the count of three. One, two—"

"You've lost it, Leslie," he said, but he was backing toward the door. "You've never acted like this. I'm worried about you."

"Then give me a real wide berth," she advised. "Three!"

He nearly fell out the door.

Conner watched as Paul Haggerty was just pulling up to the trailer. Greg Adams was standing behind his car, trunk open, cleaning his shoes with a rag he'd pulled off his golf clubs. Paul screeched to a stop and jumped out of the truck. "What the hell are you doing here?"

"I couldn't find Leslie anywhere in Grants Pass, and I heard she came to work for you, so I drove down," he said impatiently. He showed Paul his golf towel. "She shot at me with the fire extinguisher!"

Paul rocked back on his heels and laughed. He tilted his head back and bellowed. Paul was much taller and stronger than Greg. And at the moment, much happier. "Did she now?"

"What's going on here? Why would she do that?"

"Because, shit for brains, she'd like you to disappear and leave her alone. I'm sure she'd like to stuff you in a hole, but since that isn't going to happen, second choice is you go home to your new wife and leave her the hell alone. You get that?"

Greg slammed his trunk closed. "What is the matter with everyone? I'm trying to be a gentleman! Leslie was my wife for eight years! I want to be sure she's taken care of!"

"Best way to do that is to skip the cheating part," Paul sagely advised.

"I wish I could find a way to explain about that. My whole life changed in a second and it was like... Oh, never mind, what's done is done. I'm tired of saying that I'm sorry as all hell and would change it if I could, but some things just happen. Right now all I care about is that Leslie and I can be on civil terms. That's very important to me."

Paul got in his face, which meant he had to look down a little. "You better hear this, Adams. Pay attention. Go away and leave the girl alone. Copy? Now I'm going in my office and if she's upset or crying I'm going to hunt you down and beat the shit outta you."

Greg stiffened indignantly. "Threats, Paul. People get in trouble for talk like that."

"If I have to drive all the way to Grants Pass," Paul added. "Get outta here."

Then Paul went to the trailer, opened the door and stepped up. Before the door closed Conner heard him yell, "Don't shoot!"

Conner chuckled and went into the new construction to gather up his belongings and lock up.

Yeah, there were things about this place to like.

The showdown with the ex put Conner in a very social mood, and he went to Jack's Bar. He happened to run into Paul Haggerty, which was just perfect. Since Paul had seen Conner standing in the doorway of the house in progress, Conner asked after Leslie. "I didn't have any details," Conner said. "But the idea of this guy I'd never seen before going into that trailer where Leslie was alone, well, I decided to stick around to be sure everything was all right."

"Thanks for that, Conner. Around here it just doesn't occur to me we have to be watchful. I guess I forget there are people around we shouldn't trust." It didn't take Paul long to spill the basics of Leslie's story, not knowing Conner heard it. "That was her ex-husband and he's one of the reasons she preferred working in Virgin River to staying in Grants Pass, which has always been her home. He just won't go away quietly."

Jack put a beer on the bar for Paul. "Shot him but he just won't die?" he asked.

"Something like that. But I ran him off and checked

on Les. She was a little pissed, but fine." He grinned. "She turned the fire extinguisher on him."

"No kidding?" Jack asked with a laugh. "I knew I liked her."

During the course of the conversation, Paul mentioned that he'd rented Leslie a little house he'd fixed up and it was just a couple of blocks from the bar. And then, beer done, it was time for Paul to get home to dinner.

Conner had his dinner at the bar, and when he was finished and it was time to go home, he just couldn't shake off that social mood. He had an irresistible urge to check on Leslie himself; he just couldn't talk himself out of it. He drove around town, and it didn't take long to spot her yellow Volkswagen SUV in front of a small house. He parked on the street behind it and went to the door.

She opened it and tilted her head at him. "What are you doing here?"

"I was watching the trailer today, making sure the guy in the shiny Caddy wasn't giving you any trouble."

"You were?"

He nodded. "I was headed over to ask you something when he pulled up and went inside."

She hesitated for a second. "Come in, Conner," she said.

"I don't want to impose," he said. But he entered the little house quickly, before she could change her mind. He was quite impressed. It was a very homey, attractive place that seemed perfect for her, and it was completely settled, pictures hung, framed photos on the buffet, a dried flower arrangement and place mats on the dining table, a throw on the end of the sectional sofa. He followed her into the kitchen where he could see Dan's handiwork in the granite countertops and darkly stained oak cupboards.

She had been sitting at the kitchen table with the newspaper spread out and a cup of tea beside it.

"So," she said. "That was him—the cheerful ex, wondering why we can't be more chummy."

"He came out of the trailer with some white foam on his pretty shoes," Conner said, and he couldn't suppress a grin.

"I lost it. His utter lack of remorse, the way he takes so little responsibility for what happened, like we should all be grown-ups and overlook it. 'But Leslie,'" she mimicked. "'I can't help what I feel. It's not as if I planned for my feelings to change.'" She snorted. "Is that accurate? That we can't help what we feel?" she asked Conner, an imploring look on her face.

"Probably," he said. He hooked his thumbs into the front pockets of his jeans. "But we can help what we do."

She took a breath. "Would you like some tea?"

"No, thanks. But I'll sit a minute if you feel like talking. If you want to get it off your chest."

She indicated the chair opposite hers, and she sat down. "I don't know if this will make sense, but one of the reasons I took the job down here is so I could *stop* talking about it. Well, that's not true at all—I was far from done talking about it, but my friends and family were done listening. Who can blame them after a year and a half? You know, I have friends who divorced, who have kids they have to co-parent with the ex, who have very manageable relationships with exes, and I admire them for it! What is wrong with me? Why am I not the least bit grateful that Greg wants us to be friends?"

Conner shrugged before he said, "Maybe because he considers himself totally justified?"

"You're right. That whole business of how he just couldn't help himself, he had no control—that's what makes me feel like crap!"

Conner smiled at her.

"Should you smile at me when I say I feel like crap?"

He shook his head, but the smile remained. "I was just thinking, I'm not making any excuses for him— he's a dog—but that feeling? That you just can't help yourself? That's a feeling I like."

"Is that a fact?" She braced an elbow on the table and rested her chin in her hand.

He nodded. "Yeah, it's good. I can still control my actions when I feel that way, however."

"And you do that, how?"

He leaned toward her. "By being strong." He leaned back. "There's something I thought you'd want to know—I don't think it'll be a problem for you, but Paul told me and Jack that the guy who came to the trailer today was your ex and that you shot him with the fire extinguisher."

"Swell," she said.

"Jack was impressed. Paul didn't give any more personal details and I didn't let on that I knew anything. But jeez, Les, it really made me want to be a chick."

She lifted her eyebrows. "How so?"

"That was awesome. A guy couldn't get away with that. I wish I could've hosed down my ex, but I had some serious training in how women had to be treated, even if they were very bad."

"I guess I'm going to have this reputation now...." she speculated.

He gave his head a little shake. "I think you're going to have admiration. Paul obviously feels very protective of you."

"The whole Haggerty family has been really good to me, especially through this. Paul's dad, the founder of Haggerty Construction, is a tough old bear of a guy who adores his wife. They're the most wonderful grandparents, and I take it they have very strong feelings about loyalty and commitment issues."

"I hope most people do," Conner said.

She reached across the table and touched his hand lightly. "Conner, I don't think most people do," she said. "I think maybe it's a rare and admirable quality."

He felt a surge of heat at her soft touch, and he looked down at her hand. It was so perfect, her nails bleached white and filed short. Her skin was flawless. He wouldn't mind feeling those perfect, soft hands all over him.

"Here's something you might get a kick out of," Conner said. "Paul got right up in your ex's grille and told him he was going in the trailer, and if you were upset he was going to hunt him down and beat the shit out of him, even if he had to go all the way to Grants Pass to do it."

Leslie smiled happily. "He did?"

"He did. I haven't known Paul very long, but I've never seen him look so scary. I thought it was a great idea."

Leslie laughed lightly. "And to think I almost opened fire on him!"

"I heard him yell 'Don't shoot!'"

"I wasn't putting that fire extinguisher down until I heard Greg's car drive away. I should have done that a long time ago. It was the first time I got so angry."

"If he comes back and bothers you again, he's mentally challenged."

"You'd think so, huh?" she said. "Conner, I think Greg is a narcissist. He's not a mean guy, at least not overtly. But everything is all about him, I see that now. He pays a lot of compliments, sucks up a lot, strokes a lot of people—influential and even not so influential— and it's all so he gets what he wants."

"And what the hell could he possibly want with you?"

"The perfect divorce. He has lots of image concerns. While we were married he wanted everyone to think we had the perfect marriage. He said he hoped to be a role model, to be admired, in business, in relationships and hopefully one day in a larger political arena than even the City Council. It's very important to him to be respected. When I caught him cheating, he fessed up at once and all within the course of one hour explained how he'd fallen in love despite his intentions, he couldn't help it, would be divorcing me and marrying her but that we would always be best friends because he would never stop loving me. He would just have to stop being married to me because his feelings had changed and he was going through a life transition. Oh—and as he put it—I wouldn't want him to live a lie or be unhappy for the rest of his life, would I?"

"Wow." Conner thought he couldn't be more surprised by things like this, especially after what he'd gone through with Samantha. "Do you mind if I ask you? If it's none of my business, just say so. But how'd you catch him?"

"Modern technology and celebrity gossip. I thought the whole idea that someone who was cheating on his wife would have a lot of incriminating texts on his cell phone was completely ludicrous. Especially famous someones. It actually made me laugh! How could anyone be that stupid? So just out of curiosity while Greg was in the shower, I read his texts. I didn't expect to find anything. A lot were from me and his office and bingo, a lot of sexy snippets with someone named Allison. While he was blow-drying his hair, I texted her from his phone. I told her I wanted to lick her whole body, and she texted back that it was right where he left it, waiting and ready."

Conner couldn't help it, the laughter rumbled out of him and made his eyes water. "You didn't do that," he said.

"I did so. Greg was mortified."

"Wow," Conner said again, wiping his eyes. "Yeah. Mortified. He must have wanted to be caught."

"I don't know about that, but he was definitely *ready* to be caught. It turned out we had very few assets. And his new wife is an attorney."

Conner shook his head. "There must have been no sharp objects in the house...."

"I was in shock for a while. I actually thought he'd come back to me. That didn't last long." She sipped her tea. "It was nice of you to check on me, Conner. But I'm fine. Totally fine."

"You're not in shock anymore."

"Indeed not. So what did you want to ask me?"

"Oh. That. I was wondering if you were headed to that yoga class tomorrow, since it's Saturday. Because I could be headed to that coffee shop at about the same time. And maybe this time we could get off on a better foot, as in, you not furious with me."

"No," she said. "Tomorrow I'm getting my exercise in the yard. I'm planting flowers. It's spring. And I'm settling in."

Five

Saturday started with a summons to Brie's house. His landlord, Luke Riordan, the owner of the cabins, knocked on Conner's door and said, "I have a message for you to call Brie when you're up."

"I'm up," he said. "Is your phone available?"

Brie wanted him to come to brunch. He honestly didn't know if that was code for something else, he just accepted the invitation. It turned out to be code for something else.

"I'll give you breakfast," Brie said. "But you're going to call Max from my office phone. I spoke to him an hour ago. He just wants to update you."

Regis Mathis, out on bail and his case in the capable hands of one of the best defense attorneys in the West, seemed to be keeping a very low-profile. When he was seen in public, he had lots of men around him. Bodyguards, perhaps.

"How is it he's out of jail? I saw him kill a man and

then he threatened to kill me. And we know he burned down the store!"

"Unfortunately, we don't know as much about that as you might think. It's not his voice on your answering machine, which should come as no surprise."

"No, the surprise is why he would dirty his own hands in the killing when obviously he didn't need to. He was locked up when the store burned down, so we know he knows people who could do his killing for him."

"I have some theories about that," Max said. "I'm not at liberty to discuss it any further—we're still investigating. Confidentially, we're looking into some connections between Mathis and Randolph. But it's early...."

"When can we get this circus over with?" Conner asked.

"Looks like a trial date of May twenty-fifth if there aren't any more defense delay tactics, but I think you can count on the defense doing everything they can to slow the process. They've already been hammering us with motions."

"Great," Conner said.

"Listen, they're caught and they know it. The blood in the car belonged to the victim, it was a good warrant, there's an impartial eyewitness, there might have been trouble between the two men—therefore motive... There's no way out of this for him, Conner. But he's not going to go down quickly or quietly. You have to prepare yourself for that."

"How long could it take?" Conner asked.

"I'd hate to speculate. The judge is a hanging judge and won't tolerate a lot of paper delays, that's in our favor. Just sit tight and let's hope for the best. Our biggest problem is going to be jury selection."

"Why?" Conner wanted to know.

"Because aside from a little legal gambling, this guy is squeaky clean."

"I thought there were tax issues...."

"Because he's rich. And he's been exonerated. But we're on it—we have top-notch jury consultants."

Brie was more forthcoming over scrambled eggs. "The reality is, there have been high-profile cases that have taken years to get to trial. This guy of yours, he's not a big Mafia boss or anything. He must have some interesting underworld connections to get your store burned down and threaten you, but still, he's a fairly ordinary citizen. Well-known, but not well-known as a criminal. I wouldn't expect it to be that protracted."

"What about your defendant?" Conner asked. "The rapist?"

"Hah. Went straight to trial, no bail. He started out with a public defender, then scored a decent pro bono attorney, but he was nailed before they even got started. Even so, the defense had important evidence thrown out or rendered inadmissible, like the fact that I was the A.D.A. who prosecuted him and failed to convict, making him not only a random serial rapist but acting out revenge on an officer of the court. But in the end, they slipped up and that information got in. What I think, Conner, is that it might not get started before

June, but I bet your testimony will be done and you'll be reunited with your family and ready to start over by the end of summer, at the latest."

He was quiet for a long moment. "And then where are we going to go?"

"Is going home out of the question? Because once this is over—"

"When it's over, he'll forget I testified against him? You stayed here after your trial," he pointed out.

She let a small huff of laughter escape. "The rapist is a pervert and animal. He wasn't connected. And this town? My brother, Jack, and the guys around here? Mike, Paul, the Riordans, to name a few? If he even poked his head out from behind a tree, he'd be so dead, so fast. This is a place that takes care of their own, Conner. And it's not just a place of great loyalty, but of incredible strength and prowess. I think every last one of them is military-trained and at least a marksman if not a decorated sniper. I'm afraid your guy is a little more complicated than that. But still, this is probably one of the safest places I know, just based on the skills of the local population."

"Hmm," he said, thinking. "I have an army marksman ribbon..."

"You know what's wrong with that idea. Right?" Brie asked. When he didn't answer immediately, she did. "If some stranger wanders into town and looks at you funny, you could get spooked. You could run into him after dark and shoot him just because you're spooked.

I'd rather you rely on us—Mike and I. Please, anyone suspicious turns up, call Mike."

"I wish I were the one protecting Katie," he said.

"And the problem with that is that you protecting Katie brings her and the little boys into specific relief, making all four of you stand out. Conner, just build kitchens and bathrooms for a couple of months. Huh? You and Katie and the kids will be together again soon. Right now, having you here and Katie on the other side of the country just makes sense."

After breakfast Conner drove to Ferndale, a beautiful little Victorian town full of bed-and-breakfasts and shops. He sat on a bench on the main street and had a conversation with Katie, who was at the YMCA with the boys in a town very far away. Conner resisted the urge to tell her about his conversations with the D.A. and Brie. All that was important to him was hearing the happiness in her voice. She liked her job, she had friends, she thought maybe she had a crush on her boss who had taken her to dinner, and the boys were having so much fun at their new school. Andy was a little too shy and Mitch a little too not.

"Sounds like you're getting along fine," he said.

"Are you so disappointed that I'm not sobbing myself to sleep every night?" she asked him. "I do miss you, Danny."

"Names," he reminded her.

"I'm sure we're fine. I do miss you. The boys miss you and love talking to you. I'd put them on right now, but they're tumbling. They were on the trampoline and now they're on the mats. Are you getting along all right? Having fun, like you promised you'd try to?"

"Well…there is this girl…."

She choked. "Girl?"

"Woman," he corrected. "Woman. I met her at work and she's nice. Pretty. Funny."

"Well, my God, a girl," Katie said and burst into hysterical laughter.

"And this is so goddamn funny?" he asked indignantly.

"Because it's just what you need and I never thought you'd have the guts. Oh, go for it!"

"She doesn't like me that much yet," he said. "Which is probably just as well. I'd end up just leaving her high and dry with no explanation," he returned almost angrily.

"Now, calm down, that isn't what's going to happen at all. Not only will there be an explanation when you finally do your thing, there will probably be newspaper accounts and TV coverage. By the time all this is resolved, you'll be able to tell her everything and bring her along with the happy party that includes me and two tumbling-soccer-T-ball players! Even if it makes more sense for her to let you go, it's still a very good idea to enjoy yourself a little right now. You have no idea how happy that makes me."

"Because if I could just hook up, you wouldn't have to be stuck with me?" he asked her.

"Oh, my God, you can be such a drama mama. I have never been stuck with you—it's been quite the opposite and you know it. Nothing would make me happier than to hear you'd given it up to some pretty, funny small-town woman. I'm on board with that. I just wish it would go as well with the dentist."

"Are you getting involved?" Conner asked.

"Oh, no. It's very professional," she assured him. "I wasn't the only employee he took to dinner. He also invited the office manager and his sister. It's just friendly. But I think he's the kind of guy I like. Stable and reliable. He loves children."

"Don't leave him alone with the boys!"

She chuckled again. God, how he missed her laugh. "Ah, I don't think I'm going to be asking my boss to babysit."

When they hung up he spent two minutes feeling ridiculous and twenty minutes remembering how level she had always made his life. And then he saw a shop owner putting out flats of flowers across the street. It had been a very long time since he'd taken a girl flowers.

Leslie had bought a flat of peonies and a bunch of starters of Hearts and Flowers ground cover, which were sitting on her front porch. She had just begun to till the ground in front of the porch when one of her neighbors stopped by to say hello. Mrs. Hutchkins had lived in the neighborhood for thirty years and had been widowed for only two. She was a spry seventy-six who reminded Leslie of her mother, and she walked a little white Shih Tzu named Puff.

While Leslie leaned on the hoe and visited, the last thing she expected was Conner, pulling in front of her house in his big truck. He jumped out. Smiling again. Funny, when she'd first met him, one of the things that had had an impact on her was how serious he usually was. He'd seemed almost brooding. Either that or he was smiling inappropriately, like when she said she felt like crap. Now every time she saw him he was grinning like a fool.

"I know I wasn't invited to the planting," he said as he came around to the rear of his truck. He wore a cap over his short, thick, unruly brown hair, and he touched the bill with a nod to Mrs. Hutchkins. "Ma'am," he said politely.

"Young man," Mrs. Hutchkins returned. "I'll talk with you later, Leslie. Come along, Puff," she said, moving down the street toward her house.

Leslie went to the back of Conner's truck just as he lowered the hatch. The bed of the truck was filled with flats of flowers. "God above," she said. "What have you done?"

He pulled off his hat and scratched his head. "I might've gotten a little carried away."

She rolled her eyes. The truck was full of blossoming blue, yellow, red, purple, lavender, white.

"Daisies, wildflowers, peonies, lavender, garlic, bachelor buttons, poppies, lantana in three colors," he said. "I didn't get any roses or tomatoes. Roses and tomatoes are trouble."

"Are you some kind of landscape expert or something?"

He let a huff of laughter loose. "Not before this morning."

"I'm not mad at you anymore," she reassured him. "I'm over it. I was a little insulted, but then I started to think—I have my reasons for being offended that you would think I was fooling around with a married man and maybe you have your reasons for springing to that conclusion."

"Something like that," he said.

"Who's going to plant all this stuff?"

"I figured you and I would do it. And I was hoping it would take most of the day."

She put a hand on her hip. "You're getting a little obvious. Are you flirting with me?"

"Absolutely not," he said. "I'm not a good flirt. I brought my own gear. Shovel, spade, aerator. I also brought mulch and fertilizer. I assumed you weren't prepared for me to show up with, ah, stock."

She couldn't help but laugh at him. "What makes you think I want to spend the whole day with you?"

"I thought if I brought enough pretty flora, I'd grow on you."

"Conner…" She shook her head.

"Leslie…" He just smiled at her.

"All right, you can do the hard part. Make the ground ready."

"See, I haven't lost my touch after all." And he hefted a big flat of daisies out of his truck and followed her.

Several hours later Conner found himself making Leslie smile a lot, making her laugh, making her think he was a regular prince with his hard work on the yard and his flowers. It was just like riding a bike. They broke for lunch and Leslie fed him a sandwich, though she barely nibbled. When he saw the difference in their lunch plates he asked, "Are you getting enough to eat?"

"I'm a little thinner than is usual for me," she said. "Divorce diet. I've been working on keeping it off. Eating right, yoga and all that."

"You can take on quite a bit more weight before you're too fat," he said.

She frowned. "I don't know whether to say thank-you or ask you to leave."

"Are you worrying about your hips? Because a little something to grab on to looks good on a woman."

"Let me guess—you missed the class on flattery," she said.

"Seriously, Les. You don't want to be too thin. Eat. I'll keep bringing flowers for you to plant even if you grow a butt."

"Stop being such a guy, Conner," she said.

"Well, I could try, if that's what you want...."

But that wasn't what she wanted at all. Watching him flex his shoulders and arms while digging, watching him crouch so that his hard thighs were emphasized, it was all so much fun. And when he caught her looking, more fun. Leslie loved having him underfoot.

It took a long time to place all those flowers. By the time the afternoon sun was sinking in the west, most of Leslie's yard was flush with color. Flowers lined her front and back porches, her walk, her fence in the backyard, bobbed in a ring around the trees in the yard and the mailbox. And the two of them were filthy.

"Wow," she said. "You're a lot more ambitious than I am."

"Like I said, I might've gotten a little carried away. Been a long time since I brought a woman flowers."

"They sell those in the grocery store, you know. Five bucks, you put 'em in a vase, the woman thinks you're a real catch."

The smile again, dimple and all. "I didn't want to leave any doubt."

She thought about that briefly. "Listen, we can have this discussion later, about how my mission here has nothing to do with getting involved with a man. But for now I want you to put away all the garden stuff and wash your hands. I'll be right back."

"Where are you going?"

"I'm going to get us takeout at Jack's. I'm too exhausted to even make us sandwiches and too dirty to eat at the bar."

She took off her shoes, brushed her jeans free of dirt and went inside to wash her hands and grab her purse.

She returned just ten minutes later with a brown paper bag and two bottles of beer. "I have a half bottle of Merlot on the counter, but I've never seen you drink wine." She lifted the bottles. "Will this do it for you?"

"You are a goddess."

She looked down at herself. Dirty, disheveled, exhausted. "You must be more desperate than you look."

Leslie served up the dinner while Conner scrubbed his hands. While they sat at her little table with Preacher's slow-cooked ribs, potato salad and beans, they talked about safe things—being Catholic, having a sibling or being an only child, missing parents versus being close to parents. She was distracted by the deep blue of his eyes and the fact that he'd arrived in the morning with his cheeks clean-shaven and now his beard was growing in. They toasted the yard, clinking wineglass to beer bottle. They talked about work; they gossiped about some of the crew and laughed over Dan's proclivity for shedding his prosthetic leg to work and balancing with an empty pant leg flapping in the wind.

"I didn't know he was an amputee," Leslie said.

"Neither did I, until I came to work and saw a leg lying on the floor. He's better on one leg than most of us are on two." He drained his second beer. "I'll help you wash up and store the leftovers."

"No, you won't. I think you've put in a long enough day. I'll walk you to the door." And once there, she turned toward him and said, "Thank you, Conner. It's beautiful and it turned into a fun day."

He slipped his hands to her waist and pulled her in for a hug. "I had a good time," he said. She patted his upper arms, and when she tried to pull back, he held on. He buried his face in her neck and inhaled deeply, letting out a small, low moan.

"I'm all sweaty from yard work," she whispered.

"Hmm. How do you do that? Sweat, soap and flowers?" He opened his lips slightly, taking a little taste of her flesh. "Wow," he said softly.

But she didn't resist. In fact she tilted her head slightly. "Okay, this is flirting," she said in a throaty voice.

"I don't flirt," he said, giving her neck a lick, followed by a little kiss. "I just go after what I want, that's all." And he gave her several small kisses that ran right up to her earlobe. And then he pulled back and smiled into her wide eyes.

"Look, I'm only going to explain this once. It should be obvious to you. Since I'm trying to recover from a divorce—"

"And an ex-husband who's a nutcase," he added for her.

"And that. I am not getting involved romantically."

He gave a nod. "Perfectly understandable."

"Period."

"Got it," he said. "But really, how do you do that? Did you sneak a shower at Jack's? Because you look like you should taste like sweat, dirt and compost, but you're sweet."

"Did you hear me?" she asked him.

"Absolutely. I have some of the same issues. Would you like to go see a movie tomorrow?"

"No!"

"That's too bad. I think I'll go anyway. I haven't been to a movie in a long time," he said.

"So maybe you think this could work out for you

as a *non*-relationship, but I don't do non-relationships, either. Am I clear?"

"Les, I didn't propose anything. I licked your neck, which by the way was delicious. I'll see you at work Monday. Don't forget to water." He put a light kiss on her forehead and gave her butt a pat. And he was out the door, down the walk and in the truck without looking back.

She shivered. "Whew," she said aloud.

Conner's workweek was busier than usual, starting with loading the trailer that served as Paul's construction office so it could be transported across the mountain to another site. Just getting it ready for the tow took hours, the entire morning. As it got on its way, Paul and Dan talked about another project in town—the erection of a prefab building that would serve as a school. When Conner heard that it was a volunteer project, that some local men and some of Paul's construction crews were doing it without pay, he said, "Sign me up. My dance card isn't full."

"It's a project for the town," Paul made sure to clarify. "When we do something for the town, we don't take pay. It's like plowing in winter, towing a motorist or searching for someone who's lost—strictly neighbor to neighbor. We completely understand if you want to put your hours in on the clock. I'm sure you need the money."

Conner gave a shrug. "I'm sure you do, too. I'll be

glad to work on it. The more people who pitch in, the faster it goes, right?"

"That's a fact," Dan said, giving him a slap on the shoulder.

And that's when it got more interesting. Conner saw a lot of familiar faces; the bar had been closed so Jack, Preacher and Denny could help put up the school. Mike Valenzuela was there as well as many of the ranchers and farmers he'd met at the bar. He learned there had been a trust left to the town that would pay the teacher, Becca, the pretty young lady engaged to Denny. The land on which the building would sit was loaned, the building itself was paid for out of the trust managed by Jack, which made him like the unofficial mayor of Virgin River.

At some point during the afternoon of construction, nearly everyone showed up to watch. When Brie came around, Conner snuck a quiet moment. "I wish I could tell Katie about this, about how the town rallies like this."

"Better not to," she said, shaking her head. "Rule of thumb—before we get to trial, don't mention anything that can be looked up on Google."

"That's too bad," he said. "She'd really get a kick out of this. This is the kind of thing Katie loves."

For the first three days of the week he was busy working for Paul in the mornings, helping finish the construction on the school in the afternoons. Then he went with Dan to start tearing out kitchen cabinets in Redway, ready to start installing a new kitchen on Monday morning.

He didn't see Leslie all week. He spent considerable time in town, working on the school and having dinner at Jack's, and he also drove by her house a couple of times to see if she might be out watering her plants. The temptation to knock on her door was powerful, but he resisted. If he didn't leave her alone to think about things, this whole proposition would backfire.

By Saturday, he'd had enough of his exile. He helped work on the school much of the day and in the afternoon he drove to Fortuna, but he wasn't an idiot. He didn't park right in front of that silly turquoise coffee shop. Instead he parked across the street at the tattoo parlor. Then he went inside and ordered a coffee, a tea and two slices of pie.

Just as before, at around the dinner hour, the place was deserted but for one young man who appeared to be a student busy on his laptop. Conner settled right into their girlie little sitting area.

Leslie felt she had always had a confidence problem. For a while as a wife, a good wife, she'd felt sure of herself, and then Greg had answered her loaded question and said, "Yes, honey, there has been someone else. And I just can't live without her, it's that simple."

It didn't stay simple. Even though she'd been betrayed, Leslie had tried to convince Greg to try to work it out with her, to go to counseling or something. If he would just give up Allison and *try*.... But he'd been packing as he talked. And Leslie had reached one of her all-time lowest moments—she'd clung to him and begged him not to leave their marriage. She had literally fallen to her knees and grabbed his legs. Just the thought that she'd ever risk revisiting such a place in her life was more than she could bear. She would never be brought that low again—it was humiliating. So she had come to Virgin River with a very firm resolve—she'd do without a man, and if there ever was one, he would be a man she didn't care much about.

And yet, like one of those songs you can't get out of your head, she kept feeling Conner's bristly, closely trimmed whiskers on her neck. She missed him. She wanted his seduction, his power and his tenderness. She wanted laughter. She wanted to risk herself again, though it terrified her. She had fantasized about those arms around her for a week, and in each one she was wearing less. And less. *And* less...

She went to yoga to stretch out and then to her favorite coffee shop for her tea. He was the first thing she saw in the shop. He grinned at her, and her hand automatically touched her neck where she had felt his whiskers all week. He was seated at that little coffee table with coffee in front of him and tea in that place that would be hers. Her first thought was to wonder if it would be bad form to throw herself on him and taste his mustache.

"Well, look who's here," he said. "What a surprise."

Six

Leslie walked right over to where Conner sat. "What are you doing here?" she asked him.

"What do you think?" he returned. "Hoping to run into you. How was your week?"

"Fine," she said. "Do you expect me to believe you're just being friendly?"

"I haven't been anything else. I haven't seen you all week and I thought maybe you could use a piece of pie. Or something."

"I thought I told you—"

"Yes, you told me. You can't eat pie and you can't get involved and you can't be uninvolved. That's going to be tricky. Sit down anyway—I got you some tea and a slice of pie. It's apple."

"I've been trying to watch my weight…."

"I heard all about that. Just a taste," he said. "I'll eat whatever you leave. You don't have to watch your weight, Les. You're perfect. You'd still be perfect twenty pounds heavier, so don't punish yourself." He shook out a paper napkin, slid forward on his chair, put a small bite on the end of a fork and held it toward her. "Come on. I've given you a week to stew and now it's time to sort it out. With pie."

She wondered if this was a good idea, but with a fork of apple pie hovering at her lips, she let him feed her. It wasn't the pie that tempted her.

"It's been an interesting week," he said. "I worked in town some with Dan and Paul and some others, getting that school building up. Everyone who worked on that project did it without pay. It's been a long time since I did anything like that—volunteer work. Community service. Felt good. And I drove by your house a couple of times to see how the flowers were holding up—I'd say we did a damn fine job on the yard." He took a sip of his coffee. "If you're not planning to plant the back forty tomorrow, I think we should grab a movie and dinner. I helped out on that school today and they're going to be there again tomorrow but I could use a day off."

The student seated behind Conner snapped closed his laptop and tucked it under his arm to leave.

"I don't know if that's such a good idea," she said. "I wouldn't want to tempt fate...."

"Fate? No. Just you."

"Oh, that was blunt," she said.

"I know, I'm bad that way. Sometimes I'm too honest. It can make people uncomfortable. I didn't really mean what you think, Les. I understand some of your worries. They're an awful lot like mine. I haven't asked a woman out on a date of any kind for a long, long time. I haven't even asked for a phone number or bought one a drink. I just didn't want to—as you put it—tempt fate. I know you don't want to be in a position where you end up getting disappointed. Me, either. I had the same thing happen—she cheated. We divorced. I'm still pissed off about it."

Leslie was quiet for a moment. "I'm sorry we have that in common."

"Yeah, it shouldn't happen to anyone. And we have more than that in common, I'm afraid. You have parents in Oregon and you made it clear, you're going back there eventually. Well, lots sooner than eventually, I'll have to find work near my sister and nephews, my only family. I'm going to have to go home or move them. I told you, didn't I? She's alone—her husband was in the army and was killed several years ago in Afghanistan. I want to be closer than this. I want to be part of their lives, especially since the idea of a family of my own isn't on my chart anymore. So, just like you, I'm not interested in getting in over my head. As far as I'm concerned, another marriage is out of the question for me. And up until just lately, I wasn't even ready for friendship with a woman. But then I met you. I think we can be friends. I think we already are."

She frowned. "Why me?"

He laughed in spite of himself. "Seriously?"

"Why don't you hang out with Dan? Or some of the guys on Paul's crews?"

He grinned at her. "Well, let's see… Their necks

are so scratchy," he said, rubbing his hand over his goatee. "You're pretty and you make me laugh. I like the way you boss people around. That whole toilet seat mission—that kind of thing used to just annoy the hell out of me.... My sister does that. She's little, you know? But she has no trouble getting the men in her life to put the seat down."

She stiffened. "It's common courtesy when you share space with a woman!"

"That's what she says. So how about the four-o'clock show in Fortuna, dinner in Arcata after? I say four o'clock because it's such a damn long drive. Going anyplace around here is a damn long drive."

"I haven't been on a date since... I don't remember."

"Think of it as a couple of friends catching a movie and a meal," he said. And then he flashed her the dimple, and she knew what kind of friends he'd like them to be. It made her gulp and shiver in need. "I could lower my standards and make it a chick flick," he said.

"No," she said, shaking her head. "No chick flick."

His blue eyes grew smoky and dark. "Leslie, you could do a lot better than me, there's no question about that. I think it's pure coincidence we have the same post-divorce trust issues. So no expectations, just whatever good times fall our way."

"Listen," she said, "I think I know where you're headed with this idea—this friendship idea...."

"I don't think you really do, Les. Because anything beyond a movie, dinner and some laughs is entirely up to you. Your call. I swear to God."

* * *

Conner was serious about a day off. He needed to relax and enjoy himself, though he had to admit that hanging around with some of the guys from town filled a certain need. He liked the masculine camaraderie; he liked working on a project with people as opposed to alone.

But while Luke Riordan went into town on Sunday morning to help on the school, Conner helped himself to a rod and reel from the storage shed. When he made it to the river, he found Luke's helper, Art, already casting. They exchanged their greetings, and Art told him which rocks were the slippery ones.

Conner had been here four weeks and something had happened to the place since April had arrived—it had exploded with new growth and color. The sun was out almost every day, the river, as Jack had promised, was swollen, and the trout were jumping. Wildlife, from deer to wolves to bear, had begun to appear here and there with new young—in meadows, at river's edge, even in backyards. After a long, dark, snowy winter it was officially spring and the town's spirits rose with the temperature. It had been a good-natured place since the day he arrived, but now there was an uplifting mood and lots more laughter—spring fever. He'd heard all about their winter of record snowfalls and how the men of the town, including his boss, had had to get together to deliver supplies to those in need, clear the roads, rescue people who'd been snowed in.

That whole business of one for all and all for one that

they had going on—that held an appeal for Conner. As a big-city guy, he hadn't had that in a long while, not since his army days, if you got right down to it.

He caught a fish, a nice, fat trout. He briefly wondered if he'd made enough progress with Leslie to convince her to cook it and decided he'd better move slowly. "Art, you think your boss would like this fish?" he asked.

"Boss?" Art asked.

"Luke?"

Art laughed. "Luke's my partner. Luke and Shewby are my family. They found me. And kept me."

Yeah, the danger was not falling in love with a woman, Conner thought. He risked falling in love with the whole damn town.

By the time Conner arrived for Leslie on Sunday afternoon, she had already spent an entire day being tense and unsure of herself—big surprise. She had come to a few conclusions. Such as, life wasn't going to get a whole lot easier and more enjoyable if she avoided gorgeous men like Conner. And she hadn't been tempted by a man in a very long time. Very. Long. Time.

She had decided she wasn't going to try too hard. She wore her hair in the usual way—loose curls. Her makeup was the same as she'd put on for work every day. She did choose an extra nice pair of jeans, boots, crisp white blouse and blazer, however. Nothing special. They were just friends catching a movie.

When she opened the door for him, she found him

just plain dreamy-eyed. "God, you look fantastic," he said almost weakly.

And she burst out laughing.

"This is funny, how?" he asked.

"I don't look any different. Well, the jacket, that's a little different. You, on the other hand, are wearing *pants*. Not jeans but pants. Whew. Should I change?"

"Are you a little fidgety?" he asked, smiling at her.

"I haven't been on a—" She cleared her throat. "I haven't been a couple of friends catching dinner and a movie in a really long time."

He stepped into her house, slipped his arm around her waist, pulled her very close and asked, "Did I give you too much to think about, Les?"

She looked up into those vivid blue eyes. She nodded, and she could tell he smiled because the crinkles at the corners of his eyes deepened a little bit.

"Then maybe we should just get it over with," he said and came down on her mouth. He moved expertly; his bristles coaxed open her lips. His tongue tangoed with hers briefly; she made a little noise as her hands slid up his arms toward his shoulders. His kiss grew a little more penetrating; he pulled her a bit closer. Without leaving her lips, he whispered, "You taste good. Good."

"You're my first mustache," she whispered back.

He lifted his brooding, thick brows. "Like it?"

She nodded, and he went in for the kill a second time, overpowering her lips, going deep, bending her back over his arm. He gently licked her upper lip, her lower lip, then devoured her once again. That was three, she thought. Three deep, wonderful, wet, hot, amazing kisses.

She was screwed. She wanted him. All of him.

"We should probably think about that movie," he whispered.

"What movie?" she asked.

And he laughed, releasing her slowly so she wouldn't collapse. She righted herself, grabbed her purse, left a kitchen light on for later and joined him at the front door.

"It's harder now, being older and knowing the pitfalls and consequences, isn't it?" he asked her. He held the front door for her. "I remember being sixteen, going out with a girl in a car for the first time and being pretty strung out, but more excited than scared." He chuckled. "I should've been scared—she ate me alive. She wasn't happy about too much—she didn't like the movie, the food wasn't right, she didn't want to make out...."

She laughed at him. "Poor Conner."

He opened the passenger door to the truck and helped her up and in. "I learned to pick 'em better after that."

"Went straight for the ones who wanted to make out, huh?"

"Well, of course," he said, slamming the door. He came around and joined her in the cab. "I didn't pick you solely based on the making out aspect, though I do see the potential, it being your first mustache and all."

"I never dated much. I had a couple of boyfriends before I met Greg, but nothing too serious. But I bet you always had girls."

"Not always, just sometimes. I kept pretty long hours at work, it seemed. One short marriage." He looked over at her. "I am going to tell you more about that, you know. But not tonight. I don't want to spoil tonight. I want to have fun."

"I understand completely. It's been a year and a half for me, too. Not so much as a cup of coffee." She let go a little laugh. "What a couple of go-getters we are."

"But this isn't really our first date," he said. "More like our third with lots of contact in the middle. We had a couple of coffee dates, I've insulted you at least once, we had a flower planting date with a take-out dinner chaser, and this is a dinner and movie date. And we saw each other almost every day for three weeks until you moved the trailer. If we were in high school, that would equal carrying your books to class all week, then meeting you at the burger barn on the weekend with the gang…."

"Then making out," she added.

He grinned at her. "Absolutely."

Leslie found the nervousness of her first post-divorce date had gone within ten minutes of getting in the truck with him. Being with him was so easy. He had this gruff exterior and a deep sexy voice, but he had a very soft center. His honesty charmed her to the marrow of her bones. Everything about Conner seemed spontaneous and real as opposed to premeditated. He was what he was, take it or leave it.

The movie was a sci-fi thriller, very tense. When

she gripped his arm, he put it around her shoulders and pulled her protectively close. When they went to a nice restaurant in Arcata, she spent the whole meal praising the food and telling him all the things she liked to cook; he told her everything he liked to eat. On the long drive home she talked about how much she'd like to travel more than she had, which was very little, while he talked about how little wanderlust he had. Home was all that mattered to him. If he could stay in the same place forever and always know where a couple of beers and his TV broadcasting pro football games would be, he'd be content.

"I love football," she said. "But I'd still like to travel."

"I've never really had the time or money for travel, but if I did, I can think of a few things I wouldn't mind seeing."

"Like?" she pushed.

He shrugged. "The Super Bowl?"

She laughed. "I don't know if we have a lot in common or nothing in common."

"It's really too soon to tell." He parked the truck in front of her little house. He turned in his seat and faced her. "Let me come in, Les," he said.

"Oh, right. The making out part," she teased.

"Or coffee," he said. "But I'm not done yet. Are you?"

"I am not," she said, surprisingly happy about it.

He came around the truck to help her out. He lifted her to the ground. His arm around her waist both supported and hurried her, and when they were inside the house with the door closed, he swept her up to him, his lips on her lips, kissing her deeply once again as though he'd waited all night to do it. She dropped her purse on the floor and gave herself over to this kiss, wondering how she'd made it this long without it.

And that fast she decided—she was going to enjoy her life rather than subject herself to some kind of torture of denial to avoid ever being hurt again. If he wanted to devour her with these fabulous kisses, and more, she'd just have to endure it.

He backed off the littlest bit and said, "You have a very good mouth for this. Perfect, I think."

"Are you just getting it out of the way again?" she asked.

"Nope. Just getting started. Do you have to listen to messages or let the cat out or anything?"

She shook her head. "Are we going to stand inside the door and make out?"

"I could. Where do you want to make out?"

She thought about saying *the bed.* Or *the shower.* Or maybe *up against a wall?* "Sofa?" she asked.

"You don't sound too sure," he said, slipping the blazer from her shoulders. He shed his lightweight jacket and tossed them both on the living room chair. Taking her hand, he led her to the couch. "Do you need anything? A drink? A little more conversation? How's the mustache? Too bristly?"

She just shook her head, bringing a chuckle out of him. Once she was seated on the sofa he knelt on one knee and helped her out of her boots. Then he sat down and took off his. And then he had her in his arms again pulling her across his lap, going after her mouth with all his heat and power.

"I don't want to jinx this," he whispered, "but you're a natural."

"Are you saying I've missed my calling?"

He reclined with her on the sofa. "I'm saying, you're very tasty and desirable and I could do this clear into next week."

Then, with a hand on her butt pulling her against him, he pressed into her. She chuckled against his lips. "No, you can't," she said. He was hard. Ready. "All you want is sex."

He grew still and serious. He gave her lips a little peck. Then he kissed her nose. "No, Les. That's not all. But it's not a bad place to start."

Leslie could remember making out, but she certainly couldn't remember anything like this. And she'd never been romanced this way—with a truckload of flowers and comments like, *that's not all, but it's not a bad place to start.* Although Conner was a large man, they somehow managed to lie on the couch together, bodies pressed close, mouths pressed closer. And hands, gliding up and down bodies. Leslie kissed his mouth, his chin, his brooding eyebrows, his cheeks, the place where his dimple would be when he smiled. She licked his upper lip, touching the mustache with her tongue, and made him moan.

"You like that, I think," he said.

"I like it," she confirmed. She tugged his shirt out

of his pants so she could run her hands up his hard belly and over his sculptured chest. "You're hard everywhere."

He unbuttoned her crisp white shirt to find a very sexy, transparent lace bra. "And you're soft everywhere. Did you wear this for me?" He bent his head and kissed the lace.

"I might've, yes. I wasn't sure what would happen, but I did think about having the right underwear for it."

His big hand slid down to the crotch of her jeans. "I can't wait to see the matching panties."

"One thing at a time."

"You're right." He popped the front latch of her bra and enjoyed himself for a little while with her breasts, first fondling and then kissing and finally sucking. He lifted his head and looked into her eyes. "How's that bristle on your breasts?"

"It's very good," she said breathlessly, without opening her eyes.

"Les, are we gonna get naked?"

"You mean more naked?"

"It's up to you," he said. "And if the answer is yes, let's trade this couch in for a bed. If the answer is no, let's put on the coffee."

"I'm very nervous. I wonder if I've thought it through...."

He chuckled and ran a rough finger down her chest all the way to her navel. "You have no reason to be nervous. And I have a couple of brand-new condoms in my pocket. One week old."

"You planned this?"

"No, sweetheart. I wanted this. Hoped for this. Wanted to be prepared for this."

She bit her bottom lip for a second. "Will we still be friends after?" she asked in a soft voice.

"Oh, Leslie, better friends, I hope. Are you worried I'm just here for the sex? Because I'm here for the sex with you, but only because it's you. I haven't felt this in a long time. I was a little afraid I'd never feel it again. But…" He started to pull her shirt closed over her breasts. "I want you to be ready. This has to be about both of us, not just one of us. We can put on the coffee…."

She grabbed his wrists. "I'm nervous, but I'm ready."

"Are you nervous because it's me?"

"Because it's been so long and because I really like you. And because I've never done anything like this before, this 'friends with benefits' kind of thing."

"It's more than that," he said. "I think it's friends with chemistry. You really turn me on." He nuzzled her neck with a low purr that almost turned into a growl. "I'm going to take very good care of you, Leslie."

"What if I don't take real good care of you?" she asked him.

He looked surprised. "Not possible." He put his lips against hers, and then in a remarkable move, never breaking the kiss, he shifted her weight until she was sitting on his lap again. With one arm behind her and the other under her knees, he lifted her. "Which way?"

"Left," she said.

When he reached her bedroom, he stood at the side of the bed, holding her, looking down. The comforter was folded back, the pillows fluffed. "Perfect," he said. And he slowly lowered her.

Leslie lay on her bed in her jeans, socks and opened blouse and watched as Conner went through the ritual of emptying his pockets onto the bedside table. He took out condoms and wallet; his watch joined them. Then he pulled off his shirt and opened his belt. It was the sexiest thing she'd ever seen, his process of getting ready for her. But it was hard to concentrate. He had an enormous bulge in his dress pants. And when he lowered the pants, leaving only black boxer briefs, it was all she could do not to gasp.

He knelt on the bed and gently touched her, his fingertips gliding over her lips, then her neck and breasts, her belly. Then he opened her jeans and gave them a little tug. She lifted up so he could draw them off, and he groaned at the sight of her transparent lace panties. He tossed the jeans and ran a finger around the elastic. "God," he muttered.

She reached for the waistband of his briefs. "Come on," she said. "I'm cold."

"You won't be cold for long," he said. And he quickly got rid of his boxers, removing the mystery. She bit on her lower lip to keep from saying, *Wow*. It was a little intimidating. Very large. Very hard.

He sat down on the bed and pulled her into a sitting position. He pushed the opened blouse and unsnapped bra over her shoulders. "Let's get rid of this," he said, his voice gravelly.

"And these?" she asked, her hands going to her panties.

"Not yet," he said. "Not yet." He ran his finger under the elastic again. "Let me play with these awhile. God, Leslie. What an incredible beauty you are."

"Because I say no to pie," she weakly informed him.

"No, you can still take on plenty of pie and be beautiful. But, my God, I'm losing my mind." He ran his fingers under the elastic at her legs, first one, then the other. "Hmm, you're killing me."

"We can take them off," she offered.

"Not yet," he said. "Let me have my fun." And then his hands were spreading her, and his fingers were moving into that very personal territory beneath the panties. Of course she was completely ready. Swollen and hot and wet. He leaned down to her lips just as he let one finger slide into her, and his kiss carried a deep throaty moan with it. "Man, I'm having a very hard time waiting for you."

"You don't have to wait," she offered. And without meaning to, without planning to, her pelvis rose into his hand. "I'm not sure I'll be able to wait long."

"Good," he said, nibbling at her lips. "Good." He sat up again and slowly, tenderly, drew down those lace panties. She was waxed except for a small patch on her pubis. He met her eyes, smiled, lifted one brow. "Maybe I should see your barber."

She reached out and touched his mustache. "Don't you dare."

He tossed the panties and reclined, pulling her into his arms, holding her close. His hand was on her again, now rubbing that sensitive little bump that brought all the joy of the universe to her. "Stop," she whispered. "I can't wait if you do that."

"Ready?"

"I've been ready since you brought me lantana in three colors."

His laugh was a deep rumble. "I knew when it got down to it, you were easy." He rubbed more ferociously. He put a finger inside and rubbed with his thumb.

She reached for him, filled her hand with him and said, "So, you wanna play dirty?" She stroked him. Not gently. She brought deep noises from him, and he pinched his eyes closed.

He kissed her again, deeply, wetly. "Dirty is the only way I want to play." But he pulled his hands and lips away and went after that condom, suiting up. Then he covered her body with his, holding his massive weight off her. With a gentle knee, he parted her legs. "I just can't right now. I'm on a pretty short leash." And again he touched her with his fingers, getting her hotter than hot.

With slow and smooth searching, he found her and let himself inside just a small amount, checking her reaction. She nodded at him, and he pushed in a little more. Again she nodded and again he gave her more.

Then he took her mouth, his tongue playing with hers, and he slid all the way in. She gasped.

"Okay?" he asked her.

"God," she whispered. "Okay," she said weakly.

"Tell me if it's not comfortable. Don't put up with anything that feels wrong."

"God," she said again. "It feels right...."

And she saw the crinkles at the corners of his eyes along with his smile. Then he began to move in and out, slowly. Too slowly. He kissed his way down her neck, across her collarbone, over her breast and pulled a nipple into his mouth. In and out.

She rose against him. "More."

"Try this," came his throaty whisper. "Just try it this way. Let me get you there nice and easy. Let it build. Then when it's time—"

"Oh, God, it's time...." she nearly cried, pushing against him.

"You're killing me," he told her. "Almost time..."

"Harder," she asked in a whimper. She couldn't believe it was her! She'd never cried out for what she wanted before! "Faster!"

And he laughed deep in his throat. "Almost time," he said, slowly and deeply invading, one long stroke at a time, torturing her.

She moaned and rose against him. Her knees bent, her heels dug into the bed, she whimpered and moaned again and again. A cry came from her, and he must have known that her orgasm was on him; his fingers found her most erogenous spot, his lips bruised hers in a hard, possessive kiss, and he pounded himself into her. Deeper and faster. And she broke apart, exploding all over him. He growled low and with appreciation. And then he said it. "God...*Leslie*..." It went on forever, the pleasure, the whimpering and growling, and she wasn't quite done when he suddenly let go of her mouth, moved his lips to her nipple, and he grabbed her hips to plunge himself deep inside of her, holding her still but for his powerful throbbing. He groaned in ecstasy. She wasn't sure where her orgasm ended and his began, and it was beyond anything she'd ever experienced before. Then he grabbed her chin in one big calloused hand, tilted her mouth toward his and took her mouth with almost the same force.

She thought it was a wonder she didn't faint.

Seven

She felt herself smiling and yet on the verge of tears. He held the bulk of his weight off her, his eyes closed. Then his features slowly relaxed, and he kissed her several times, on the lips, the cheeks, the neck, chin, forehead. She reached up to his thick eyebrows with her fingertips and smoothed them, and he opened his eyes.

He took a deep breath. "That was the most amazing..."

"Oh, my God," she said. "I had sex on the first date!"

"You and I had very good sex on the first date," he said with a laugh. Then he frowned again and wiped a thumb along her temple. "Hey, forget what your mother said. It's not a bad thing! We've been over this—it wasn't really a first date! Are you crying?"

"Sorry... I might be a little emotional or something...."

"Leslie, was I rough? Did I hurt you?"

She shook her head. "You were wonderful. I think I might be a little crazy," she said. "I can't believe I was worried. I was so worried...." She gave a little hiccup of emotion.

"Because it was so long since the last time?" he asked.

"More than that," she said. "Oh, Conner, you just can't imagine the kinds of things I've believed about myself. That I wasn't much of a lover, for one thing..."

"You can't be serious. You put me on another planet...."

She laughed through a tear. "I'm just overthinking things again." She put the palm of her hand against his cheek.

"Tell me," he insisted.

"I've been told I..." She took a breath. "That I could be more interesting."

"That's ridiculous," he said. "Whoever said that probably needed practice."

"I've always wondered...you know...if that was one of the reasons..."

"That he strayed? That he left?" he asked.

She gave a weak little nod.

He laughed in spite of himself. "You're wonderful, Leslie, you can trust me on this. You make love like a goddess. An angel. A very wild, wonderful angel." He laughed again. "Jesus, what a mean way to undermine a woman's confidence. From what I could tell, we worked together just great. Hmm?"

She let out a shaky breath. It was one of the most exciting, intense moments she'd ever had with a man, but she'd hold on to that information a little while. "Are you uncomfortable? Holding yourself up like this?"

He shook his head. "I don't want to move. Ever."

"Me, either. I think it's the mustache that makes the difference."

"Oh, we haven't even put the mustache to work yet." She shivered, and he laughed, a low rumbling. She put her arms around his neck to hold him and just closed her eyes, comfortable and relaxed like never before. "Do you need to fall asleep?" he asked.

"Nope. Not tired."

"Good. I'm not tired, either," he said. "I'd like to check and see if it can get better than perfect...."

Her eyes opened in surprise. "Really?"

"Oh, really," he said. And then he clutched her close and rolled with her until they were on their sides, still locked together.

In the early morning, Conner pulled Leslie close and nuzzled her, kissing the back of her neck. She mewled and snuggled closer, and he splayed a big hand over her belly. He wanted her again, but he didn't want to wear her out. They'd made love three times in the night, and while it seemed she slept, curled up against him, he didn't sleep much. Instead, his mind was working.

She was perfect. Sweet, funny, passionate, smart. He couldn't imagine what more a man could want. She should want a lot more than him, that was his next thought. And he was a little angry, too. He hoped it hadn't shown, but the very idea that a man would tell her she wasn't enough, it roared inside him with a carefully held fury. He knew who that would have been. She hadn't been with many men. It would have been the cheating ex, the bastard. It made Conner want to mess up his face because it was becoming clearer by the hour just how much that asshole had hurt her. And hurt her. And hurt her.

People hadn't acknowledged her hurt; they'd wanted her to move on. People did that because they get tired of hearing about it. No one ever knew what to say or how to help. He'd gotten a lot of sympathy after Samantha, but then they'd divorced, she'd gone into a treatment facility in another state, and in the mind of his few supporters, it had been time for him to let go before he made them any more uncomfortable.

He and Leslie shared another trait—he, too, wondered how badly he'd been lacking that his wife had needed others, so many others. He hadn't revealed that to anyone and probably never would, but it made a man wonder. He would have given her anything she wanted, everything she wanted.

But no more. Now he was all for getting past it and hoped Leslie felt the same about her situation.

He was holding in his arms one of the best reasons to move on he'd rubbed up against in a couple of years. And it surprised him that he had absolutely no doubts about her. He wasn't the least bit afraid that he'd come home someday and find her bouncing up and down on the cable guy. In fact, Leslie was so different that he instantly knew if he'd met her first, his entire life would have been different.

In fact, he wanted her like he'd never wanted a woman, *including* his wife. But he'd be very good to her, and when the time came, he'd tell her the truth about his dilemma and leave because he valued his life. And the lives of his sister and nephews.

She turned in his arms, facing him, burrowing her face into his neck.

"I woke you," he said. "I didn't mean to, but I have to get up."

She made a protesting noise and snuggled closer.

"I have to drive to my cabin, shower and change. It's Monday morning." He pushed her curls away from her eyes. "Maybe you should call in...."

She giggled a little. "Call in what? Orgasmed to death?"

"You did say you were dying at least once," he reminded her.

"We're putting framers on the new construction today. I have to go." She lifted her head. "When will I see you now that we're not working on the same site?"

"When do you want to see me?"

"Will I scare you off if I say soon?"

"I don't scare easy. Want me to sleep with you tonight?" he asked, running a hand down her spine.

She nodded. "I'll make us dinner. I'll even buy a six-pack to keep in my refrigerator."

"What if you make me too comfortable?" he asked. "Could be as bad as feeding a stray cat."

"If you're worried about getting too involved…"

He shook his head. "I don't think we can get too involved—we're both in this weird place, trying to overcome having been in even weirder places. But I'm not worried about it. When I first saw you, I knew you were special."

"You thought I was involved with a married man!"

"I'm jaded. Cynical sometimes. I apologized for that, didn't I?"

"Yes, quite nicely, I think. So…? Dinner?"

"Yes, tonight. I have to get up now."

She slid a leg over his hip, wiggling closer. "It doesn't feel like you want to leave me yet."

He smiled and gave her a kiss. "I didn't dare ask. Now lie back and let me make you really late for work…."

The next night, very unlike the way a typical man thinks, Conner was relieved that they made love only once. Superbly, but once. He had serious reasons to be suspicious of a woman who would take it to the obsessive level.

And a few nights later, because she had mentioned she liked it, he found himself stopping in Fortuna for Thai takeout to bring for dinner to her house. It was Conner's intention to have a serious talk with Leslie over dinner—

But he was barely in the door before that plan changed. She was standing in the doorway wearing a pair of snug jeans, a blue chambray shirt opened almost to her waist with a little white tank under it. He caught that scent—soap and flowers. Her hair was all those dark blond, streaky curls that made her look so cute, and her cheeks were flushed, which made her look already ravished, and he said, "Oh, my Jesus..."

"What?" she asked.

"God, you turn me on. Just seeing you."

"Is that the same as hello?" she asked with a smile.

"I don't know. How fast can you get naked?"

"Conner," she said and laughed. "Wanna tell me what's in the bag?"

"Thai. It's for dessert...."

"And the main course?"

"I'm thinking mustache rides."

"I guess that means you missed me," she said. And she took the bag off his hands, and no sooner had she deposited it in the kitchen, than she headed straight for her bedroom. He caught her there, spun her around and fell with her on the bed, covering her mouth in a searing kiss.

It was an hour before they could get to the Thai takeout, and when they finally did, they sat on her sofa. He had pulled on his jeans and T-shirt, and she wore a robe. She put the cartons on a tray between them, and they ate directly out of them—she using chopsticks while he had to have a fork.

"I can teach you to use chopsticks," she offered.

"Why would I do that? Nah. But I wanted us to talk."

"The talk?" she asked, digging into the Nam Sod—

minced chicken with ginger, peanut and onions. "About expectations and stuff?"

His eyebrows lifted curiously. "You want to give me the talk?"

"I know how men think. You think that if I've slept with you, I'll expect you to marry me. And you want to be sure I don't."

He tilted his head and thought about this. She was damn close. "Well, not exactly. Being with you is good—but I'm afraid I'm going to let you down. I have serious baggage. Things to overcome, work through, you know."

"I know."

"I should tell you about my ex-wife…."

"Only if you feel like it. I don't think she has anything to do with me. With us."

"Well, she might. You're trying to get over a divorce after what you thought was a good eight-year marriage. My marriage lasted a year. I only knew Samantha for six months before we got married. And she cheated, too, but with something like a hundred guys…."

Leslie coughed and choked. Conner slapped her back until she recovered.

"I know. It's a lot to swallow, no pun intended. I thought I had a great marriage, too. It worked for me. But my wife cheated, we had a confrontation and she said she was…" He paused. It was still hard to say. He cleared his throat. "She said she was a sex addict."

Leslie's eyes grew very large. "Is that so?" she asked cautiously.

He gave a nod. Then a shrug. "Maybe that's correct, that's what her problem was. My sister didn't exactly forgive her, but she did kind of defend her, saying she was dealing with a compulsion. She went into a treatment program, though. I have no idea if it worked. She asked me to come to some kind of family week session so I could understand her and the disease, but I couldn't. I was done. I said that I wasn't family anymore and wouldn't be. In the one year we were married, she was unfaithful more times than she could count. Or remember."

"Oh, Conner, I'm really sorry."

"So as you might expect, I have world-class trust issues. Not the way you think—I really don't have a single problem trusting you. But I sure don't trust me. I never thought I was the kind of guy who couldn't see what was right in front of my face. I never suspected a thing. I never even had enough imagination to suspect something like what was going on right under my own nose."

Leslie left her chopsticks standing in the Yum Woo Sen.

"Listen, I've been divorced almost two years and I've been completely checked and checked and rechecked," he assured her. "There hasn't been anyone since. I'm safe." At least in that regard, he thought.

She was quiet for a moment. Finally she said, "It must have been awful."

"I'm one of those guys like your old boss—I have strong feelings about that kind of commitment. My parents married for life. My sister married her husband for life, though his life was cut short way too early. I assumed any woman who made those promises meant them. I guess I can be naive. Put it another way—I had no idea how naive I could be."

She smiled. "I know exactly how you feel."

He smiled in spite of himself. "Well, you don't know exactly. You caught a text message. I came home early and found her banging the kid who delivered bottled water."

Leslie gulped, trying to imagine.

"When I think back about it, it's pretty ironic. I actually delivered bottled water part-time during my one semester in college." He snorted. "No one ever met me at the door naked."

She let herself give a short laugh. "I guess she hasn't been in touch."

"There have been letters, but I didn't open them, just put them right in the shredder. I had made it pretty clear to her it was over for me, no grudges, nothing. It was a lie, of course—I was mad and I was carrying a grudge. But really, she needed to pick up the pieces somewhere else."

"I'm shocked," she said. "I can't imagine a woman attached to you even having enough desire leftover for another guy. You're pretty efficient."

He lifted his eyebrows. "Is this where I say thank you?"

"Not yet. Let me tell you a couple of things. You're not the only one with a few revelations. Moving here a little over a month ago was the first time in my adult life I didn't live in the same town with my parents and husband or my ex-husband and his perfect new little wife. And you know what happened? I immediately started learning a few things about myself. For years I had wondered if I deserved Greg, the fabulous future governor he thought he was, and now that I've had some distance from all that, it's pretty clear I deserved much better. I give you a lot of credit for that, by the way, for really *seeing* me, and not just seeing me as a reflection of you. With my husband, I was always fading into the background, like an overexposed photo. Even though I was the one who did most of the work in our marriage, from the scut work around the house and yard to paying the bills to constantly supporting my wonderful spouse, I had a hard time thinking of myself as valuable. As competent. I didn't even feel competent between the sheets!"

"No," he said, shaking his head. "Les, you're way past competent. Trust me."

"Since I've been here, I've been liking myself a lot more. I like my little rented house, all the new flowers, my yoga classes, my job in the construction trailer. The crews respect me and do things my way, my boss already needs me. I have a kind-of boyfriend," she said, pausing to grin at him, "who lets me call the shots. I'm getting to know myself, Conner. It's okay that you don't feel like marrying me because I don't feel like marrying *anyone*. I feel so good being on my own. Take care of your issues, I'll take care of mine and if we meet along the way and have a good time, more the better.

"Oh, and one more thing. I trust this isn't going to be a problem, but while we're having fun together, there will be only one man's shoes under my bed and I expect to be the only pair of high heels—"

He held up his hand. "It goes without saying."

"I assumed so. Now, are we squared away on the expectations? Because I'll miss you if you go, but you shouldn't worry you're going to let me down."

He took in her bright eyes, her confident smile, the flush of happiness which included him but wasn't only about him. She was remarkable. "I'm not going to let you down," he said. And he wasn't sure how he'd manage that, but it had suddenly become the most important thing in the world.

"Of course, there is one little issue that's getting in the way of my striking out with complete independence...."

"Oh?" he asked.

"I don't want to mention it if it's going to make you all clingy...."

"Throw it on out there, Les," he said.

"I'm having trouble with the garbage disposal...."

He smiled broadly. "It will be my pleasure to have a look at your garbage disposal. Don't get any ideas, though."

"Part of learning real independence is knowing who to ask," she informed him.

"Then, if you've had just about enough shrimp curry, why don't you ask me back to bed."

Leslie had always been close to her parents, both of them, and talked to one or both of them at least every couple of days. But they had been married for ten years before she'd come along and to say they were tight as a couple was the understatement of the century; they made good role models for a successful marriage. In fact, it would occasionally occur to her to worry what would happen if one of them passed. Surely they would fit into that classic model of the spouse who followed his or her partner to the other side rather quickly.

When Leslie married Greg she had wanted that kind of relationship. She'd always known she didn't have it, but until it was over she hadn't realized how far from that ideal they'd been. "In fact," she had said to her mother during a recent phone conversation, "it's only since I came here that I've really begun to see how much was missing from our marriage. Greg had the kind of marriage he needed and I helped him achieve it by going along with everything he said he needed. Isn't that what a good wife tries to do? No wonder his defection was so hard on me. I couldn't figure out what more I could've done for him!"

"Oh, Les, it sounds like you're finally getting ready to really let go of him," Candace Petruso said.

"Not just getting ready—I have!" She told her mother about Greg's surprise visit and her fire-extinguisher

attack on him, which sent Candace into a fit of laughter.
"And," Leslie confided, "I'm kind of seeing someone."

"And who might that be?"

"Oh, one of the carpenters who works for Paul. Very
nice man, very handsome. He's helped me with a few
things around the house—helped me with some land-
scaping and fixed my garbage disposal. We sometimes
grab a movie or go to a restaurant or just hang out together. I've cooked for him a few times and recently
he surprised me with a small backyard grill so he can
cook for me. You'd like him."

"I can't wait to meet him," her mother said.

Leslie's conversations with her parents were usually dominated by all that sixtysomething Candace
and Robert were doing to stay busy, which had saved
Leslie from revealing too much about Conner or her
deep fondness for him. Her parents were so busy that
sometimes they joked they had to take a vacation to get
a rest from retirement. The latest thing they'd taken up
was learning Italian in preparation for a Mediterranean
cruise in a few months. Some of their friends would
also be going, and Leslie's parents were in a fever of
excitement.

Now, as Leslie mentioned Conner to her parents,
she tried to cover the subject quickly. She couldn't help
sharing news, but wanted to keep him to herself for now.
Her connection with Conner seemed strangely wrong
yet miraculously right. Wrong because she shouldn't
have that kind of rapport with someone she'd barely met

when she couldn't find it with a spouse of eight years. And right because it just *was*.

Leslie thought the best of both worlds suited her magnificently—an independent life and a man who was free to spend two or three nights a week with her. Sometimes she'd sit on the back porch with Conner and just admire the setting sun and the flowers and the fragrant spring weather, talking. It was rather amazing how much beyond a couple of crappy marriages and divorces they had to talk about. In fact, once the facts of those had been shared, they found many more interesting things to discuss, from global warming (on which they did not agree) to *American Idol* (upon which they did).

Many of their conversations, whether over dinner, breakfast, on the back porch or cuddled up in bed, touched on values like honesty, loyalty, just plain knowing what was the right thing to do.

"How about being unfaithful in a marriage?" she asked him.

He grunted before he spoke. "Look, it's too easy to say just plain never do that, even though that's what I want to say. I know all marriages aren't made in heaven. Sometimes there are circumstances that are hard to understand."

"Like Greg falling in love for the first time after eight years of marriage?" she asked.

"I was thinking of my own shortcomings, to tell the truth. Giving your word on something usually requires a sacrifice, and it's the measure of a man by how much he can live up to his word. I gave my word, Les, but I wasn't able to keep it when it came to my ex-wife. A stronger man would've tried to understand and give her a chance to at least make amends, but I couldn't. Wouldn't. And Greg stepping out on you like he did? Not only do I think he was wrong, I think he was a fool. But damn, did I end up getting the good end of that deal or what? Because now that I know you, I know you wouldn't have looked at me twice if you were married."

After a moment of thought, she said, "I think the best happened for me, too. You, naturally. But a lot of other useful lessons, as well."

There was a lot going on around Virgin River as April neared May and the Virgin River School neared completion. The town had big plans for a grand opening. People around town were furiously scouting secondhand stores, closing schools with content to sell, eBay and other resources for items to stock the school with. Dan and Cheryl's house was finished, thanks to the help of many friends, including Conner, and they were planning a party, immediately after which they were headed north for that fishing trip Dan had mentioned.

"I spent a lot of time in charity work," Leslie told him while they were lazing around in her bed late on a Saturday morning. "It's good but not quite as fulfilling as actually helping out a friend, you know? It's fun helping Dan and Cheryl plan their party or helping Becca look for furnishings and supplies for the actual school in which she'll teach."

Her doorbell rang, followed by a rapid knocking.

"I'll get it," she told him. "I think the kid down the street has been selling candy for school. Stay where you are. I'll be right back." She got out of bed and grabbed her terry robe.

"We should probably get up," he said.

"Just give me a minute." She tied her robe and blew him a kiss.

The doorbell rang again; the knocking followed.

"Hold your horses," she said, throwing open the door.

And there stood the sixty-eight-year-old fun couple she knew so well. Her father had that oddly colored, thinning hair and her mother's short blond was all teased up and spiky, Ms. Modern. They were dressed… in evening clothes? Cocktail party attire.

"Coffee on?" her father asked, beaming.

"Mom? Dad? What are you doing here?"

Eight

"We missed you," Candace Petruso said. "And we have a surprise."

"Why are you dressed like that?" Leslie asked.

"Part of the surprise. Leslie, I thought for sure you'd be up. It's…" She looked at her watch. "My gosh, it's ten!"

"It's Saturday morning!" Leslie protested, a little flustered.

"You're usually an early riser," Robert said, pushing his way into the house. "Where's the kitchen? I'll put on the coffee. Candace, you get the music ready and we'll push a little furniture back, make space." And he was off in the direction of the kitchen.

"Music? What is going on?" Leslie demanded. "Did you get up at five to make this drive from Grants Pass?"

Candace came in and looked around. "Oh, Les, this is just as adorable as the pictures you sent. I think it's really *you*. You know your father—he can't sleep past four-thirty even though he has nothing in the world to get up for. And he can't seem to be quiet, either. We had something we wanted to show you so we decided on the spur of the moment. It's a nice drive."

"Must have been kind of uncomfortable in your fancy clothes," she observed.

"Don't be silly, we stopped at a service station and changed," Candace said. She put her iPod with speakers on Leslie's coffee table.

Robert was back, brushing his hands together. "There! Coffee's on. Let's make a little room here." He pushed the chair back against the wall, the coffee table against the sofa, the dining table back, chairs pushed in. "You're going to get the biggest kick out of this, Leslie," he said.

"I'd better." Leslie crossed her arms over her chest.

"It's spectacular," Robert promised. "Now stay right there. Candace, press Play."

Just as Candace pushed the button, before the music even started, Conner stepped into the room looking like pure sex. His short hair was mussed, and he had a scruffy growth of beard surrounding that tight, trim little goatee. He'd pulled on his faded jeans that hung low on his delicious hips, his feet bare. He wore his white T-shirt and had carelessly stuffed a handful of it into the low waist of the jeans right at the center, over the zipper. The hair on his chest was visible in the V-neck, and she wanted to run her fingers through it. His eyes were sleepy and his smile small and one-sided. He came to stand next to Leslie.

"Oh!" Candace said, startled. A tango began to play,

and Candace looked at her husband. "Robert, we should have called! We're intruding."

"No problem," Conner said.

Candace smiled. "You must be Conner," she said.

"Luckily," he said, causing Leslie to laugh.

Candace grabbed Robert's hand and said, "We'll be along now and call you in a couple of hours. Maybe we can get together for lunch or something...."

"Don't be silly," Leslie said. "You're here now. Let's see your surprise. Then we'll plan lunch."

"Are you sure?" Candace asked.

"The tango, I presume?" Leslie asked, lifting a brow.

"I guess we got a little excited. We've been taking some dance lessons."

"Getting ready to knock 'em dead on the cruise! You're the only one we're showing," Robert said. "This sort of thing was a lot easier when you lived in Grants Pass."

"Well, let's see, then," Leslie said.

"Are you absolutely sure, honey?" Candace wanted to know.

"Go for it, Mother. Believe me, you have my complete attention."

Candace started the music again, Robert swept her up in the traditional embrace, and they glided back and forth across the living room floor. Nicely, as a matter of fact. They were very agile and coordinated, and their moves were well matched. They looked into each other's eyes like practiced partners ready for *Dancing with the Stars*. Her mother's short, spiky blond hair even looked professionally done. Leslie tilted her head and glanced up at Conner. He lifted his brows in amusement.

After watching them dance for a couple of minutes, Conner turned and pulled Leslie into his arms. He put her arm around his shoulder and tucked her hand into his chest. Then with his cheek against hers, he simply rocked back and forth, dancing his own slower dance, keeping time with the music. Sort of.

"Your parents are very interesting," he whispered in her ear.

She laughed. "Aren't they?"

"Your mother is gorgeous for almost seventy."

"I know. I hope I got her genes."

"I do, too. Otherwise you might find yourself dying your hair with some reddish-black concoction." She giggled. "Your dad has the worst dye job I've ever seen."

"I know. Mom fusses about his thinning hair all the time, but apparently to him it looks good."

"He got a lot of it on his bean," Conner said. "I think he stained it good."

"I know," she said as she chuckled.

"They're fun, aren't they?" Conner asked.

"Sometimes a bit too much fun," she answered.

"Look at them," he said. "They're having the time of their lives, doing the tango in their daughter's living room. How long have they been married?"

"Forty-three years."

"When the dance contest is over, here's what we should do," Conner said. "I should go home to shower, shave and change, you should have coffee with your folks and get dressed, and then we should meet at Jack's for lunch so they can interrogate me a little bit."

They turned and looked as Robert dragged Candace across the floor in a wicked tango move. They turned back.

"Okay," Leslie said. "But you don't have to be interrogated."

"I don't mind a little bit," he said. "Basic information, you know. Name, rank, serial number. Let's not tell them I was married to a sex addict, okay?"

"I still haven't told them I was married to a guy who had trouble getting it up."

Conner's eyes flew open wide. "He did?"

"Shit. I was going to be classy and keep that to myself. Naturally I thought that was mostly my fault."

He ran a knuckle down the curve of her jaw; his blue eyes got all dark and smoky. "No way."

"Thank you," she mouthed.

Candace and Robert ended the tango with an elaborate flourish that left Candace draped along the floor at Robert's feet, one arm extended into the air.

Leslie and Conner parted and applauded while Robert helped his wife to her feet. He bowed and Candace dipped into a curtsy. "What do you think, honey?" Robert asked.

"I think you're awesome, provided one of you doesn't break a hip." She stared pointedly at her mother. "You might want to go easy on the collapsing to the floor part, Mom."

"I'm very careful and my bone density is excellent,"

Candace said. "All right, we'll get out of your hair. If you really do have time for lunch, just tell us—"

"I have a better idea," Conner said. "I'm going home to shower and change. I'll meet you at noon, if that works for you three."

"Perfect," Leslie said. "See you at Jack's."

As Conner drove to his cabin to change, he saw it as very strange indeed that he should consider the tango debut of Leslie's eccentric parents absolutely normal, but he did. Sure they were a little out there, but they were clearly enjoying life and each other. And they loved Leslie.

When Conner had been twenty and Katie a mere seventeen a heart attack had dropped their mother like a stone. She'd only been fifty-three and hadn't seemed the high-risk type at all—she had been trim and fit and very energetic, much like Candace. Three years later their father passed after a short, difficult battle with colon cancer—he'd been sixty-three.

Not only had they lost their parents too young, Conner and Katie had been left the house they'd grown up in and Conner's Hardware. Twenty-three and the owner/operator of a substantial business. If he hadn't had a few trusted employees who had worked for his father for a long time, he would surely have sunk out of sight. Now he found himself wondering what his parents would be like, had they lived. Nothing like Candace and Robert, that was for sure. His mom hadn't ever been very fancy and his dad had been a real stick-in-the-mud. They wouldn't be taking tango lessons or going on cruises. But his dad had had a dream of a retirement cabin on a lake that was full of fat fish. They both had looked forward to grandchildren...and had never met the boys.

Had Conner relocated to Virgin River for some reason other than this particular one, his parents would have enjoyed this kind of place. But he was living a whole new life in a whole new world, and he found himself hoping Leslie's parents would like the new him.

Leslie jumped in the shower, then pulled on some jeans. With her hair still wet and wildly curly, she grabbed a cup of coffee and went in search of her parents. She found her mother sitting on the back porch enjoying a lovely late-April morning. Candace had changed into slacks, and Robert was nowhere in sight.

"Where's Dad?" Leslie asked, joining her mother.

"He wanted to walk around the town a little bit. Leslie, I apologize again. How naive of me—I knew you had a young man in your life...."

"Don't give it a thought."

"Well, we're so foolish. We might've come all this way and found you weren't even at home! I promise, I'll think ahead in the future."

"I was home and everything is fine."

"Conner went home to shower," Candace said. "Does that mean he doesn't exactly live here with you?"

Leslie laughed. "He doesn't at all! Conner has a very small cabin by the river and I've never even seen it. His stay in Virgin River could be even more temporary than mine."

"And what brings him here?"

"He has an old friend who found him a job with Paul after the contractor he worked for in Colorado Springs filed bankruptcy and shut down. But Conner has a sister who's still back in Colorado Springs. She's a young widow with a couple of little boys. Conner has mentioned more than once that he misses them, that he wants to be closer. They're his only family."

"He's close to his family."

"He is. And from what I hear from Paul, he's a very talented finisher and carpenter. Great with cabinetry, stone countertops and such. No matter where he goes, he'll land on his feet with work."

"And the two of you?" Candace asked. "Is it serious?"

"In a way," Leslie said with a little lift of one shoulder. "As you can tell, we're very close, but we're realistic. I came here to rebuild my confidence, and Conner is here to work until he can either go back home or find a place that's right for himself, his sister and the kids. Our paths might only converge for a while. But he is such a good man, Mom. And I am so happy I met him."

"And your confidence?"

She chuckled softly. "This is the best totally accidental move I've ever made. Not even two full months and I have friends, a great job, a good man in my life and I have a much better feeling about myself. Mom, I didn't realize how Greg's expectations of me hammered my self-esteem until I broke away from Grants Pass entirely! We were supposed to both be playing on the Greg Adams team, getting him all the things he wanted in business, in the city. And then he expected me to be the perfect ex-wife and wanted me to continue to play on his team. In fact, if he had things his way, it would be a bigger, stronger team—one including his new wife and their baby!"

"Phhhttt," Candace said in disgust. "He was always like that. He was such a pain in my ass while we planned the wedding, I wanted to knock his block off!"

"He was?" Leslie asked.

"Oh, Lord! As if it was all about showcasing *him!*"

Leslie wrinkled up her forehead as she tried to re-member the details.

"You know," Candace went on. "We had to run about five suggested venues by him before we found one that was good enough for him! Your father finally asked him if he was picking up the tab, because his family certainly wasn't stepping up—they don't have a pot to piss in!"

"Mother, I've never heard such language from you! I mean, I can swear like a truck driver but you're usu-ally—"

"Greg Adams doesn't bring out my best behavior," Candace said with a definite curl of the lip.

"But, Mom, you were one of many people who said I should let go, move on!"

"Yes, sweetheart. And do you know how hard it was

not to say you caught a break when he walked out on you?"

Leslie choked. "I thought you loved Greg!"

"Leslie," Candace said, leaning toward her daughter, "*you* loved Greg. Therefore I couldn't say anything negative about him."

"Not even when he cheated on me and left me for another woman?"

"You *still* loved him. You were in terrible pain. How could I say you were crazy to love that weasel in the first place? Saying something like that makes *you* look foolish, and you are not foolish. At least not about most things. I have to be honest, I always thought you saw more in Greg Adams than there was."

Stunned, Leslie took a moment to absorb this. "You did?"

"He was never good enough for you."

Oh, God, life was strange, Leslie thought. All that time she'd had the feeling she wasn't good enough for him, it was the other way around? But that was her mother—mothers always felt that way. "You should have said something...."

"I couldn't. Marriage rule."

"Huh?" Leslie asked.

"You know. I can call my husband an idiot and asshole but no one else can. It's a rule. It's almost a *law*."

"There is that...."

"Besides, you wouldn't have listened. And you would've gotten mad at *me*," Candace said.

"Possibly. But okay, in the future, will you please risk it? Because I spent so much time…"

Candace was shaking her head. "I don't know, my angel. I was at odds with so many of your decisions and really, you blew me off. Like the whole idea that Greg's political career—" And right there a bark of laughter came out of her petite mother's mouth, and she covered it with her hand. "Hmm. That his political career was so important you'd decided not to have children so you could focus on that. You, who had always said an only child wasn't a good idea, and when you got married you'd have at least two, maybe three, maybe even four. And *what* political career?"

"He thought he was going places. He was the Chamber of Commerce president and aspired to—"

"Phhhttt," Candace said with a wave of her hand. "Your father was president of the Chamber, the Rotary, a dozen city organizations. And I'm no slouch—I headed the Junior League for three years! In fact, I was asked to run for City Council but I just didn't have the time."

Leslie mentally checked her memory book. That was all true. Her parents had had more political influence before she married Greg than Greg had to date. *Was I in some kind of romantic fog?*

"I never put these things together," Leslie said. "I thought he was wonderful for such a long time."

"He had his fine points," Candace said. "When you first met and were first married, he fussed over you. He definitely romanced you and treated you like the First Lady he wanted you to be. Of course he also treated you like his administrative assistant. *Give Leslie a call and ask if I can squeeze that in. Check with Leslie and ask if we can make a donation. Leslie will know if I can speak at that event.*"

"God! He did!"

"It was so annoying!" Candace said. "We had a fight once, you know."

"You did? You and Greg?"

Candace nodded. "I didn't want you to ever know. It was not my finest hour. You know how we had to split holidays with his family? One of us got Christmas Eve and the other got Christmas day? And it was every other Thanksgiving? And the Adamses always had first choice. Well, I always had a problem with that whole idea—I didn't know why we couldn't all be together. I welcomed his mother and father and even his no-account brother and that whole crew. But I called your house, and he answered when you weren't home yet. I told him I wanted to nail down the holiday schedule, the plans for when we'd get to host. He very sweetly told me that you were managing his schedule because *he* was in such demand that he didn't even know which days were free, and you were the manager of *his* 'events' calendar. What a load of crap—all he did was go to meetings and dinners and play golf with potential investors."

"That doesn't sound like a fight…."

Candace looked down briefly where her hands with the perfectly manicured nails were folded in her lap. "I told him to kiss my ass. And then I just called you at the office."

Leslie laughed with delight. "Really? That's awesome. I wish I'd known that."

Candace was quiet for a moment. Finally she said, "It was a long eight years of you promoting him, Les. He knew how to choose restaurants, music, order from the menu, and his plans for his future were a priority. Not your future, but his. Your dad and I sometimes wondered if we'd have to have you deprogrammed." She shook her head. "He must have been some kind of wonderful in the sack."

A burst of laughter shot out of Leslie, not because her mother had been so candid but because she'd been so *wrong*.

"How would you have felt about us if our marriage had lasted?" Leslie asked her mother.

"Leslie, it doesn't matter how other people feel about your spouse! Don't you see? You chose him, you had to live with him, he was your package to adore or be fed up with! Once you made your choice, I didn't have a right to an opinion. Your grandma Petruso never much cared for me and she let me know it—I learned a very important lesson from that. And I made a vow never to be that kind of mother-in-law.

"But he's not my son-in-law anymore and I don't have to pretend to have any hero worship. All I care about is that you find the happiness in life you deserve."

Leslie felt her eyes mist. "Every time I saw him with Allison it felt like a knife. I wonder how long I would have suffered like that if I hadn't decided to leave Grants Pass...."

"It was obviously a good decision," Candace said. "And I dreaded it so much...."

"It's temporary," she said. "I'm sure I'll be back eventually, and in the meantime we'll visit. I'll admit something, Mom—I was thinking of coming up for a weekend and I hated the thought of not spending my time off with Conner!"

Candace ruffled Leslie's curls. "Speaking of Conner, we don't want to keep him waiting. Go tame your wild hair—your dad should be back any second."

When they were all seated for lunch at a table in Jack's bar, Leslie's parents first asked Conner where he was from and whether he had any family. Right after that Leslie redirected the conversation before it could turn into Twenty Questions.

"Mom, tell Conner about your last cruise and the friends-for-life you made."

Candace was only too happy to comply, and now, at the age of thirty-two, Leslie was rediscovering her mother. Candace was not the least bit wrapped up in herself, despite allowing the conversation to revolve around the activities of this retired couple. In fact, she gave Leslie a little wink before she embarked on a description of their Alaskan cruise.

Candace used the excuse to talk as a way of not having an opinion about Conner. And Conner asked questions. "Did you fish while you were in Alaska?"

"No, but we definitely ate some of the best fish imaginable. We nearly had to fight bears for it. We went to an outdoor restaurant built along a river where the bear fish!"

"You can see that here all summer," the eavesdropping Jack said while delivering drinks to the table.

"Is that a fact?" Robert asked.

And of course Jack hung around a while to extol the scenic virtues of Virgin River. And while he did so, Conner slipped his arm around Leslie's shoulders and gave her a squeeze.

After lunch, Leslie asked her parents if they couldn't stay through the weekend.

"Not this time, honey. But if you get some furniture for that second bedroom, we'll happily come back. I wouldn't mind learning to fish if there's a bear sideshow to go with it."

After lunch, the Petrusos left Virgin River, and Conner went back to Leslie's house. Once there, he pulled a shovel and stakes out of his truck.

"Paul ordered cement for your drive and I asked him to let me get it ready. I'm going to trench it out so he can have it poured this week."

"I'll help," she offered.

"Nah," he said, giving her a kiss on the forehead. "Go find something relaxing to do. Read a book. Knit. Do you knit?" he asked. She shook her head, and he laughed. "Take a nap, then. I'll be about two or three hours. Then I'll grab a shower and make you a burger on the grill later, if you're interested."

"Always interested," she said. "Why did you take this on?"

"I heard him mention it to Dan and I said I'd be happy to do it. I didn't have plans. I guess there's going to be a little building here, too. He wants to add on a covered carport with a storage closet. You knew that, right?"

"I knew that," she said. "I didn't know it would fall to you."

"It didn't, babe. I asked for the job. Now go find a way to kick back."

So for the next three hours, while Conner sweated in the driveway, digging a wide path for concrete, Leslie sat on the porch with her feet propped up on the rail and a book in her lap. She didn't get much reading done. She found herself watching Conner more than the book she held. And she smiled a lot. Because despite all their proclamations of finding themselves and working out their issues without becoming too involved, there was one thing she knew in her heart.

He was hers.

Nine

As Brie walked into the bar in the midafternoon she found her brother had removed all the glasses and liquor bottles and was giving the mirror and glass shelves a good cleaning. This was the sort of chore Jack liked to do during the time of day there were few patrons.

"Sparkling up the place, Jack?" she asked.

"Hey," he said. "What are you doing here?"

"I had to drop a load of old clothes off at the church. They're getting ready for another rummage sale."

"Haven't they sold enough rummage yet?" Jack asked.

"It's only disguised as a rummage sale. They hold back a lot of stuff they can just give away as needs arise, and what they sell, they sell so cheap it's the same as charity. But the women's group gets a little something for their kitty. Ness is playing with your kids, or hopefully taking a nap with your kids, and I thought I'd let you buy me a Diet Coke."

"My pleasure," he said, leaning over the bar to give his sister a little peck on the forehead.

"I'm not interrupting your cleaning binge, am I?"

"You are, but I don't mind. I don't get to visit with you that often." He poured and served her the drink. "Seems like you've been busier than usual lately."

"The county has kept me really busy. My part-time job is taking more than full-time. Just as well," she shrugged. "There aren't enough cases around here for a private practice anyway."

"But that's how you like it," he said. "The days of the overworked A.D.A. are not all that far behind you. You've always loved to work."

"As a consultant for the local D.A., I usually don't have such a full plate. It's usually just here and there."

"I haven't seen much of you, that's for sure. You must be over in Eureka all the time."

"Plenty of domestics and sexual assaults right now for some reason, my unfortunate specialty. Anything interesting happening around here? Anything more upbeat than my line of work?" she asked.

"This is an upbeat kind of place," he said. "Sometimes I feel like frickin' Cupid. I think we got ourselves another romance, and man, I never saw it coming. But now that I think about it, it makes sense."

"Oh?" she asked, taking a sip.

"Yeah. That friend of yours, Conner. And Paul's old/new secretary, Leslie."

Brie sputtered and choked. She tried to recover, but she coughed until her eyes watered; the cola went down the wrong pipe. It took her a couple of seconds, and then in a weak voice she said, "Really?"

"You all right?" Jack asked.

"Swallowed funny. Tell me about the new romance. You sure?"

"Yeah, I'm sure. They were in here for lunch today with Leslie's parents. Her folks drove down from Grants Pass for a quick visit and, I assume, to meet Conner. And it was a pretty cozy lunch. Conner had his arm around Leslie the whole time and the four of them seemed to hit it off. Another one bites the dust." And then he laughed.

Brie cleared her throat and tried to appear nonchalant. "You said it made perfect sense. Why is that?"

"Oh, they seem right, but that's just me talking. But here's the gist—he's here alone for work and she's here alone to put some distance between her and her ex-husband. I assume they met at work and boom— hormones. Those really fun hormones—remember those? And there was the definite scent of satisfaction in the air. Those two are getting it on."

"And that's it? You saw them together and you assume…?"

"No, Leslie stopped by for takeout for two a couple of times and so did Conner, so I knew they were seeing some action with someone. I just didn't realize it was each other. Seeing them together? It looks just right. I've always had a good eye for that sort of thing."

Brie was stunned silent for a moment. Then she recovered and said, "Oh, gee, look at the time. I better get going."

"You haven't been here ten minutes! What's the rush?" Jack asked.

"If I get home before Ness wakes up from her nap, I might get a couple of things done without the constant interference. Thanks, Jack. You're a dream brother."

"Oh, yeah? You could stay ten whole minutes if I'm such a dream."

"I know you want to get back to your spring cleaning…"

"Oh, yeah, I was dying to do some more clean—"

But Brie wasn't listening, she was on the move. She barely knew Leslie; she'd run into her a couple of times at the bar, but on neither occasion had Conner been with her.

She wasn't quite sure where to go. To Leslie's? She didn't know where Leslie lived. She headed for the Riordan cabins, though she knew on a Saturday Conner might be spending his day off with his new girlfriend!

She was going to kill him!

When she pulled into the Riordan compound, it was just after four, and she saw him fishing in the river with Art. She pulled in, parked and plastered a cheerful expression on her face as she approached the two men.

"Hey," she called. "Hi, Art. Hi, Conner."

"Hey, Brie," Art said. "You wanna fish?"

"Gee, thanks, Art, but I'm gonna pass. I wanted to talk to Conner for a second."

"You sure?" Art asked. "I have another rod…."

She smiled at him. "You're so generous, thank you. Not today."

"I never seen you fish, Brie," Art pointed out to her.

"But you've fished with Mike many times."

"Uh-huh," he said. "He's good, too."

"Conner," Brie asked. "A minute?"

"Sure." He reeled in his line and turned to exit the river. "Save my place, Art."

He stood on the riverbank looking at Brie.

"Your cabin, please? It won't take long," she said, smiling the whole time. And then she turned to walk slowly back toward the cabins.

He caught up with her, his waders making a scrunching, squeaking sound with each step. "Everything okay?" he asked.

"Sure," she said. "Which one is yours?"

"Number four," he said. When they got there, he leaned the rod against the outside wall and took off the waders. He opened the unlocked door and held it for her.

When they were both inside and the door closed, her expression went south in a hurry, and she punched him in the shoulder. It was not the force of the blow but her angry expression and surprise that caused him to take a backward step. "Hey!"

"Have you lost your mind?" she snapped. "You have a thing going with Leslie? Didn't we talk about this?"

"Not exactly," he said. "If you're referring to telling me this wouldn't be an ideal time to hook up with someone, I heard that. I couldn't agree more. In fact, when you get down to it, it's not an ideal time for *anything!*"

Brie got right in his face. "What are you thinking? You're supposed to be flying under the radar as much as possible!"

"Yeah? Then you brought me to the wrong place! I've been helping erect the school, finish a friend's house, hang out at the bar with your brother and work overtime for your friend Paul. I've been fishing with Art every week. Art depends on me fishing with him. And that's the tip of the iceberg. This isn't the kind of place where you stay a stranger for long."

"But a *girlfriend?*" she said, an accusing tone to her voice.

"I didn't plan that," he said.

"Where's this going? You going to just leave her high and dry when it's time to testify?"

"No," he said. "At the very least I'm going to tell her. Everything."

Brie palmed the top of her own head and dug her fingers into her scalp, massaging. "Oh, God. And make her collateral damage, too?"

"How?"

"If the other side ever finds out who's important to you here—"

"The list would be long," he said flatly. "And it might even include you."

"No. No, you don't understand. The rest of us have a lot of other links—like for example, I'm married to a cop. Jack's not exactly someone you love even if you like him. Lots of people worked on the school. But Leslie is alone...."

"No, she's not. Paul and Dan look out for her, too. She's not that alone and I'm not going to leave her stranded and like a sitting duck. Not going to."

"You shouldn't tell anyone anything until your testimony is complete and you're finished with the court!"

"You know where I am, so what if the bad guys snatch your daughter? Would you tell them?"

"I'm not going to know where you are after then, which makes what I'm putting out for this effort the ultimate sacrifice!"

"You're going crazy," Conner said. "Stop it, it's my job to go crazy."

"Can you break it off?" Brie asked. "Before it gets any more serious?"

"No."

"Conner, this could be bad for you. Emotionally bad, if you have to cut and run. It could be bad for her if anyone on the other team ever figures out there's someone here you really care about. They could leverage her to get to you."

"Then maybe we should change the game plan...."

"Huh?" Brie said, startled.

"Just thinking out loud, maybe Danson Conner disappears forever and Conner Danson grows a new life in Virgin River. I have a hard time believing any of Mathis's connections are going to figure out I'm here."

"People will make the connection when you testify...."

"Maybe I won't testify, then," he said. "I can't believe they won't make a conviction without me—they have the car, the murder weapon, forensics.... Max said there's other evidence, he just wouldn't tell me what."

"And an eyewitness, who led them to all the other evidence! Max will pull the plug on you! He's not going to help you maintain this cover—he can't. It costs the state money."

"I'm working. I'm paying the rent on this cabin," he argued.

"You think transferring all your identity and bank accounts was free? You think that truck you're driving is free? And if you try to sell your Sacramento properties without a middleman like the D.A., Mathis is going to find out. At least we have to assume he knows how to get that information, even though it wouldn't be through legal channels. Besides, you know it's the right thing to do! If you don't testify, you're setting a murderer free, and even though he looks upstanding, if he'd kill once... Conner...!"

"Settle down. I know it's the right thing to do. It also might be right to stare him in the eye while I do it."

"And what the hell does that mean?"

"Hey—didn't you tell me you looked the man who almost killed you in the eye and said, 'He's the one'? And did you change your identity? Hide in Virgin River? No, you pointed at him, put him away and got on with your life."

She was shaking her head. "There was no evidence

he was connected to dangerous people, people he could commission to come after me for revenge!"

Conner chuckled. "Don't you watch TV? He's been in prison for years now. If he wanted to, he could make a partnership. I doubt he will, but he could. Revenge is a hot poker, kind of hard to forget. Now don't get me wrong, I'm not trying to scare you or anything. I bet I'm not telling you anything you haven't already thought of."

"I'm just trying to help keep you safe. And you're making me very nervous."

"You're not the one who should be nervous. I've been thinking a lot and I think maybe what I'll do is ask Max to unload all that property. Sell it. The furnishings and personal property in the two houses. He can launder the money, so to speak, so the proceeds of the sale aren't made out to Danson Conner. We'll liquidate, make a fresh start. It's what we were going to do anyway. When it's time, I'll go to Sacramento and testify and come back here. I'll start over here with my new name and my family."

"Your family?"

"I don't know what Katie wants for herself and her boys, but we've talked. We know we're not going home. But I want them here. This is the right kind of place for them. Maybe I'll work cabinetry for the rest of my life. Maybe I'll do something else."

She took a step toward him. "And Leslie, as well? Mathis had your store burned down! Your life was threatened!"

Conner looked down. When he lifted his eyes, they were blazing. "I never saw it coming. He won't take me by surprise again."

"Conner, what you're proposing is dangerous to you and your ancillary connections, like Katie and her boys. Like Leslie. I think what we should do is move you. I'll call Max and tell him we have a complication and have to get you away from here before anyone can make the connection."

"No. I'm not going."

She shook her head. "If you care about her, you have to reconsider."

"I care about her, and before I make any moves, I'll give her the choice." He lifted one shoulder in a half shrug. "Maybe she'll tell me to be on my way. She's not here to find the right guy, she's here trying to get her idea of the right guy out of her head—that ex-husband who cost her so much. Besides, she's close to her family—no way she's going into hiding. I wouldn't even ask her to."

"You love her."

"Don't get ahead of me. We're enjoying life. We haven't said those kind of things to each other." He swallowed. "I don't want to crowd her."

"You're talking about just ignoring the threat Mathis and his people impose."

"No, sir," he said. "I'm talking about defending my loved ones, something I never knew I had to do before, something you and the D.A. have made a point of suggesting is impossible for me to do. I have a gun and I have—" He broke off and laughed cynically. "I have the Virgin River posse. Even though all I've done for these good people is help out here and there, I have no doubt they'd back me up."

Brie was quiet for a long moment. Finally she said, "They deserve better than that."

"I haven't done anything yet," he reminded her. "I haven't told anyone. I haven't changed our game plan. But if you push this, I will. Because Les and I deserve a break. Just a break to see if maybe we found something worth the risk. That's all I'm saying."

"You're not in charge," Brie said forcefully.

"Yes," he said. "I am."

That night, as Conner held Leslie, the temptation to tell all was overwhelming. He didn't, but he wanted to. He wanted to say, *This thing happened and testifying is the right thing to do and I can keep you safe. I know I have to keep the people I love safe.*

Instead he said, "Your parents are nice."

"Yeah. The fun couple. They're wonderful. Sometimes their antics are a little embarrassing, but I have to remember how supportive they are."

"Antics?"

"Oh, they love dressing up funny, getting into fund-raising things like pie-throwing contests or dunking booths. For their fortieth anniversary they went bungee jumping off a bridge in Oregon. They're kind of *Where's the party?* all the time. But I have to say, they've never let me down. Maybe I've let them down...."

"That's hard to imagine."

"I'm just realizing… I was pretty caught up in…other things for the past few…okay, for the past decade or so. I might've kept them at arm's length. I'll never do that again."

"You shouldn't, Les," he said. "You don't know how much time you'll have with them. They're a little wacky, but in a good way. Enjoy."

"Do you understand everything?"

He laughed. "Oh, hell no. But I lost my parents when I was young. And even though yours are a lot more fun than mine were, there are times I still miss them. And my life would be totally different if they hadn't died prematurely. Just be glad you have a chance to spend some more time with yours." He coughed. "That dye job, though…"

"I know…."

Conner sat in front of The Loving Cup in his truck and phoned Katie. He talked to Mitch and Andy for a few minutes, but, with the typical attention span of five-year-old boys, that didn't last long. Then Katie was back on the phone.

"I want to ask you something, and I want you to be honest."

"I'm always honest," she said.

"Are you afraid of what's going to happen after I testify?"

"We've been over this, but if we have to go over it again, okay. I know life will never be the same, Conner.

I knew the morning the store burned down that life as we've known it is over. I knew then—I can't live in Sacramento again. I'll look over my shoulder like I never have before. I'm doing it already. But it is what it is—there's no changing it. It happened to us—and you have to follow through. You can't let that man win. You know what the worst part is? Having no choice. There's no choice, Conner. We have to go on. Forward."

She was brave. She'd always been brave. "I'll be honest—I've been giving a lot of thought to not going to court—"

"Your woman," she said immediately.

He just grunted. "Not her. Me. But she's like you. I haven't told her anything, but she'd expect me to do the right thing even though it might cost her in the end."

"I like her," Katie said.

"I'm in a good place. I don't know where you are emotionally, but I'm in a sweet little town off the grid. I want you and the boys here."

Dead silence filled the space in the conversation.

"Katie?"

"Because of the new girlfriend?" she asked softly.

"No, honey. Because of the town. Because of the kind of place it is, because of the people. The woman might not even be here long. But this is the place to settle. I feel more strongly about that every day. The only downside is—it limits your prospects for a new man in your life. But the boys would do well here. And it would be easier to keep a close eye on them and you."

Again, silence.

"Katie?"

"Little complication," she said. She took a deep breath. "I think I have a crush on the dentist."

"You mentioned that before…."

"Yeah, but… Seriously."

"Are you involved?" he asked.

"Not romantically, not yet. But we spend more and more time together and gosh, Danny… Oops, sorry. *Conner.* I like him so much. He wants the same things I want—a stable home, kids, family. He's so sweet and smart and ethical. I think he's trying to maintain a professional relationship, but I swear if he even leans toward me like he wouldn't mind being kissed, I'm going to devour him. I'm sorry, but I am."

"This is happening at work?" Conner asked.

"At work, after work, at lunch and we've done a little extra time on the weekends. He's wonderful with the boys. He's gone to some of their soccer games, and they think he's so much fun. I cooked him dinner one night. He had us over for hot dogs and burgers on the grill one Sunday afternoon."

And now the silence was his.

She was in Vermont. Could she get any farther away? And they had both met people of interest, to put it lightly. Of course, she was working up a crush while he was in all the way, though he had no idea the degree in which Leslie was committed.

"Danny?" she whispered.

"Yeah. Here."

Those boys meant the world to him. Hell, Katie

meant the world! When their mother died, Conner had tried to fill the gap. When their father died, Conner had tried to be both mother and father to her. Katie's husband hadn't even seen the boys enter the world, but Conner had been there, at the hospital, spending the night there to help his sister with these newborn twins when they'd been less than a day old.

"I was kind of fantasizing you'd come here," she said. "I really like it here. I know, I know—we couldn't get farther apart and be in the same country."

He laughed. "We could if you were in Florida."

"Maybe this will work out...."

He'd always known that this could happen one day. He hadn't expected it to happen like this, with Katie moving away and meeting the man of her dreams because he was an eyewitness in a crime. But he'd always known she could fall in love with a man who could take her away, making the end result the same. And by damn, she deserved to fall in love again! Her short marriage to Charlie had been filled with intense love lost too soon.

"It'll work out, honey," he said.

No matter what he had to do, it would work out.

Ten

When the kitchen remodel work was finished on the house Dan and Conner had been concentrating on for the past two weeks, Conner volunteered to drive over the mountain to Paul's new office location to pick up the specs for the next job he wanted them to tackle. The trailer sat on the property for the big custom job; the foundation had been poured, the house was framed and huge.

Inside the trailer he found Paul, not in his office but perched on a sawhorse at the big plywood-fashioned table, his laptop and a lot of paper spread out. And the look on his face was, frankly, frustrated. "What's up, boss?" Conner asked.

"Fixtures, that's what. I've got a big renovation in Clear River and I don't know how I can make the owner happy and bring it in on budget. They have pictures from *Architecture Monthly*—top-of-the-line stuff—and I can't find most of it at builder's cost anywhere."

"Let me see," Conner said.

Paul handed over magazine cutouts.

Ah. This was what Conner did. He sold to custom builders. He looked at the pictures. "Nice. Monticello brass. Tuscan accents. Brushed nickel faucets, I like that. But this brass basin? I'd try to talk them out of that if I were you—pretty, but a godawful pain in the butt to keep from spotting. I don't like brass around water so much, but I'll be the first to admit it's classy. Brass accents is one thing, but... Hmm, and nice lighting—this shouldn't be hard. You wouldn't think Italian accents would work in a mountain house, but in thinking about it...perfect. Let me use the laptop a second, I think I know where we can find some of this stuff. Manufacturer prices."

"Really?" Paul said, turning his computer toward Conner.

"I'll try. I know some wholesalers who carry some of this stuff, or damn close replicas." He did a search, and in minutes he found the widespread faucets, the chandeliers, the spigots and showerheads, the cupboard knobs and handles. He scribbled down the order codes and prices. He launched into one item after another, found them, wrote down the specs. Some items were tougher than others—some weren't available at cost. "Try this alternative on the client—it's good quality, equal in value and, if you ask me, a fine-looking showerhead. Might even be better—it's a Koen and comes with a kick-ass lifetime guarantee." And he went on, through the kitchen and a few bathrooms, finding the actual items or good alternatives at even better prices.

"How'd you do that?" Paul asked.

"Paul, it's what I do. Kitchens and bathrooms."

"Yeah, but you do it like a contractor, not a finisher."

"The boss relied on me a lot. This is the kind of stuff I looked into all the time. Good hardware and contractors' prices."

"Thanks," Paul said, staring at a sheet of paper with lots of prices, order numbers and internet addresses. "Next time I'm not going to waste so much time. I'll just call you."

"Absolutely," Conner said. "I'd be happy to help."

Paul looked at him a bit oddly. "Sometimes I think there's more to you than meets the eye."

Conner laughed. "You have no idea. Do you have the specs for the next kitchen job? Dan and I will get started tomorrow if the owners are ready."

"Right here," Paul said, handing over some rolled-up architectural plans. "You'll tear out the existing kitchen in the next two to three days, get your flooring, raw cabinetry, granite cut to size, hardware and fixtures delivered over the next ten days. Make it happen."

"Big job," Conner said, looking through the plans.

"Good bid, too. We want to be on time. If you need help, let me know and I'll send over extra crew. I want these folks happy. They have a lot of friends."

"You bet."

"And, Conner, I wanted to talk to you about something else."

Conner lifted his eyebrows.

"Leslie," Paul said. "She's not here right now. She's

gone to Eureka for supplies for the office. But I wanted to talk to you about her."

Conner thought for a minute and then said, "Shoot."

Paul took a breath. Whatever it was, it wasn't easy for him. "I like you. Brie vouches for you. Dan says you're a good worker and conscientious. Dan trusts you and he's a hard sell. I don't have any reason to doubt you or suspect you, so it's not about that. But Les has been almost a part of the family for ten years and she's been through a lot lately. I don't want her to go through a lot more."

Conner gave a short nod. Word traveled fast; no surprise there. "Perfectly understandable. But you should talk to her, not me. Tell her what worries you, because I'm not looking to complicate anyone's life."

One corner of Paul's mouth curved. "She seems happy."

Conner almost smiled. "How about me? Do I seem happy?"

Paul laughed. "I couldn't read you if my life depended on it."

"Let me ask you something. Don't read anything into this, but when you were dating your wife, did a lot of people question you? Have a lot of opinions about your motives and behavior? Your intentions? Before you were even sure yourself?"

That brought a really big laugh out of Paul. "Yeah," he said. "Everybody and their brother. And have you met my father-in-law?" He shook his head with another laugh. He stood and stuck out a hand. "Good luck, buddy."

Conner took the hand. "Thanks. I think."

"Don't mess her up."

"She doesn't seem like the kind of woman who's real fragile or neurotic. In fact, I think she's the most normal woman I've dated. Ever."

"I just hope you're the most normal guy she's ever dated," Paul told him. "Because I met the last one, and she's due a normal guy."

April disappeared with a shower, and May arrived in the mountains with enough glowing sun to set the roadsides and hills on fire with color as the wildflowers took over. Conner borrowed Luke Riordan's Harley and took Leslie on a ride through the hills one Sunday afternoon. They rode through the mountains out to the ocean cliffs, through the redwoods and down through vineyards.

They stopped for a while on a hilltop to enjoy a breathtaking view, but the view only occupied them for a little while, and soon they were reclined on the grass, making out like teenagers.

"You're tempting," he told her. "I could get you naked right here, but there'd be a risk."

"Oh?"

"Well, there's a road for one thing. We could get into each other, like we do, and not hear an approaching car or truck until it's too late. Or, we could get fire ants in our underwear and really pay."

"Let's stop at the grocery, get a couple of filets, two potatoes, some mushrooms and asparagus and go home. You can grill the steak and asparagus and I'll be in charge of the potatoes and mushrooms."

"Deal," he said, standing and helping her up.

Later, when they were enjoying an after-dinner libation—her Merlot and his beer—she said, "I hope this doesn't scare you, but I can't remember ever feeling this calm."

"Why would that scare me?"

"I know you aren't really into the idea of any kind of permanence. But I feel so much better than I can ever remember feeling."

The idea of permanence sounded great. It just wasn't a luxury he could afford at the moment. A lot had to be worked out first. "Why do you suppose that is?"

"I don't know. Maybe because I'm not dancing as fast as I can. Conner, I seriously didn't realize how hard I had to work at my relationship with Greg. I was used to people saying marriage was hard work and I bought it. I don't think I understood what they meant—I think what I didn't get was that *both* people were supposed to be working at it, not just one of us."

Oh, man, am I going to upset her calm world, Conner thought. "All couples are going to have issues," he said. "We just haven't had any lately."

"Somehow I think it's going to be different with you."

"Why is that?"

"You seem to enjoy the calm as much as I do."

He took a swig of beer. "Oh, baby, I do. But that doesn't mean trouble won't find me."

She just shrugged, happily oblivious. "Well, I guess if something comes up, we'll play the hand we're dealt."

I can't put this off much longer, he found himself thinking. Even though he wasn't supposed to tell anyone, he knew he could trust Leslie with his life. He couldn't help it, he'd wait just a little longer. Because the respite from the hard life was just too good to give up prematurely.

Jack Sheridan was wiping down the bar at about three-thirty in the afternoon when a man he'd never seen before came in. Nothing unusual in that—people were passing through all the time. But this guy wasn't the usual—this guy was not a hunter, camper, fisherman or hiker. Not a mountain guy, but more of a *Gentlemen's Quarterly* kind of guy. He wore a starched white shirt, open at the collar with the sleeves rolled up. He had pleated pants, fancy loafers and carried a sports coat or blazer or something.

"Hey," Jack said amiably.

"Hi." He jumped up on a stool. "Beer?"

"Absolutely. You have a preference?"

"Not really. Something imported?"

Jack laughed. "Sure thing," he said, pulling a Heineken out of the cooler and popping the top. "Glass or bottle?"

"Chilled glass, please," the man said. Then he pulled

out his cell phone and thumbed through his panel of selections.

"You're not going to have a lot of success with that. Our cell reception in town isn't so good. Down 36 toward Fortuna it gets better. I have a landline, if that would help."

"Do you mind? I have to call my wife."

"In the kitchen, help yourself. Don't let the cook scare you." The man froze. "Kidding," Jack said with a wry smile. "He looks a little scary, but he's a pussycat. Honest."

With a slight hesitation, he made his way to the kitchen. In just a couple of minutes he was back, and within seconds, Preacher was tailing him standing behind the bar next to Jack. Preacher's white apron was a mess today, which made him look slightly scarier than usual, plus he was frowning darkly. It took Jack only a few seconds to decide Preacher hadn't liked what he'd overheard the man saying on the phone or he wouldn't be here.

Jack poured himself a cup of coffee and a seltzer for Preacher.

"So, I'm Jack. Passing through?"

The man immediately put out his hand, which was very soft and pretty. "Greg," he said. "Yes, just here for an hour or so."

"What kind of mission brings a man to Virgin River for an hour? Buying property for someone?" Because, surely not for himself.

"Well, not that it's any of your business, but I want

to talk to my wife. Ex-wife. She lives here. We have a couple of things to discuss and I thought a public place might be more agreeable to her than having me drop in on her. Unannounced."

"Excellent idea," Jack said.

Preacher crossed his arms over his chest. He glowered.

"She'll be stopping by?" Jack asked.

"Hard to say," Greg said. "We were disconnected."

"Ah," Jack said. That was fancy-man talk for *she hung up on me.* "Anyone I know?"

The man tilted his head and narrowed his eyes. Then he shot a quick glance at Preacher. He cleared his throat. "Leslie Adams." He cleared his throat again. "Petruso. Leslie Petruso."

"Ah, Leslie," Jack said, grinning. "Sure. Good friend of ours, right, Preach?"

Preacher glared at the guy briefly, then turned and went back to the kitchen.

Now Jack wasn't a genius, but he knew Preacher. This guy, Greg, must have said something ungentlemanly to Leslie to warrant Preacher following him back into the bar. And of course Jack knew this was the guy Leslie had nailed with the fire extinguisher. Jack would've paid to see that.

"Leslie's well liked around here, as you might guess," Jack said.

"She's well liked everywhere," he said. "I've been a little worried about her since she's been down here. Alone."

"She's not alone, my friend. Paul Haggerty looks out for her, as do others. She seems to be getting along very well."

"I heard she's seeing someone," Greg said. "I wonder, do you know who that might be?"

Jack decided to lie. "People don't normally run their romances by me. Couldn't tell you."

Greg shook his head solemnly. "I wish she were back home. Where I could look after her better."

"Unless I misunderstood you, pardner, not only are you divorced, you indicated she has someone new to look out for her now."

"That's not a good thing, Jack," he said. "No one knows Leslie like I do."

Jack gave the counter a nice, serious wipe-down. "Interesting that the two of you divorced. Sounds like you were pretty close."

"We're still close. We'll always be close. You don't spend almost ten years with a woman without being extremely bonded. That's what we are, Jack. Bonded. Leslie needs me. Oh, sometimes she doesn't want to admit it and I get that—I am remarried. But I know what's good for Leslie even if she doesn't."

Jack was silent for a moment. A long moment. He was thinking about how his wife would make him pay for a comment like that, and they were still married. That wouldn't float too well at his house. Mel didn't like being "managed." "You must be a very insightful man," Jack said.

"I have my moments," he said, lifting his beer to his lips.

Yeah, but I don't think now is one of those moments, Jack thought.

Leslie answered the phone on her desk. "Haggerty Construction, Leslie speaking."

"Leslie, it's Greg. We need to talk."

She took a deep breath. "Has there been a death in the family?" she asked crisply.

"No! Of course not!"

"Have you decided to give me a big pot of the money you hid while we were divorcing?"

"No! I mean, I didn't—"

"Then we don't have anything to talk about."

"Leslie! Wait! Listen, I've been visiting with your parents!"

She was struck silent for a moment. "Whatever for?"

"I've been checking on them and keeping tabs on you. They tell me you're seeing someone now. We better talk about that."

"All right, now listen," she said sternly. "Who I might be dating is none of your business and I don't want you pestering my parents. They don't *like* you!"

"Don't be ridiculous," he said. "They're very nice to me!"

"They're nice people! You better leave them alone or…or…or I'll sic Paul on you."

"Watch that temper, Leslie! There's no reason to be so defiant, just listen to me a second. I'm here. I'm in

Virgin River at that little bar in town and I'm not leaving until you meet me. I thought a public place might suit you better, make you feel less threatened...."

"Make *me* feel less threatened?" She laughed out loud. "Bullshit, Greg! You think I won't hurt you in a public place? But you wasted your time. I'm not meeting you. We have nothing to talk about."

"If you don't, I'll find out where you live and come to your house. Seriously, I'm not leaving without seeing you. We have to discuss this man you're—"

She disconnected the cordless. "Goddamn it," she muttered. And she wondered how she'd been married to him for so long without realizing what an idiotic pain in the ass he was. She briefly wondered if he had slipped drugs into her tea throughout their marriage.

She did not want to see him, talk to him. She was a little bit afraid that if she *didn't* go to Jack's, Greg was just going to make her life here so much more complicated. She did not want him to upset her relationship with Conner. She was truly happy for the first time in so long. She banged the phone on the top of her desk several times and swore.

Paul was quickly standing in her doorway. "Problem?"

She grabbed her purse and keys. "I have to run out, Paul." She looked at her watch. "It's late—I'm not going to make it back here today. I'll come in early tomorrow...."

"You don't have to come in early. Something wrong?"

"That man is getting on my last nerve," she said.

"Conner?"

"God, no. Conner is a gem. Conner is perfect. Greg Adams."

"What's he doing now?"

"Waiting for me at Jack's. Apparently my parents told him I'm seeing someone and he wants to discuss it with me."

"Why?"

"I don't have the first idea, but he's threatening to wait me out or even show up at my house. I better get over there before Jack's fills up with people and there's an audience."

Paul stepped aside so she could pass. "Want me to go with you?"

"Don't be silly, Paul. I can take him."

If Jack's had been an old Western saloon and Leslie had been wearing six-guns on her hips, her entrance would have blended perfectly. She blew in, loaded for bear. By the time she arrived, there were a couple of men at a table by a window sharing a pitcher, but thankfully that was all. Within a half hour, the dinner crowd would begin to arrive.

Greg turned to see her enter. He smiled. She scowled and walked up to the bar, but she didn't sit down.

"Drink, Les?" Jack asked.

"No. Greg, I don't want to discuss anything with you unless you're here to give me a big check. I want you to go home. And I want you to leave my parents and me *alone.*"

"Leslie, Leslie... Honey, I know this transition is difficult—"

"Don't call me *honey!* It is not a transition and it is not difficult. It's a divorce and I've discovered it's the best thing that ever happened to me. Now, listen to me, *please.* We're done. We're over. You left me! You have a pregnant wife in Grants Pass. You—"

"Pregnant wife?" Jack repeated. Jack being Jack, he wasn't far from the conversation.

"Don't you have something to do?" Greg asked him.

"No," Jack said. "Buddy, you gotta let go...."

"You don't understand," Greg said to Jack. He turned to Leslie. "This doesn't have to be so adversarial, Leslie. I only want to help because I care about you. I just thought maybe we should talk about this guy you're seeing because, well..." He reached for her hand, and she snatched it away. "Okay, well, this may be hard to hear, but you're on the rebound. People can make serious mistakes on the rebound."

"I. Am. Not."

"It's not the length of time that's the deciding factor, Leslie," he said. "It's really about the emotional investment. And believe me, I know how hard our divorce was for you."

"It's not hard anymore. I feel like you did me a monumental favor. Now go."

"Just tell me who he is, Leslie. Tell me about him. I don't want to worry about you."

"You lost that privilege, Greg. I no longer discuss my personal business with you."

He shook his head. "Your bitterness speaks for itself. There must be something about this guy that worries you or you wouldn't be so defensive."

"There's something about *you* that worries me. If you come down here one more time I'm going to call Allison and suggest she have you committed."

"Seriously," Jack said. "I'm a little worried about you, too, buddy. You got a bun in the oven up there and you're still hanging around here, bothering the ex?"

Greg turned sharply toward Jack. "Can you go find something to do?"

Jack shrugged. "I could, but this is fascinating. And it's my bar." Then he smiled.

Greg sighed in frustration. He turned back to Leslie. "Let's get right to it."

She rested an elbow on the bar and let her head drop into her hand. She groaned. She swore under her breath.

"The fact is, whether you realize it or not, you've had a blow to your self-esteem, and you're in no condition to get involved with some guy you don't really know. I knew when I made the hard choice to leave that I would have to be prepared to help see you through it, and I will, Leslie. Because I care about you. Because even though I don't love you as my wife, I love you as my best friend and always will."

"I am *not* your best friend. I am not even your casual friend. And my self-esteem has never been healthier."

"And so even though it's reasonable for you to be in denial, I know that losing me destroyed you. It was like hitting bottom for you and I don't want you to reach out to a man who isn't good for you. Not when I'm prepared to help you through the crisis. We both know you've never had a strong self-image, that you've always struggled with your perception of yourself. All I want to do is help. You have more potential than you realize, Leslie. Let me help."

She stared at him in dumb wonder for a minute. The irony was—not only did *he* believe this to be true, there was a time it actually had been. His leaving *had* shattered her. Every time she'd seen him with the new pretty, smart, accomplished young woman, it had hurt. He thought he was God's gift to women, and if he left his wife, she must be devastated.

Oh, how it pissed her off that she had been!

She turned her back on him and stomped away, charging through the swinging door to the kitchen. Preacher looked up from the stove and lifted his eyebrows, wondering what she was doing there.

She looked around. Then she saw it. The fire extinguisher was mounted on the wall in the kitchen by the back door. She rushed to it, snatched it off the brackets that held it and made for the bar.

If Jack hadn't been following her to see what the devil she was up to, he might not have been in time. He was right near the door as she came back through; she was freeing the hose and positioning her hands on the handle. She was aiming. Preacher was right behind her, but not fast enough.

"Whoa! Whoa! Whoa!" Jack said, circling her waist

with one arm and lifting her clear of the floor. "Hold on there!"

"Did you hear what he said to me?" she ground out angrily. "That his leaving destroyed me? That I now have no self-esteem because he left me?"

"Yeah, I couldn't miss that. He's an idiot. I'll throw him out for you," Jack said.

"No! This is the only thing he understands!"

"Aw, Les, it's so messy...."

"It's not as messy as me killing him!"

Jack smirked. He stole a look at Greg, who was backing away a little nervously, unknowingly making himself a better target.

"You have to help clean up the mess," Jack said to Leslie.

"Certainly," she said.

"All right, then." He let her go.

She ran around the bar and fired. This time there was no warning, no countdown, no compassion. She hit him square in the chest, face, arms, legs and in the back as he ran away, yelling.

"You are an insane fucking bitch!" he screamed, looking a little like a snowman as he ran into the street.

Leslie turned back to the bar. Laughing.

"It wasn't that messy," she said. "I got most of it on him. I'll have that drink now."

Jack served her up her preferred Merlot and handed her a rag from behind the bar. "He seems to have forgotten his sports coat."

"Church rummage sale," she said, lifting it with one

finger and handing it over the bar to Jack. She propped the fire extinguisher on the bar stool beside her, as if it was her date. "I don't think he'll be back for it. Too bad they'll never get what it's worth. I'm sure it's expensive."

She turned toward the door just in time to see Conner and Paul enter the bar together, no doubt having seen Greg. She lifted her drink toward them in a little toast.

"She did it again," Paul said to Conner.

"That's my girl," Conner said to Paul.

Eleven

Leslie hated to sacrifice time with Conner, but she couldn't wait to get home and call her mother. She asked him to give her an hour, then if he wanted to see her later, the price of admission was takeout from the bar.

"Why didn't you tell me Greg's been pestering you?" she said when she got her mom on the phone.

"Oh, I thought I mentioned…" Candace said.

"I knew he called or something to ask where I'd gone when he couldn't find me in Grants Pass, but I had no idea he'd continued bothering you."

"Well, I knew it wasn't your doing, Leslie. I didn't want you to worry about it. And I thought I finally got rid of him."

"How long has this been going on?"

"Oh, really since you moved," she said. "At first I thought he was only stopping by because he wanted to know where you'd gone, but then when he kept it up after he finally knew where you were, I was a little confused. I finally told him, in a nice way, that he just couldn't drop in on us anymore. I said it was a requirement that he call ahead. In which case I always said we were just on our way out. But the doofus just kept calling."

"What is up with him?" Leslie asked.

"Well, at first he said he didn't want his relationship with us to be lost just because the marriage was over, but I knew that wasn't true. The conversation always came around to you very quickly. He wanted to know how you were. So I told him you had never been better, that you were seeing a wonderful man and were so happy."

"When did you do that?"

"Just last week," Candace said. "Why?"

"He came down here to Virgin River. Again!"

"What on earth…"

"He wanted the details about this man I'm seeing. He wanted to help me through the rebound crisis because he's certain I'm devastated over losing him."

Candace laughed into the phone.

"What's funny?" Leslie asked.

"He has such a high opinion of himself, that's what's funny. How'd you get rid of him?"

"I shot him with the fire extinguisher. This time I got him good."

"That's getting to be quite a habit, isn't it, sweetheart? I just had the scariest thought—you might be getting more like your parents…."

She sighed. "That wouldn't be all bad, especially if I could have as much fun as you do. I'm going to get a fire extinguisher for the house. You know, if I weren't afraid of the message it might send to Greg, I'd call Allison and ask her if she can keep him home."

"Hmm. Maybe the new marriage isn't working out so well—have you thought of that? He has far too much time on his hands."

"Oh, please be wrong," she said. "I need him to be happily married and not my problem."

"There was a time such a thought—that his marriage was on the rocks—would have filled you with joy," Candace reminded her.

"Well, I've discovered something very important over the past couple of months. The only thing worse than feeling rejected and devastated is feeling like a damn fool."

The second week in May, Conner received a message from Brie to give her a call when he had a minute. She told him she had information for him and to come to her house around six in the evening, by which time she expected to be done working for the day. To kill time, he went to Jack's for a beer.

If Conner had any fantasy of flying under the radar in Virgin River, it was gone by now. He was made as the man in Leslie's life. It only took one bartender, one cook, a couple of local guys sharing a pitcher and one general contractor whose loose lips had the story all over town. Within a week of Greg's visit and the fire extinguisher dousing in the bar, it was a legend. Virgin River, he realized, loved a good story. They had plenty of them, too. There wasn't a lot of entertainment in town besides those stories, and they lapped them up.

"Small town," Jack said. "We live for stuff like that."

"And the latest story on me?" Conner probed.

"Nothing all that interesting. Just that you're gonna have to get Leslie away from her ex-husband to have her." And then Jack grinned.

Conner eyeballed him for a moment while he considered the grim truth—that he had much more interesting facts still under wraps. "You people," he said, shaking his head, "need to get a life."

"This is the life, man. As a rule we like as little excitement as possible."

Conner could relate to that.

"Where is the little lady tonight?" Jack asked.

"I believe tonight is yoga night," Conner said.

"And what do you do on yoga night?"

"A little computer time and early to bed. Being gossiped about is very tiring."

Jack laughed. "I guess you're not as tough as you look."

Conner went from the bar to Brie's house. She'd said he was to come to her front door at six, not her law office door which was an addition to the side of the house. When she let him in, he was struck by how much she reminded him of his sister. Brie was tiny in her snug jeans and bare feet. Her sleeves were rolled up, and she had a child's cup in her hand. Her hair was loose and long, and she looked so much younger than she was. If he was correct, she was over thirty-five.

"Come in," she said. "I'm giving Ness her dinner."

He followed her to the kitchen. He watched her pull a bowl of mac and cheese from the microwave and blow on it. Ness was seated at the small kitchen table on a booster chair, squealing and reaching for her dinner. "All right, all right, hang on to your britches," Brie said, putting the bowl in front of her. She filled the cup with milk and put it on the table, then leaned against the kitchen counter and let out a breath.

He chuckled and shook his head. "It's sure hard to picture you kicking butt in a courtroom," he said.

"She was terrifying, too," Mike Valenzuela said as he came into the kitchen. He didn't look like a cop in his denim shirt, jeans and boots. But then as Conner had learned, he didn't want to. He rarely carried a sidearm, though he kept a rifle in the rack in his truck. "Can I get you something to drink?" he asked, opening the refrigerator.

"No, thanks. What's up?"

"Couple of things," Brie said. "First of all, they'll be starting jury selection soon—looks like they're running close to the time frame Max suggested. I bet you'll be called by late May. Possibly sooner. That should come as good news. And this was forwarded to you from the D.A.'s office to me." She handed him a white envelope.

He looked at the handwriting and return address and handed it back to her. "This is my ex-wife. I've gotten letters before. I don't read them."

"Read this one, please," Brie said. "We'd like to know

how she knew to send it to the D.A.'s office, if she mentions that."

He pressed it on her. "Go ahead, knock yourself out. Read it."

"It could be personal, Conner," she said as she took the envelope with reluctance.

Of course the D.A. knew the story even if Brie didn't. "No, it couldn't be. We've been divorced almost two years and we divorced because she had a problem with sex, as in she had a great deal more of it than I did. With many, many partners."

"Oh," Brie said. "Sorry."

"So go ahead. It's probably one of those amends letters—there were quite a few before the fire, before the murder in my back alley."

"Amends?" Brie asked as she ripped open the envelope. "I take that to mean…?"

"Some kind of program," he answered. "A very long, expensive program. My parting gift to the lady."

"Wow," Brie said under her breath, unfolding a long letter. "Wow," she said again, taking in the neat, close, tightly constructed and lengthy penned letter—three pages, both sides. It was written so densely. Obsessively. "This could take a while."

"Take as long as you like, it's all yours."

"You're not wondering how she tracked you down to Max? The D.A.'s office?"

"Not really. She was a smart woman. About most things."

Brie scanned the first page. "Well, we're in luck—

it's up front. After she heard about the killing and your store being burned down she decided to take a chance and see if the D.A.'s office might know where you could be. She's very worried about you and hopes you're all right."

"That's Samantha," he said. "She was worried about me before all this happened, too. She wants dialogue— it's not going to happen."

"Maybe she wants to be forgiven," Brie suggested.

"That, too, so I told her that I forgave her, but that we weren't going to have a relationship. It just isn't a good idea, not for either one of us. I wish she'd quit writing me letters."

Brie scanned some more. "She says she's been straight for a long time and that she's sorry and that she misses you."

"Hmm," he said. "Good for her. That she's fixed, I mean. So, there are a couple of things I need to talk to you about. First of all, when do you think I'll be asked to go to Sacramento?"

"A few weeks, I think. Give or take."

Ness tried to get her cup of milk, just out of her reach, and Conner automatically slid it closer to her. "There you go, honey," he said. "That's good, isn't it?" he asked her gently. Then he straightened and looked at Brie. He was glad they were all in the kitchen together with Ness eating her dinner. That alone would probably keep Brie from having a little hissy fit.

"Before I testify, I'm going to see my sister," he said. "I'll drive to San Francisco, leave the truck in the long-term lot and fly to Vermont. I haven't asked her if I can visit yet, but I'm sure she'll be happy to see me. We're very close. I'm close to the kids."

"Not recommended," Brie said, shaking her head.

"I wasn't asking for a recommendation," Conner said. "I don't know what you know about me, Brie, so let me fill in some gaps. Our parents died when we were young—both of them were gone when Katie was twenty and I was twenty-three. We took over a family business we didn't know how to run, and although she thought she was all grown-up by then, I had to be a parent to her. She married a great man, Charlie, when she was twenty-six—he was like a brother to me. Less than a year later, a couple of months before Katie's twin boys were born, he was killed in Afghanistan. That was five years ago. I took care of her and my nephews right up to the day the D.A. sent her in one direction and me in another.

"Now I talk to Katie every day, and guess where we are? She likes where she is. There's someone she's starting to care about there. She's talking about staying there. She thinks she and the boys might have a future there. She was kind of hoping I'd end up there, near them. But what do you suppose happened? After all these years, after all the crap, I find myself wanting to give a little more time to the best thing that's ever happened to me."

"Conner, look, I'm totally sympathetic, but—"

"I don't know what your concept of family is, Brie, but Katie and I and the boys are tight. We've always known we might not live in the same town all our lives—hell, she was married to a military man. She was going to be moving around as an army wife—I can live with that. We can make do on visits. But like I said, we're tight. The boys don't get why they haven't seen Uncle Danny—that's how they've always known me. And before I testify, before I put my life on the line or make another major change in my life, I'm going to do two important things. I'm going to tell Leslie what I'm up against and that I'll come back here after the trial if she thinks she can handle that. And I'm going to go see my sister to be sure she and the boys are all right. And that they'll be safe and happy if they stay there."

Brie looked down. She slapped the effusive blue-inked letter against her thigh. She looked up at him. "Now look—"

"Brie," Mike said. He didn't say it loudly or sternly, he just said her name and she looked at him. He lifted his cola can, and on the way to his lips, he gestured toward Conner.

"There are risks. No matter what I do. That son of a bitch could have me capped as I'm walking up the court-house steps. In fact, that's the only thing that makes sense. And I bet he'd still get convicted."

Mike gave a shrug that was nearly a nod.

"I'll keep the new name, all the new ID, and if the D.A.'s office will help, I'll sell everything and start over. I'd be willing to sell it all, but it probably makes more sense to put it all in crated storage in Sacramento until we have a destination. The houses...?" Conner shrugged. "We'll have to sell them. We know we're not going to live in Sacramento again. Not after what happened there. I'll pay for the truck I'm using or get a new one, whatever. Katie's share will give her a fresh start. But that's it, that's all I'm doing. I'm not going to run for the rest of my life. If Regis Mathis doesn't get me before I can help lock him up for life, I find it hard to believe he's going to go to too much trouble and expense to scour the entire frickin' United States for me or Katie. Not just for revenge. His money would be better spent on lawyers for his appeal."

"Think about this," she said. "Please."

"Thought about it. I've seen you with your brother, your husband, your daughter. There's no way you'd do what I'm doing. You'd have Mike wearing his pistol to bed every night before you'd go through this."

"I'm not sure how Max is going to take this," she said.

"Well, he's a good man," Conner said. "He might get a little unhappy with me, but he's not going to retaliate by giving my current address to Mathis. I haven't done anything wrong."

Brie took a moment to turn her back on him as she poured herself a cup of coffee. She turned back to him. "You really thought about this. What did it? What changed your mind? Made you put together all these plans? Leslie?"

"Leslie is so awesome," he said. "But seriously, it's not like we're ready to make a commitment or anything—we haven't known each other too long and we both have some pretty kinky exes to overcome. That's why I want more time with her—I'm not tossing this away before it's had a chance. It was your husband," he said. "Mike."

"Mike?"

"Decorated police officer. According to Jack, not only a bunch of medals in the Marine Corps but a commendation as a sergeant in the gangs unit. Here's a guess," he said, looking at Mike. "You've testified against a lot of bad guys. And you didn't go into hiding."

Mike gave him a small smile. "A ton of bad guys. And I did keep a very discreet profile. Still do. But I do agree with you about one thing—if Mathis doesn't stop you before you testify—I think the revenge factor is fairly slim. He might be that kind of criminal, but I'm sure he'll have bigger things on his mind. Mathis is a businessman, not a psycho. Killing you afterward isn't going to get him much—just maybe scratch an itch. He might be too busy for that."

"You face the same threat every day," Conner said. "The revenge possibility."

"As does Mrs. Valenzuela," he said. "She put away a lot of felons."

"There you go," Conner said.

"One of them escaped conviction and attacked me," Brie said. "Remember that."

"I'll never forget it," Conner said. "I'm so sorry that happened. I really am. And I still think my plan is a good one."

"Everything changes, of course, if he somehow gets

another trial and you are once again the only witness that can hurt him," Mike said.

"I guess I'll have to count on Max to run a tight prosecution and make it stick then, won't I? I'll take my chances. I'll let you break it to Max."

"Oh, gee. Thanks."

"We just gotta get this over with," he said. "Really."

"Well, how about this compromise—wait till after the trial to visit your sister…."

He was shaking his head. "Sorry. She's my only family. Those boys are like my sons. The risk is now, not so much after the trial. I need to see them before something…" He dropped his chin and didn't say, *before someone gets to me to keep me from testifying.* "Now. Before the trial. Who's gonna know anyway?"

"At least do this for me—fly out of an airport that isn't real high-profile. A smaller airport—Redding, maybe. Avoid the big airports if possible, especially the ones near Sacramento where associates of Mathis's might happen to be."

"I can do that."

Conner emailed Katie. He asked her to email him her address, using their new, secure email handles and accounts. Katie was in Burlington, Vermont. And then he called her.

"But you can't come here, Conner! You've been told not to do that!"

"I'm going to slip out of here in a couple of weeks," he said. "I'll let you know when to expect me. I'll spend a few days to a week with you. By then it will be time or almost time for me to go to court. After that it will be over and we can get on with our lives. But, Katie, you and I have things to talk about. *Where* we'll get on with our lives, for one thing. There are so many things to think about. The boys being a first priority."

With a little catch in her throat, she said, "You are so wonderful. No matter how complicated things get for you, you always put them first."

"It isn't hard to do that, honey. I'll always do whatever I have to do to make sure they're in the best possible place."

Their conversations were always pretty brief, so after a few minutes on the phone, they said their goodbyes, leaving Conner time to think about the future. Despite the fact that it caused a little ache in his heart to think of his only family living on the other coast, if they were happy there, he'd manage. He might end up spending more on travel expenses than he could afford, but the most important thing was that his sister and the boys have a good life.

The second most important thing was that he tell Leslie the truth and give her some time to consider the fact that she was lied to. He gave himself permission to wait until the weekend, when there would be time to talk it all out. While she went to her Saturday yoga group, he went to her house, cut the grass and watered her flowers. He bought himself a steak and the sea bass he knew she loved, along with all the other dinner trimmings that would please her.

When she got home and saw what he'd done, she smiled and said, "Someone wants something...."

"Understanding, that's what I want," he said. "Les, I've never lied about my feelings for you—they're real and they're real powerful. But a lot of the rest of my personal history is a lie."

"Oh, God," she said. "Oh, Conner...what?"

"It's actually Danson Conner," he said.

Conner was surprised by the weight it lifted off his shoulders just to be able to tell Leslie the whole story, even though she was shocked. Stunned. Pretty much blown away.

They were seated at her little kitchen table, facing each other, because this wasn't a conversation for bed or for the porch, where they might be overheard. When he got to the part about being the only witness in a murder trial, thus the name change and low-profile existence in Virgin River, she let her head drop to the table with a groan.

"I'm sorry, Les," he said.

She lifted her head wearily. "It's not like you planned it...."

"When I said I had baggage, it was more than a divorce and those trust issues."

"No kidding."

"You would probably be smart to cut your losses here and now."

"What does that mean? You mean kick you to the curb?"

He gave a little shrug. "The reason no one knows where I am or who my close friends are is because I've been threatened. My store was burned down. And the reason no one but me and the D.A. knows where Katie and the boys are is because we can't take the chance that they would be threatened to get to me. We won't be going back to Sacramento, where we've lived almost our entire lives, because we'd make too visible a target in the unlikely case of revenge."

"Where will you go?"

"Not sure. Katie likes it where she is, but that's not a final decision. I like it here, but that's not a final decision, either."

"And after the trial? Is your life in danger after the trial?" She wanted to know.

"Always possible, if you consider revenge. But I'm not a mobster testifying against mobsters.... I'm just a guy who was taking out the trash. I'll keep this new identity and start over, but I'm not planning to hide in deep cover like secret witnesses in a marshal's program. You know—like never make a phone call to friends or visit them. Every witness to any crime faces the possibility of revenge, I guess. But if the guy is locked up, getting rid of me won't help him. Might even make things worse for him. I think I'm at risk before the trial. Which is why I'm going to visit Katie and the boys before I have to go testify. While I can..."

"You should," she said.

"It would be hard to give you up, but like I said..."

"Right—cut my losses. Well, not before you cook and serve me that sea bass, that's for sure."

He smiled at her. "Maybe after I finish the dishes?" he asked.

"Maybe after you finish me," she said. "But unlikely. If you decide to go away, I won't try to hold on to you. You're free to go, you know that. But I'm not going to give you up just because you come with a few complications. You're too good in the kitchen."

"I don't want to put a strain on you...."

"Oh, I think we'll manage. Now before we enjoy a splendid meal and some wild monkey sex, is there anything else you should tell me?"

"You mean other than a crazy ex-wife and a murderer who could be after me? No, that probably covers it."

Twelve

Jack actually heard the motorcycle pull into town before he saw the biker. The Harley had a fierce rumble, like someone had poked a screwdriver into the muffler a few times. On purpose. He glanced out the side window behind the bar and saw a roadster with high handle bars parked right next to the bar. Seconds later its rider ambled in.

He was a big guy with a lot of leather and hair, long retro sideburns and a shaggy goatee. And it kind of surprised Jack to note a wedding band.

"Afternoon, pardner," Jack said.

"Hey," the guy answered. "Just a cup of coffee while I think about food. And while you're pouring that, can I trouble you for the restroom?"

"Absolutely. Right through the kitchen there. Be sure you hit the one with the sign on the door and don't make a wrong turn into the cook's residence."

"I'll do my best," he said, making his way through the door.

He was back momentarily, looking a little spruced up. His long hair, which had been a little matted down where it wasn't wild and crazy, had been combed into a fresh pony tail; he might've washed his face.

"Get the bugs out of your teeth?" Jack asked.

"Pretty much," he said, lifting his coffee cup. "It's a beautiful day out there."

"This place really lights up in spring," Jack said. "Where you headed?"

"Don't know," he answered. "Just around. What's good today?"

"There's the irony," Jack said. "There's no choice, but it doesn't matter—everything is good here. It's whatever the cook dreams up. Today it's a seafood bouillabaisse—there was a special on lobster and scallops."

"Damn," he said. "That sounds awesome!"

"It is. Has a coconut base and Preacher said to be sure to tell anyone who's gonna eat it, there are peanuts in it. Not a lot, but they're there. The way he tells it, people who are allergic to peanuts can't take the smallest amount."

"No problem. I love peanuts." He looked at his watch. "Am I too early for some of that?"

"I think I can talk him out of some even though you're a little ahead of the dinner crowd. Excuse me a second." Jack went to the kitchen door to ask the question. "Fifteen minutes," he said to the biker. "Can I get you some bread and butter to tide you over?"

"I'll be okay, thanks," he said. "But I'll have some with the bouillabaisse, if you don't mind."

"My pleasure. Your bike was pretty loud coming into town...."

"Hope I didn't wake anyone from a nap," he said. "I have a couple of problems with the engine and muffler. I could work on it now, but it's safe, and after I eat, I'm headed home." He got up, took off his leather jacket and hung it on the hook by the door, ready to get down to some serious eating. When he came back to his stool at the bar, Jack couldn't help but notice the tattoo of a naked woman on his forearm.

"Where's home?"

"Sacramento. How long you been up here?"

"Jeez, seven or eight years now. Best move of my life," Jack said.

"You get a lot of bikers through here?"

"Just now and then," Jack said with a shrug.

"I'm surprised you don't get a lot of big groups. The roads up this way are just the kind riding clubs go looking for. In fact, that's what I'm doing—scouting. We have a group ride coming up and I'm putting together a plan for a road trip. From the mountains to the coast, challenging roads, incredible views. I don't get this far north too often."

"You're welcome to spread the word, as long as we don't attract gangs," Jack said.

"I don't belong to a gang and I don't hang with 'em."

"Some of the riding clubs can get a little wild, can't they?"

The man shrugged. "Maybe. What's wild?"

"Get drunk, start fights, tear up the town," Jack speculated.

"That sounds awful," he said. "I wouldn't hang with a group like that. That sounds like jail time and a big fine, not to mention a bill for property damage."

Jack grinned. "We don't look much alike, but it turns out we think a lot alike."

"Looks like you just got out of the service. Seven years up here, you say?"

"I guess it's always going to look that way," Jack said, running a hand over his head. "Twenty in the Marine Corps. You get used to combing your hair with a washcloth and it's hard to change. You do any military service?"

"I did not," he said. "And I thank you for yours." He put out his hand.

"My pleasure to serve," Jack said, shaking his hand. "I'm Jack."

"Walt." Preacher came out of the kitchen with a steaming bowl and basket of bread on a tray. Walt actually rubbed his hands together. "I'm really looking forward to this."

That brought a slight smile from Preacher. "I've only made this once before, but it was a hit."

"No menu, huh?"

"I can't keep this kitchen on budget if I cater to the town. I do try to keep in mind what the hunters and fishermen like, but that's so easy it's almost embarrassing. It's wet and cold—they have favorite stews, soups, chili, and of course, they want something like their kill or catch—venison stew or chili, salmon or stuffed trout."

While Preacher talked, Walt dipped his spoon into the bouillabaisse. The first sip of the creamy broth had him rolling his eyes back in his head and humming with approval. "When's hunting season?" he asked. "I don't hunt, but I eat like a champ."

"You cook?" Preacher asked.

"Not at all. The two best things about riding are the views and finding the best places to eat. There are hidden gems like this place all over California—the back roads. My wife won't even ride with me more than once every couple of weeks anymore—she loves to eat as much as me, but says I'm making her fat." He shook his head. "Women are funny that way."

"I have a wife and four sisters," Jack said. "There's a lot of talk about butts and thighs."

"I hear a lot about that, too," Walt said, dipping into that bouillabaisse again. "I don't know what she's worrying about, but whatever makes her happy. Look at me? Am I Tom Cruise or something?" He fished out a scallop and popped it in his mouth.

"Happy wife, happy life," Preacher said.

"Preacher, this is inspired. You have a gift."

Jack and Preacher both watched as Walt fished a lobster tail out of the stew and halved it with his spoon.

"There's this little hole in the wall in Paradise owned by this Hungarian guy. He and his son do all the cooking. It's amazing—one of my favorite places. Pull up to it and you think it's a shack, a lean-to. Inside? Crystal and white tablecloths and the best food I've ever eaten. Then there's a really small restaurant in Napa I love. I think they only seat about a dozen patrons, but it's fantastic. Fancy and pricey, but they earned it." He chewed, swallowed. "That's pretty much my hobby—road trips and restaurants."

"I could get into that," Preacher said.

Walt grinned. "Get a little more hair on you, you'd be a natural."

"I don't want to interrupt your meal," Jack said. "But I'd sure like to hear about your bike club."

"Well," he said, chewing, swallowing. "Well, I'm associated with a few bike clubs through the shop. This group I'm scouting for—they're a little rough around the edges—these are not IBM sales reps out for a weekend ride. They take their bikes and rides pretty seriously, and they're safe as babies, but I think they'll appreciate it if you act a little scared when they show up." Then he grinned and went after the stew again.

"Might have to practice that," Preacher said, and Walt chuckled through his mouthful. Preacher gave him a half smile. "Give him a discount, Jack. The man shows the proper reverence for my work." Then he went back to the kitchen.

"There should be four to six of them in this group," Walt went on. "We'll be back about a month from now. We can camp, but if there's lodging around here that would make for a good base, point me to it, will you? These guys are not as into the restaurant part of the trip as I am. I'm planning on spending some quality time with Preacher."

The door to the bar opened, and Conner came in, dragging off his hat as he entered.

"There are some cabins along the river, owned by a friend of mine. I have no idea how booked he is. Conner here stays in one. Conner, meet Walt. Walt here is a front man for a group of riders, checking out the area for a road trip."

"Hey," Conner said, putting out his hand. "Where are you from?"

"Sacramento area. You?"

"Colorado," he said a bit uncomfortably. "Road trip, huh?"

"We do that kind of thing a lot," Walt said. He dove into his stew again. When he came up for air, he asked Jack to write down some directions to the cabins for him and Jack slipped down the bar a bit where he had a pad of paper and began writing.

"And what do you do when you're not planning a road trip?" Conner asked.

"Work in a bike shop. Big surprise, huh? I'm pretty good with a wrench. You?"

"Build and remodel kitchens and bathrooms. I'm pretty good with a hammer and saw. That your bike out there?"

"Not exactly," Walt said. "I've been working on that bike for a customer. Kind of a pet project. I'll be riding my own bike when we come back up here, but I told my customer I wanted to take his bike out on the road for a long ride before turning it over. Good thing I did, too. That bike isn't ready." He plucked out some fish, ate it, wiped his lips and beard with a napkin. "Gave me a pretty good ride, though. I'll give him a break on the repairs."

Conner tried to keep the suspicion from his eyes. "I took a friend's bike out on some back roads along the Pacific cliffs recently and I have to say—I liked that. If I wanted to buy a good bike and was willing to go to Sacramento, where would you recommend I shop?"

Walt stood up to reach inside the pocket of his jeans. He had chains around the heels of his boots, a long chain connecting the wallet in his back pocket to a belt loop and keys attached to the opposite belt loop. He pulled out a pretty limp business card, worn from a long ride in the pocket of his jeans, and handed it to Conner. It said, *Walt Arneson, Maintenance and Sales, Harley-Davidson.*

"Call me at that number. I'll meet you at one of the dealerships and show you some good stuff." Then he put out his hand. "I'm Walt. And you're?"

"Conner," he said. "Conner Dan...Conner Danforth."

"Look forward to it, Conner." Then he turned back to the bar and put his hand out to Jack. "Thanks, man. That was outstanding. Thank Preacher for me." He took Jack's directions to the cabins, stuffed it in his pocket and shook his hand. Then he pulled out his wallet and put a couple of twenties on the bar.

"Whoa," Jack said. "Put one of those back and I'll get you some change."

"Keep it," Walt said. "The company was almost as excellent as the food. See you in about a month."

"We'll be here," Jack said.

Walt left, and it was only a moment before the loud rumble of the cycle filled the afternoon.

"Okay, that was a little weird," Jack said. "Your last name is Danson."

"Yeah. Right at the last minute I didn't feel like giving him my name." Conner shrugged. "He looked a little, I don't know, like a Hell's Angel or something."

"Yeah, he looks that way but I didn't get a bad vibe off the guy. He's got a job, he loved Preacher's bouillabaisse, in fact, he was a nice guy for a big, hairy, tattooed biker. But then, I've gotten used to all kinds of strange characters up in these mountains."

"Did I offend you?" Conner asked.

"Well, no. But that was a little weird. That you would be skittish like that. You got me and Preacher if you get scared." And after saying that, Jack grinned.

Conner slapped a hand against his chest. "Oh, man, I forgot about that. Next time I'll remember and offer the strange dude my phone and social security numbers."

"Wiseass. You in here for a reason?"

"A beer, if it's not too much trouble. You want ID?"

Jack served him up a beer. "You and Leslie going out to Dan and Cheryl's this weekend for their housewarming?"

"Absolutely. I was wondering, what do you think I should give them as a gift? Do you think they'd like some good wine?"

Jack grinned. "Nah," he said. "Dan has an occasional beer and as far as I know, Cheryl doesn't drink alcohol." The door to the bar opened, and the first of the dinner crowd ambled in. "Something for the house. Or something nonalcoholic. Hey, folks," Jack greeted the newcomers. He moved away from Conner.

Conner drove down the mountain in search of bars for his phone for two purposes—to call Katie and the boys and to call Brie.

"Hey, Brie, Conner here. This is probably nothing, but I ran into a biker at the bar—big, kind of scary-looking guy from Sacramento. He said he was scouting out the area for a road trip. I got his business card—he works for Harley-Davidson. He asked my name and I fudged it a little bit."

"Did you get the impression he was looking for you or something?" Brie asked.

"Not really. But it seemed an interesting coincidence. Can you check him out, make sure he's not a hit man or something?"

"Finding out who he is won't be the same as finding out if he's a hit man, Conner. Hit men usually have a nice, legitimate cover."

"Jack liked him," Conner said.

She laughed. "Jack likes most people. What's his name?"

"Walt Arneson. And here's the address and phone number." He read it off the business card. "Thanks. I appreciate it. Oh, and before I forget, I explained things to Leslie. And I told her you were my contact in case she gets worried or needs to talk to a woman."

"How'd she take it?"

"I'm a lucky guy," he said. "She was everything I expected. Supportive and understanding, if a little shocked out of her mind."

"Then don't let her get away," Brie said. "I'll call Max with this name. He has detectives assigned to the prosecutor's office."

"Appreciate it," he said. "Better to be safe than sorry."

"Of course. And, Conner? I'd like to tell you this over the phone so I don't have to look you in the eye. I read that letter from your ex-wife, laborious though it was. I wasn't nosy, I had to be sure she didn't reference something we should know—like if she learned you were the only witness of the crime or something like that. Many things are easy to assume—it was your store, there was a threat from an unknown source, the police were called immediately, et cetera—"

"Brie, I don't care that you read it," he said. "I gave you permission anyway."

"I thought you should know something. What you do with it is entirely up to you, but you should know. She knew she was sick, Conner. When she met you and married you, she thought she could tame her wild compulsions by being hooked up to you, and she has regrets about that, about the position she put you in. She didn't suddenly learn she was a sex addict when you caught her with another man. She thought you were the kind of man who could ground her, slow her down, keep her happy, so to speak. That was before she knew very much about her disease."

"Disease," he said in a grumble.

"Did you know that? That she married you with that agenda?"

"No. And I don't know that I buy that whole disease thing, either."

"I know," Brie said. "I don't really get it, either. But then there are a lot of things I have trouble understanding. I don't understand why smart, strong women let men hit them, and yet I end up helping a lot of them. The human condition, Conner, is complex and often confusing. But there's one thing I do know—holding a grudge isn't going to help. I hope you can let it go soon. I realize you didn't feel the need for any information from her letter, but I wanted to be sure you knew that. Conner, it wasn't your fault in any way. She knows it and you should know it."

Leslie hadn't met Dan's fiancée, Cheryl, even though she'd helped Dan with some of his housewarming party details. She called Cheryl just the same. "Let me come over a little early on Sunday and help you around the house or kitchen," she said. "You probably have a lot of people coming and tons to do."

"That's so nice of you," she said. "It's appreciated."

So Leslie, armed with her favorite Merlot and a bunch of flowers, headed to Dan and Cheryl's new house. They'd built in the countryside, far enough up the side of a hill to afford them a decent view. It was a small house at the end of a long, curly drive, and while there was still plenty to do around the yard, it was a nice-looking brick-and-wood ranch. There were a few pots of flowers flanking the front door.

The front door was opened by a lovely, smiling woman. "Hi, I'm Leslie," she said, cradling the wine and flowers in one hand and sticking out the other.

"Gee, it's nice to finally meet you. Dan is one of your biggest fans."

"And I'm one of his," Leslie said, entering. She held out the flowers and wine. "These are for you."

"You're so sweet," Cheryl said, taking the flowers. "I don't drink, but if you'd like a glass of that... I don't even know if there's a corkscrew in the house.... Maybe Dan has one on that fancy knife of his. Want me to ask?"

"Gee, I never even thought to ask," Leslie said. "Since I've seen Dan at Jack's..."

"He likes a cold beer sometimes," Cheryl said, heading for the kitchen. Once there she put the wine and flowers on the counter; the work island was full of food trays in progress—a veggie tray, potato and corn chips still in bags sitting in big bowls, a couple of large Crock-Pots, bags of buns, condiments, relishes such as pickles, onions, tomatoes. "He doesn't overdo it," Cheryl went on. "He's one of the lucky ones. An amputee doesn't want to throw himself off balance." And then she laughed. "Have you ever seen Dan on one leg?"

"I've heard," Leslie said.

"He's pretty amazing. He says it's a survival instinct. And me? I don't drink because I'm a recovering alcoholic."

"I didn't know," Leslie said, somewhat embarrassed.

"Then you're probably just about the only one. I had quite a reputation back in the drinking days. I've been sober three years."

"Congratulations. Is that the appropriate thing to say? Congratulations?"

"I'll take it," she said with a laugh. "They knew they had a tough one when they saw me coming." Cheryl opened a cupboard and pulled out a vase for the flowers.

"They?" Leslie asked before she could stop herself.

"Sorry, I spend so much time talking to other people in recovery sometimes I forget there are people who haven't faced all that. AA. Rehab. And I've been taking courses toward a counseling degree. I work at the college, get discounted courses, and my dream job is working with people in recovery."

"Wow. I'm surprised Dan never mentioned any of this. I mean, I knew you had a job at the college, but…"

"Oh, Dan wouldn't say anything. He's very good that way. These are my issues to talk about or not talk about. He leaves that entirely up to me and I appreciate it. A couple of years ago I couldn't talk about it. Now I can't shut up about it." She arranged the flowers in the vase. "How's this?" she asked. "I'm completely untrained in domestic skills."

"Looks great. I know there's a lot going on at the

moment and we should get this food together, but I'd love to see the house if there's time. Dan talks about it all the time. He's so proud of it."

"He should be—it's almost entirely his project. He stays off ladders and scaffolding, but everything else has his fingerprints all over. Come on, it won't take a minute—it's a small house." And with that she led the way. First, they walked through the living room/dining room to a large master bedroom and bath. The master formed an L-shape with the living/dining so that doors in that room opened onto a deck also. There were also two more small bedrooms—one set up as an office. "This is for me," she said. "Some women dream of a sewing room—I wanted an office with a computer so I could research and study. This is something I never imagined possible when I was a kid!"

A small powder room separated the two small bedrooms. Back in the living/dining room, Cheryl opened the doors wide onto the wooden deck as they walked outside. The house had a short yard that backed right up to the hill and the trees. "We have all kinds of animals that wander right up to the house. Deer, bear, puma, you name it. This is the most relaxing spot in the house, right on this deck. If you're real quiet in the early morning or early evening, animals might come close enough for you to count their eyelashes."

"Okay on the deer," Leslie said. "You might want to be real careful of the others."

"I'm careful," she said. Cheryl looked up at the trees that surrounded her house and took a deep breath.

"I'm careful not to take this for granted, too." After a moment, she turned to look at Leslie. "Let's get the food ready. We'll have company pretty soon, I think."

Leslie didn't realize the significance of the day for Cheryl until Paige Middleton explained it as best she could. According to Paige, Cheryl felt as though she'd left the town in shame, having been driven out of town to an alcohol treatment facility. Mel, Jack's wife, was the one to find her a program that the county paid for, the beginning of the rest of her life. Then she'd stayed in Eureka for months, living with some women in a halfway house and slowly but surely falling in love with Dan Brady.

"She's been very slow, probably reluctant to come back to us, as if she couldn't shake her reputation. I'm pretty sure she expected to be judged harshly. Plus, I'm sure she has a lot of negative memories of growing up in Virgin River, the place where she got into so much trouble as a youth." Paige shrugged. "There are plenty of people ready to take that judgmental role, I guess. Most of us, though, are just so grateful she was able to save herself. Cheryl is an amazing woman. She's going to be a great counselor. I have no doubt she'll help many people."

When more people started to arrive, Leslie positioned herself in the kitchen so she could help them find paper cups and paper plates and then be sure the discarded made it into the trash. From around two till five, friends both from Virgin River and Cheryl's college made their way to the house. They didn't come in droves but in manageable numbers. There were perhaps twenty from town, and Leslie knew them all, from the Haggertys to the Sheridans. There were a few of Haggerty's crews—men Dan had worked with. And the rest were Cheryl's friends from Eureka. And people didn't stay long—an hour, hour and a half. Just long enough to see the new house, have a bite to eat, congratulate the happy couple.

When Conner arrived, Leslie was aware of him the minute he entered the house. Her eyes went to him, and the feeling that came over her was like a swelling in her heart, a shudder of instant desire and love. He was such a beautiful man, so tall and strong, and those blue eyes were instantly on her. Then his lips curved in a smile only for her, and he was quickly at her side. He slipped an arm around her waist and touched her temple with his lips.

Cut her losses? What losses? He was the best man she'd ever known.

All around them people noticed their intimacy and smiled.

These people didn't realize that in addition to being a good man, a handsome man, Conner had the courage of ten men. She was so proud of him.

After helping Cheryl get the kitchen under control, she was only too glad to say goodbye to her new friends and whisk him away to have all to herself. Every minute felt as if it went by too quickly.

Thirteen

Conner and Leslie tried very hard not to amp up their courtship just because Conner's upcoming testimony loomed. It would be easy to dive in, to virtually move in together and spend every waking moment in each other's company. Tempting, but not practical, not when both of them were still coming to terms with who they were in this new, second life.

"Like putting on a new skin," Conner said to her. "We're going to end up together, I'm pretty confident of that. And when we do, I want you to feel secure about what you're getting yourself into. We're not going to take any chances. I don't want you to ever regret your choices."

Still, if they were together at the end of the day, they were usually still together first thing in the morning.

"One of these days, we're going to take the next step," Leslie told him. "The sheets on the bed in that little cabin aren't getting much of a workout."

For the time being, they spent at least a couple of

nights a week on their own. On one such night, Conner sat at his laptop in his cabin and worked on an email.

Dear Samantha, I saw the last letter you sent. It's the first one since our parting of the ways—I shredded the previous ones. Maybe I was afraid to read them, I don't know. I'd like to share where I am in life right now, so we can both put this behind us. First of all, I've moved on. I'm happy in ways I was never happy before, and that has nothing to do with any failing of yours. Second, I don't have any hard feelings toward you. True, I did for a long time, but I really feel free of that now, free enough to tell you I wish you all the best. And third, now that we've both had that chance to clear the air, to forgive and forget, to get things off our chests, I'd like to move on without the baggage, without further explanations or contact from you, without reminders of everything that went on before. I want to think of you as a woman I was once close to, a woman who has moved on to a new life that doesn't include me. And if I could ask one favor, I'd like you to remember me as a man who once cared about you, and who did the best he could with a difficult set of circumstances. Believe me, I know that's asking a lot; I know it can't seem like I tried, but I did the best I could at the time.

I'm letting go of it now, Samantha. No grudges, no obsessive remembering, no self-pity.

Good luck to you. Be well.

Danny

When he was done and mostly satisfied, he created a new, free email account and sent his email to her email address. He waited a little while to see if the email bounced back as undeliverable and was not surprised when it didn't. She was keeping things the same in case he ever succumbed to the urge to reach out to her. He didn't give it much time—an hour or so. When it didn't bounce back, he closed and canceled that email account.

Done.

The very next morning, it began. He was not prepared, though he should've been. The pretrial jury selection started a rush of press about the crime he'd witnessed and speculation about the trial.

Conner spent a lot of time reading the news online before he went to work. He was working with Dan Brady on a kitchen renovation. He kept his ears sharp all day, but the news of a murder trial in Sacramento didn't seem to spark any interest in Virgin River. He even stopped by the bar before heading over to Leslie's house just to see if anyone was talking about it.

He had to give the press some credit —there was speculation about witnesses and even some curiosity about whether the prosecution's witness might have any connection to the hardware store where the crime was committed, the hardware store that had burned to the ground. But unless there were articles he was unaware of, they were not putting names to their speculation. He didn't see his name in any press, yet they would have known it was him—his name had appeared as probable cause on the search warrant that was used to search Mathis's car and home and arrest him.

A name he did see quite a bit of was Dickie Randolph, the victim. Randolph had been pretty well-known for dabbling in the underworld of drugs and prostitution.

Yet there was more—Randolph had invested in some of Mathis's condo properties, and it was speculated that Mathis could be a silent partner in some of Randolph's businesses. And of course a sleazeball like Dickie Randolph had a lot of ancillary characters involved in his businesses, as well.

Motive? The press hadn't uncovered one yet, unless there had been some sort of bad blood between the two that had gone unnoticed thus far. In fact, if Conner hadn't seen Mathis do the shooting, there would have been many other individuals who would have been suspect.

As the police had told Conner a long time ago—everyone in this case was dirty. But as far as what they could prove in a court of law, only Regis Mathis had committed murder.

Conner was a little uncertain how to handle the flood of news where Leslie was concerned. In the end he told her to get out her laptop and log on so they could look at some of it together, while he was still in town to help her understand the details and what he knew about the stories. They sat at her kitchen table, and he ran the search, bringing up pictures and articles from the Sacramento newspaper.

Most of the pictures that would be used as evidence, such as the blood splatters in the car that were illuminated by the luminol the police used, were not available to the press, but there were photos they couldn't control. The Dumpster where the body had been dumped, for example, with the long streak of blood running down the side and the yellow crime-scene tape stretching across the area. The covered body on the gurney that was being loaded in to the ambulance.

"Where were you?" Leslie asked.

"I had just walked out the back door of the store," he said. "I heard the car door, noticed a man walking around the front of the car to the passenger side. He was pulling a gun out of his pocket at the same time he opened the passenger door and he shot him in the head. I ducked behind the Dumpster. It was fast and brutal. Over, body dumped and car backing out of the alley, in a couple of minutes or less. I looked in the Dumpster first—the man's hands and feet were bound with duct tape, a strip across his mouth."

"And you called the police right away?"

"My cell phone was on my belt," he said. "The dispatcher asked me if I could check for a pulse. He was very dead."

And of course there was a picture of the skeletal remains of a once large and prosperous hardware store.

"Do they *know* it's you? That you're the witness?"

He shrugged. "Of course they know—my name appears on the warrant. Before this is over, my picture will be in the paper. If there's a leak in the D.A.'s office, they might know where I am. Either way, the burned building is a message sent to anyone who might be considering testifying against Regis Mathis. I had a more direct message, left on my voice mail at home. Just in case I wondered if they knew where I lived."

"And if you didn't testify? Would you be forgotten?"

"There are way too many unknowns," Conner said. "I called the police within minutes of the murder," Conner said. "If no other witness appeared, would they consider their warning had scared me off? Or would they try to ensure I remained scared off? Because what I saw, Les, was horrible. If that happened to a member of my family, I'd hope to God someone had the balls to step up."

"Of course you have to," she said.

"And the hard part for you, Les, you have to act like you didn't even notice any of this has been happening. At least until the trial is over."

She laughed softly. "Do you think I'd have trouble doing that if it means keeping you and your family safe?"

"If you get overwhelmed or freaked out, you can talk to Brie."

"But I'll talk to you, too. Won't I?"

"Sure we will." He put down the laptop screen, blocking the stories and images, and gently traced the line of her jaw. "Yes, we'll talk. Probably every day." He leaned toward her to give her a light kiss. "Let's be done with this for now. Let's sit on the back porch and talk about regular things. Let's pretend life is normal."

He pulled her to her feet and walked her outside. They sat side by side in chairs as the sun sank and the sky above the trees grew lavender. He asked her about high school and her friends when she was younger. She told him about a best girlfriend who moved away when they were both sixteen, and it had been so traumatic, she had cried for days. And there were the sorority sisters in college—they stayed in touch, got together every year or so. She'd had a close friend during her marriage, but they'd grown apart as her girlfriend had children and Leslie didn't. And, Leslie admitted, it was her own longing for a family that kept her away.

He wanted to know about boyfriends, and she told him there had been a couple of pretty unexciting ones. And then he wanted to know who the first one had been, the one who had captured her long enough to lay claim to her virginity. "That would be Pete," she said. "And I suspect I was his first, too, because neither one of us was very good at it. And it happened at my house when my parents were out for the evening. On the couch. I was unimpressed."

And he pulled her onto his lap. He kissed her in that teasing way he had. "What does it take to impress you now?" he whispered against her mouth.

"Now?" she asked with a laugh. "Now it takes the perfect man."

"Don't know any of those," he said, running his hands up her sides. "Sometimes it pays to be imperfect. I'm willing to try harder."

She wiggled into his lap. "Take me to bed, Conner. The whole world goes away when you take me to bed."

Conner didn't know how many women he'd been intimate with in his life. It didn't seem like that many. There had only been a couple who had stood any kind of test of time—one when he was in the army, away from home, young and lonely. One was later, when he was working all the time and felt the stress of trying to operate a business he was too inexperienced to run. Both of those had probably been six-month relationships. He was grateful for them—they were nice women and the relationships hadn't ended badly. There had been others here and there before his wife, very brief liaisons.

Nothing in his life had prepared him for this woman, for Leslie. The way she came to him was magic; she unfolded for him, drew him in as if absorbing him and surrounding him with her love. Words of love had not been spoken, but he felt it to the marrow of his bones. He liked to lay her gently on the bed and slowly undress her. Every time she grew impatient when he got to the snap on her jeans, and every time she would go after his belt buckle, even more eager for him than he was for her.

"Wait," he said. "Tonight you're going to wait."

She groaned and said, "I hate to wait. I love to wait."

He drew down her jeans very slowly and revealed red lace panties that were barely panties at all. "These are new," he said.

"Mail order," she whispered. "It's nice to buy for someone who appreciates it so much."

"Oh, I do, sweetheart." He ran a finger around the elastic below the waist and at the legs. "I'm going to eat these. I'll buy you more...."

That brought a deep moan from her and a low laugh from him. He bent his head to her red panties.

"No!" she said, pushing him back. "Not until you take off the jeans! You have to play fair!"

He didn't even hesitate. He shucked those jeans so fast, it was like sleight of hand. Then he started over, from her lips to her chin to her breasts to her belly and then lower. They hadn't been a couple long, but he knew what she liked, knew what her favorite adventures were, and one of them included his tongue teasing around the edge of her panties until he couldn't stand it any longer and had to go in for the kill.

Tonight, he decided, he wasn't taking the red lace off. He was going to move it around. Until Leslie, he'd had no idea how much he enjoyed a little lace that barely covered her. He gently spread her, licked her thighs, pulled the panties to the side and enjoyed the most private part of Leslie. Enjoyed her *deeply*. Wanted her wildly. And she made those beautiful sounds for him, lifted herself against his mouth, begging. When her moans came in breathless gasps, closer and harder, he pulled away from her and rose to her lips. "Not yet," he said. "Not yet."

"I think you have a mean streak," she rasped out.

"You like this. This is your favorite. Deny it."

"I can't deny it."

He kissed her in a way that said he owned her, and she wrapped herself around him, trying to hurry him, but he couldn't be hurried. This was going to be like the first time. Then if he had the energy, he might take her through all the times....

He changed his mind and got rid of the red lace, leaving her beautifully bare.

"Please," she whispered against his mouth.

"Not yet." And then he entered her slowly, so slowly. He held very still because when he was inside her like this he wanted time to stop. This felt natural and right to him, to be cocooned with the one woman in his life he loved with all his heart and mind. Loved.

He dipped his head and gave her nipple a lick, then a tug. And he moved, very slowly and deeply. And she said exactly what he expected her to say. "More. Come on, harder."

He chuckled. "Not yet. I want you to let it build. Slow and easy. Try to lie still and let me get you there, from the inside, let it build."

And she groaned. She couldn't do it. She tried moving her hips against him, but he wasn't allowing it. He held her still and took his time, pumping, kissing, sucking.

It wasn't long before she began to lose control and pant, squirm, dig her heels into the mattress and lift against him, slam against him.

"Okay, baby," he said. "I guess it's time...." He covered her mouth, accepted her tongue into his, grabbed her hips, fixed the friction just right and pounded into her, fast and rhythmic, hard and even, deep and perfect. And she rose, cried out against his mouth, wrapped her legs around him to hold him and erupted into a liquid heat that sent him out of his mind, clenching in the most delicious spasms. He tried to wait her out, let her finish before he gave it up, but he could only do so much, and he went off like a rocket, a beautiful rocket.

"God," he said. "God. Les…"

She eventually collapsed beneath him, panting. He buried his face in her neck and tried to even his breathing, but it was as if he'd run a sprint.

She played with the hair at his temples while she floated back to earth; he liked that part. When he could finally lift his head, he looked into her hot, dark eyes and said, "Do you have any idea how much I love you?"

She smiled at him and said, "I think I do. About as much as I love you."

He smoothed back her hair. "We're going to be all right, Les. We'll just get through the next few weeks and then we'll get on with our lives. New lives for both of us."

"Here?" she asked.

He gave a little shrug. "This is as good a place as any. And if the time comes, we can take care of your parents." He grinned. "The fun couple."

She was momentarily stunned into silence. "You'd do that for me?" she asked in a whisper.

"I'd do anything for you."

* * *

Conner spent the weekend. He went back to his cabin for a change of clothes, but had all day Sunday with her. They went to a movie and brought home Thai food Sunday night, watched the sky turn lavender again and went to bed together. Early.

When Conner lay beside Leslie, he found it difficult to sleep. She felt so good against him, and he didn't want to miss a second of it. Everything in his life had changed in the past couple of months. Everything he *wanted* for his life had changed.

Witnessing a brutal crime was a helluva way to have an epiphany, but that's probably where the changes began. When it had first happened, his resentment for his circumstance had been so enormous it had almost been suffocating. When his store had burned down, when the threat had come, hatred had risen up in him, and he'd felt like killing someone himself. When the D.A. had decided the most reasonable and safe thing to do was separate him from his sister and nephews for at least a few months, it had felt like a small death.

Slowly his perspective began to change. It was so slight at first he'd barely noticed, and he certainly hadn't understood what was happening to him. He understood now. He'd been a slave to his business; there hadn't been room for much else. It hadn't been unusual for him to put in sixteen-hour days. When he had spent time with Katie and the boys, he'd often done so during a work break. He'd leave work to go to their preschool program or T-ball game or birthday party and then go back to the store to clean up, to lock up. He would have dinner with them and then go back to the store. He had rarely taken days off; he'd even built the boys' race car beds at the store in the stockroom and then delivered them in one of his trucks. It had been all about filling up the days and making things work.

When he'd lost the store, the shock almost broke him. He'd had nowhere to go, nothing to do. When Katie and the boys had moved away to their own hiding place, he hadn't been sure he'd ever sleep at night again. "Just a few months," he'd told her. "Just to be safe, and then we'll get it all back the way it was."

Now he realized he didn't want it the way it had been. He wanted to be able to give quality time to the people he loved. He wanted to teach the boys to fish, to camp, if he could even remember how himself. And while he'd always told himself he'd be okay with the idea of not living within a couple of blocks of them, he hadn't really accepted it. Not really. Now he knew that would be okay. He also knew that he'd make even more time for them under such circumstances. He would visit; he would bring them to him.

He wasn't going to work himself to death anymore, either. Hard work was good, all work was destructive. He wasn't sure what he was going to do when this current mess was behind him, but there were lots of options. He could be happy working on bathrooms and kitchens for a long time to come. He could buy or build a hardware store in the area, though it wouldn't be the same kind. He could order parts, fixtures and accessories for Paul, but there was no market around here for a store full of high-end, custom items. But for other hardware from lumber to nails—that might actually work.

He dozed off amid thoughts of a life in which work was balanced with fun and relaxation. The sun was coming up as he opened his eyes again, still in possession of the woman who had helped change his perspective, whether she knew it or not. He pulled her tighter against him, spooning her, and kissed her neck and shoulder.

"It's very early," he whispered. "I should sneak out of here and head for my cabin, then to work."

"Hmm," she hummed. Complaint was clear in her murmur.

"You know I'd like to stay in bed forever. And you know we can't."

"I know," she said.

And then the phone rang. She turned in his arms and gave him a startled look. Who would call her house so early in the morning? She reached over him and grabbed the cordless on the bedside table. She muttered a sleepy hello.

"Sorry to call so early, Leslie. This is Brie. Is there any chance Conner is there?"

"Right here," she said, passing the phone to him. "It's Brie."

"Brie?" he said into the phone. "What's wrong?"

"Nothing wrong, Conner. Max called just a few minutes ago and got us all out of bed. They're going to want you in Sacramento soon to prep you before the trial. You should be there in a week at the outside. Get there by next Monday morning."

He sat up and rubbed a hand over his goatee. "How long is that going to take?"

"A couple of days to prep, tops. You'll be put up in a hotel and you will have protection, so don't worry about that. I don't know when they'll put you on the stand—whenever it's most strategic, I imagine. What I'm saying is, I don't know how long you'll be stuck in Sacramento. But you should be there in a week at the outside. Which gives you a little less than a week to see your sister and get to Sacramento."

"I should go directly from my sister's to Sacramento?" he asked.

"That's the best idea, I think. Then you won't raise any eyebrows in Virgin River. And another piece of information you've probably been wondering about—your biker is safe. All good. He works in a Harley dealership and there are a lot of group rides out of that shop. He's clean as a whistle."

"Not a hit man, huh?"

"Doesn't appear to be, no. Now, can I suggest you pack and tell your boss you have a family emergency back in Colorado?"

"And what am I going to say it is?"

"Just tell him you're not real comfortable talking about it right now as you don't have all the details, but you'll stay in touch and be back as soon as possible. If it seems safe and appropriate, I could have a word with Paul."

"Please, if you can," he said. "I want the job, if I can still have it after the trial. And do this for me, Brie. Check on Leslie."

"Certainly. Tell her if she needs anything at all, call me."

"I already have."

"Then say your goodbyes and get going. It'll soon be over, Conner."

Of course Conner had known that he'd be headed to Katie's home soon, but not quite this soon. He'd already purchased a ticket for a departure a week from now, but he'd wisely chosen a refundable one that, for a fee, could be changed to a different flight, just in the event something like this came up.

Thank God it was only five in the morning. That gave him a little time.

He put the phone back on the bedside table and rolled over, pressing Leslie down into the bed. "In a couple of hours I'm going to drive to the job site to tell Dan I have to leave town. Then I'm going to drive out to the office to tell Paul. Then I'm going back to the cabin to check flights and pack up. I'll call you when I get to Katie's."

"And now?"

"Now, I want to love you one more time before I go."

"Please, don't act like it could be the last time. I don't want to be afraid."

His eyes bored into hers. "It's *not,* Les. It's *not*—don't even think that way. It's just an inconvenient piece of business that has to be handled. That's all it is."

She ran her fingers through the short hair at his temples. "Serious business," she whispered.

"Don't worry," he said. "Just kiss me." And with that, he devoured her with one of his possessive kisses.

An hour and a half later, his hair still damp from his shower, he was standing at her front door, with Leslie pressed tightly against him. "I'll talk to you later. Tonight, if I don't have any problems getting flights changed and make it to the East Coast. But if you don't hear from me tonight, don't worry—I'll call first thing in the morning."

"I hope you find out your sister is in a good place," she said.

"I'm sure you're perfectly safe, Les, but don't take anything for granted. Lock your doors and pay attention to what's going on around you." He put a kiss on her nose. "I love you."

"I love you more," she said, letting him go very reluctantly. "Come back to me soon."

There were things Conner had not thought to ask Brie, like when, if ever, they could share the truth of this situation with close, trusted friends. When Conner told Dan there was an emergency back home in Colorado, true to his character, Dan said, "Oh, man! Is there anything I can do to help?"

"I just have to get home right away. Sorry to leave you without any help here."

"Don't worry about that, buddy. I'll snag some crew off another project and pull 'em over here. Won't be as talented as you, but family comes first."

"Sorry for the inconvenience."

"Don't say another word. You have my home number, right? Because if things get hairy or you need help, call me first. I'll do whatever I can."

He'd only known Dan since early March and it was now late May, yet this was as close as he'd felt to a friend in a long, long time. One more reason not to be owned by a business that left no time for quality friendship. He wished he could say how much it meant to him. He settled for, "Thanks."

"It's what friends do," he said. "Travel safe. Don't get in a hurry and wreck or something. Just let someone know you're okay."

"I'll let Les know when I get there. I'll probably call her tonight if I can."

Then there was Paul. "Oh, jeez, Conner, that's too bad. You okay for cash? Need an advance or loan or anything?"

He was speechless for a moment. He hadn't even said why he had to leave without notice, yet his boss was offering him money. What was to prevent him from taking advantage of that offer, accepting a tidy little wad and never coming back? "No, I'm good. Sorry to take off like this, but—"

"Hey, if you were going fishing I'd dock your pay,

but you gotta take care of your people. If you run into a problem, call me. I can always find some way to help out. If you get on the road and decide you were a little hasty and you do need some cash, I can wire you money. Don't stand on ceremony."

"That's terrific of you. I have enough money, but thanks."

"I hope you get things worked out."

"I'll do that as fast as I can."

"I'm not worried about how long it takes you—I'll hold your job for you. Just make sure you don't come back here too hastily. Settle things. Family business can get complicated—I know that."

Now this was a nosy town, Conner knew that, yet neither one of them had asked him what was wrong or what was going on. They might be curious but they showed a respectful restraint when it came to personal family business. He hadn't offered extra information, and they hadn't pried.

Conner felt this kind of loyalty and support was more than he deserved. The day would come when he'd return the favor. He'd make sure of it.

Fourteen

Conner had a long and tiring day traveling from the West Coast to the East Coast, and even though it was late by the time he arrived in Burlington, Katie had kept the boys up and insisted on meeting him at the airport. Katie stood in the baggage claim area with a little boy on each hand...a *cranky,* tired little boy on each hand.

She looked like a teenager to him, like a little girl with her long, soft brown hair, makeup-free face, large blue eyes. And when she saw him, she started to cry. Her mouth twisted, her nose reddened, and her eyes grew very wet.

He kissed her forehead. "Don't," he said in a hoarse whisper. And then he fell to his knees and pulled the boys into his arms. "I missed you!" he told them, nuzzling their necks.

"You're itchy," Andy complained.

"Why do you have this?" Mitch asked, touching his goatee.

"I want to be cool," Conner said, fighting emotion. "Look at you. You grew. Which one of you is bigger?"

Andy giggled. "We're identical. We're the same."

"I don't know," he said, frowning at them. "I think Mitch is getting taller."

"Naw, but I'm smarter," Mitch said.

"Are not!"

"Am so!"

"Can we fight at home, please?" Katie asked, emotion tugging at her voice.

Connor stood and enfolded her in his arms, hugging her close. "It's so good to see you, to know you're okay. Let's get these monsters home."

She nodded, tears in her eyes. "Let's get Uncle…" She stopped and looked around, clearly giving a second thought to saying his name out loud in a public place. "Let's get the bags and go home before you two turn into pumpkins."

"I never done that, but she says it all the time," Andy said to Conner.

"You better look out. You just might one of these days. Honey, take one of them to get a cart. I'll take the other one to get the bags."

"You have a lot?" she asked.

He looked down at her. "Everything. I have everything. I'll explain later."

Her eyes got round for a moment, but then she was all about business, taking Andy with her to get a cart while Conner grabbed Mitch and went to the carousel, praying his duffels made it, and he wouldn't have to deal with lost baggage.

Once they had three large duffels and a carry-on, they made their way to the car. Conner insisted on driving; Katie seemed emotional and tired. She gave him some directions to get them started, and they were hardly underway five minutes when both boys passed out in the backseat.

"Everything?" Katie asked softly. "You brought everything?"

"I'm going straight to Sacramento from here. They want to prep me for the trial, which should be starting soon. There was no point in paying rent on a cabin just to store my jeans and boots."

"But you're going back, aren't you? You love it there!"

"I hope to, but one day at a time…."

"What about your girlfriend? Couldn't she hang on to it for you?"

"I'm sure she would've been happy to, but I didn't want to load that on her. She's a little stressed about this whole thing as it is."

"Aren't we all! I'm still a little nervous about you doing this, coming here. We weren't supposed to see each other until this was over. More to the point, we weren't supposed to be seen together, the four of us. A big guy with a short woman and five-year-old twin boys—we stand out."

"Look, I know Mathis must have a lot of connections, but I find it hard to believe any of them have traced us to Burlington, Vermont. Thinking about it, I agree it's smart to get us out of Sacramento—that's a hot potato. And they did demonstrate they'd burn down a building to make a point. But I doubt they have a huge interstate network of thugs and investigators trailing us both." He reached across the console and squeezed her hand. "Why do that when they can wait in Sacramento for me to show up for the trial? That's where I could be a sitting duck."

"I'm so scared, Danny."

He squeezed again. "Don't be. This will be over before you know it. And, this might be hard for a while, but I'm keeping the name Conner now. We're going to change. You don't have to, but I am."

"Why?" she asked, surprised.

"Well, all my new ID is in that name and while I don't plan to hide forever, I think it makes sense to leave Danson Conner behind...." He looked over at her. "And that's what Leslie calls me. I'm keeping it. It's convenient and it's who she knows."

"Wow. I think you're in love again."

He shook his head. "Not again. In love for the first time."

Anyone would have had to be blind to miss Leslie's melancholy, and she knew it. Conner had only been gone twenty-four hours, but she'd pulled into herself the minute he'd driven away from her house. Paul was good enough to ask if she was all right, and she said, "Of course, I just hope everything is all right with Con-

ner's family." Brie called her at work and asked how she
was holding up, and she said, "I miss him, of course,
but I can live with that easy. Is he in danger?" Brie answered that he'd benefit from the best protection law
enforcement could offer. Leslie stopped by the bar for
a glass for wine and takeout, and Jack said, "So, your
boy had family business. He okay?" And she said, "He
made it there safely and said everything is going to be
fine. He should have things sorted out in a week or so."

"What kind of family business?" Jack asked, because
he was Jack. "I hope there isn't illness involved."

"He didn't give me any details. He left pretty quickly.
But I understand there's some kind of domestic situation."

"Ah," Jack said. "Sounds like a divorce brewing or
something."

"It does sound like that, doesn't it? We'll get the full
story when he's back, which hopefully won't be long. I
sure got used to having him around in a hurry. I admit,
I miss him already."

So due to that and a nagging worry that she simply
couldn't ignore, she was quiet and knew it. She also
knew she wasn't going to be able to spend a lot of time
talking to Conner while he was away, so she'd have to
suck it up and think positively.

The very next morning before work, she was out
in the front yard, pulling dead blossoms off some of
the flowers they'd planted together, every thought on
him. She heard someone coming down the street and
looked up to see an elderly woman walking with a

young woman who held the tiny hand of a two-year-old and carried a pudgy, smiling baby in a backpack. She'd seen them before; sometimes the young woman had one of the kids in an umbrella stroller. She stood up and smiled at them.

"Well, hi," she said, brushing off her knees.

"Hello," the older woman said. "I've been meaning to get down here to say hello. I'm Adie Clemens and this here is Nora and her babies. Nora forces me out of the house almost every morning."

Leslie lifted her eyebrows. "Is that so? I'm Leslie." She put out a hand to the older woman first, then the younger.

"Doc Michaels said she should walk every day and if I don't walk her, she manages to forget. Nice to meet you."

"Are you two related?" Leslie asked.

They looked at each other and laughed. "No, I'm just a thorn in her side," Nora said. "Adie's blood pressure and cholesterol have come down since she's been eating less pound cake and walking. And now that spring is officially here with summer right around the corner, the girls and I sure can use the vitamin D. Your flowers are so beautiful. Adie and I have admired them every morning since you planted them."

Leslie surveyed the yard with a longing in her heart. "My boyfriend, Conner," she said. "This was his idea of bringing a girl flowers. I've never seen anything like it."

"The young man with the great big pickup truck?"

"The same. We work for the same construction company. I assume your husband works around here?" she asked, looking at Nora.

Adie laughed. "Not a husband between us," she said, trading smiles with Nora. "Maybe that's why we lean on each other a little bit."

"I work part-time at the clinic and will work more part-time at the school when they open up. They're going to do summer school with preschool just to get started and test the waters. Adie and Martha Hutchkins sometimes keep the girls for me."

"She's excellent with children," Adie said, giving her arm an affectionate pat.

"I apologize. It was silly of me to assume..."

"No worries, I probably would've assumed the same. This is Berry," she said, ruffling her little toddler's curls, "and this is Fay Lynne. You have the most wonderful front porch. Best one on the block. And the weather is so great—we should christen it with some lemonade and cookies one of these afternoons. Are you up to some old lady chatter?"

"Excuse me, madam," Adie said indignantly, drawing herself up to her full five feet.

Nora just laughed. "Like I said..."

And Leslie immediately thought, a friend in the neighborhood sure wouldn't hurt, especially right now when she was feeling too alone. "I would love that. I usually get home by five. Six if I stop off at Jack's for dinner or takeout."

"Ah, Jack's," Nora said almost wistfully. "Back in

the days before motherhood, I had been known to stop at a tavern or two. I vaguely remember...." Then she laughed.

"I would love to have you over to test the porch. Invite Mrs. Hutchkins and Puff," Leslie said.

"We'll be in touch," Nora said. "Come on, Adie, let's log those miles! See you later, Leslie."

She watched them go and thought that Nora couldn't be twenty-six, and here she was, a mother of two with no husband. Of course she hadn't asked if there was a man somewhere, but she got the impression there wasn't.

And then she heard the phone in the house ringing and dashed for it. Only two people called her—her mother and Conner.

"Hey, baby," he said in his low, sexy voice. "I caught you before work." He laughed. "Caught you alone without work crews in the trailer, so you can talk dirty to me."

"Conner!"

"I'm alone at the moment, which is hard to manage around here. What are you wearing?" he teased.

"Oh, stop," she said with laugh. "Tell me about Katie and the boys."

"Ah, the boys—not a real quiet pair, that's for sure. We've been doing a lot of wrestling and I think my sister is about to throw us out of the house. This is a small house, about the size of yours—just two bedrooms and a small living room, which we manage to fill up completely when the three of us are rolling around on the floor. And they get wound up and can't settle down. She's gone to run them around the park to see if she can wear them out a little. She took the day off today to spend time with me and to cook a nice dinner for me and her boss...the boss she says is keeping things very professional while she's working up a crush on him. I'm going to get a chance to look him over." Then he chuckled again.

"You sound...you sound so wonderful," she said. But the image she conjured of him hugging his younger sister and rolling around on the floor with his nephews made her wonder how he was going to make himself leave them. "It must feel so good to be reunited with them."

"They should have me completely worn out by Sunday, when I leave. Speaking of Sunday—are you checking the news?"

"I look online every day," she said.

"They published my name before the preliminary hearing, but I haven't seen it again in reference to the pending trial. And no picture. At least not yet."

"Why would they publish your name?" she asked with a tinge of anger.

"It's not malicious, Les. It's part of public record. They needed the name of the witness to get the search warrant to collect all the other evidence. It was news. Once something like this happens to you, you begin to notice things, like the names of victims published, if they're not minors. I'm just grateful they haven't run a picture yet, because I look an awful lot like Danson

Conner. And if I can keep all my Virgin River friends from figuring this out before the trial…"

"But, Conner, no one from around here would wish you any harm!"

"Of course not. I just don't want pretrial publicity to lead to you."

"I don't know what you mean…."

He took a breath. "I don't want your safety compromised to get to me. You don't watch cop shows, do you?"

"No. Lately I haven't watched anything but you."

"Well, don't start watching them now. In another week and a half, this will be over, and I'll be back."

"Are you sure, Conner?"

"What do you mean, am I sure?"

"It's going to be so hard for you to leave your sister and nephews."

"It was always going to be hard," he said. "When she married Charlie, she was only twenty-six, and off she went to Fort Bliss in Texas. Less than a year later he brought her back to me, pregnant, and left her with me while he deployed. For the past five years I've tried to prepare myself for the day she'd meet the right guy. The chances have always been good that she and the boys would move away."

"You sound more like a father than a brother," she said.

"I felt like that sometimes," he said. "Maybe I got a little stodgy—I had a lot of responsibility at a young age…."

"You're not stodgy now...."

"Until now, I was tied to that store. It was our legacy—I had to make it work to ensure the future. Not just mine, but the whole family's, because there was an equal chance Katie *wouldn't* meet the right guy and move away...."

"It's different now," she said. "You're free to go anywhere."

"Yes, I am. And I'm coming back to you."

Conner felt as if he could've stayed on the phone with Leslie for a long time, but not only were Katie and the boys coming up the walk toward the house, Leslie did have a job to attend to. He reluctantly said goodbye with a promise to call her at his next opportunity.

He saw them from the living room picture window— they were running, of course. They didn't walk anywhere. Katie was bringing up the rear, much more slowly. The boys blasted in the front door and tackled him, one kid on each leg. He laughed and said, "Yeah, you're tired out. Right." When Katie came in the door, he smiled at her and said, "You did a good job of wearing these guys down."

"I need a nap," she said. "Where do they get the energy?"

They ran off to the TV, firing up their current favorite movie, *Avatar*.

"I think we should stop feeding them," he said.

"I'm going to make lunch, then with any luck we'll have some quiet time! Sandwiches?"

"Anything, honey," he said. "What can I do?"

"You can tell me what you think of the house, the neighborhood, the area."

"I think it's great and have no trouble understanding why you feel comfortable here. But once the trial is over you probably can't stay in this house."

Her hands full of cold cuts from the refrigerator, she turned slowly toward him. "But I can," she said. "I checked. This was a six-month lease, which is available again when I move out. It's a warm, friendly town, Danny. I mean, Connor."

He smiled indulgently at her struggle with the new name. "And there's a guy here," he reminded her.

"It's not like we've dated or anything, but we have a couple of complications. One—I work for him. I get the sense that there are lines he won't cross and that's one of them. But I like that. If I'm going to be involved with anyone, he has to have really strong principles. Like Charlie had. Like you have."

"I have?" he asked.

"You have definite limits," she said, pulling out the mayo, mustard and lettuce. "There are things you just won't compromise."

"I think you have an idealized vision of me," he pointed out to her. "Right now I'm getting it on with my boss's secretary. And have absolutely no guilt."

"Tell me about her," Katie said. "All. Tell all." And she began dealing out bread on the counter to make sandwiches.

"Well, she's beautiful. The second I saw her, my

knees started to feel soggy. She has blond curls—big, loose curls. Brown eyes—when she smiles her eyes get almost black, they're so dark and wet. She's not short like you—she's a few inches taller and when I dance with her—"

"You went *dancing?*"

He chuckled. "Long story—I'll tell you later. Les is beautiful, but the best part about her goes way beyond looks. She's very feisty—she runs that construction company and all those men, and believe me, they don't give her any trouble."

"Is she bossy?" Katie asked.

He shook his head. "She's confident. Funny thing is, she told me she's always had a confidence problem. Maybe in other parts of her life, but not with me, not with her job. And she's very funny. She's kind of a wiseass. I like that. And this might seem kind of incongruous—she's very kind. There was a house-warming party for one of our guys and his fiancée recently, and even though Leslie hadn't met her, she called her and offered to help out before and after the party. Thoughtful. Sincere. She's sweet but very strong. I didn't even think about how much I like strength in a woman until I met Leslie."

"I'd like to be stronger," Katie said.

"Oh, sweetheart, you're strong enough," he said. "You've really made lemonade with what life handed you. Better than anyone I know."

"I've always had you," she reminded him.

"And you always will have me," he said. "Even if we end up on opposite oceans."

She was quiet for a second. "So, are you saying there's absolutely no chance Leslie would consider a major relocation?"

He put his hands in his pockets. "She's an only child. Her parents are a long way from needing her, that's my guess, but they are in their late sixties and it's something she thinks about. She's close to them—yet another thing about her I love. With any luck they'll be in their late eighties before they call on her for help, but I think Les and her parents need each other emotionally. I know if Mom and Dad were alive, I'd feel that way."

Katie's head tilted to one side, and she smiled. "Did you finally find someone who feels the same way about family that you do?"

He leaned his big hands on the breakfast bar. "Katie, even if I live in California and you live in Vermont, you can always depend on me. You know that, right? That you'll never be stranded and alone? All you have to do is call me."

"I know that," she said. "Keith is like that, too. He's very close to his mother and his sister and he looks out for them. You'll like him, I know you will."

Of course Conner liked Keith. He was easy to like. He arrived on time, brought a nice bottle of Chardonnay, because that's what Katie liked. The boys ran to him, hugging his legs, and he bent to receive them. When he stood up he was holding Andy with one arm under his rump and ruffling Mitch's hair while he had a bottle of wine tucked under one arm. He stuck out his hand toward Conner. "Nice to meet you," he said. "Katherine can't stop talking about you."

Katherine? he wondered. That wasn't an alias, but her given name, the name that appeared on her driver's license. Katherine Malone—her married name. "Don't believe everything you hear," he said with a laugh. "Nice to meet you, Keith." And then he reminded himself that not all men had hard handshakes; not all men did hard physical labor for a living. In fact, there were many times Conner wished he didn't have to toil so hard, wished he could take it a little easier.

Keith Phillips wasn't a large man like Conner. He was around five-ten and had the slim build of a runner/ skier and a dental perfect smile. He seemed just right for Katie, who was a little five foot four. And like Katie, Keith looked young.

"You sure you went to dental school and everything?" Conner asked him.

He chuckled. "And everything," he said. He put a hand on Katie's shoulder, gave a squeeze and smiled at her. He handed over the wine. "Rombauer Carneros Chardonnay—2009. I think you'll really like it," he said.

"How sweet, Keith, thank you!"

"Do you have a favorite vineyard?" he asked Conner.

"Not much of a wine drinker, actually," Conner said. "More of a beer connoisseur."

"Imported beers?" Keith asked.

"Pretty much any beer," he said. "My first choice

would be a Mich, but if push comes to shove, I'm not all that fussy."

Keith laughed and said, "Caught me—I'm trying to impress Katherine."

"Well that's pretty easy," Conner said. "One of her virtues is that she's easy to please. She takes great pleasure in every little thing. She's the one person I know who is so completely positive and happy it puts me to shame. In fact, it's pretty hard to bring her down."

Keith smiled appreciatively. "What a gift," he said. "That's how it is around the office. And that's why everyone loves her. Katherine, can I help with dinner? Do anything for you?"

"Not a thing. If you two wouldn't mind keeping the boys busy for a little while, I'll finish setting the table and we'll have dinner in just a little while."

This was a good idea, Conner decided. It would give the men a chance to talk without Katie listening. So they took the boys into the small backyard. Andy and Mitch lit out for the play set. It wasn't quite as nice as the one that had been left behind in Sacramento, but it worked. It was a heavy wooden bar supported by four legs and sported hanging rings, a climbing rope, a bar to swing on.

"Look at them go," Keith said. "What a couple of monkeys."

"No children in the family?" Conner asked.

"Oh, I'm an uncle. My older sister has two teenage daughters, age thirteen and sixteen. It's a whole different ball game."

"I imagine. And I have no experience with girls."

"Katherine told me you're like a father to these boys," Keith said.

He gave a nod. "Pretty much. What else did Katherine tell you?"

"That you're in Colorado working. Sorry to hear about your company going out of business—it's a rough economy right about now. Hopefully we're headed for a recovery."

"It's not going to be quick," Conner said.

"But we all do what we have to do. Even dentistry has taken a hit, Conner. People tend to put off things like that as long as possible."

"But you're doing all right?" Conner asked.

"Not bad, considering. Pediatric dentistry isn't exactly a high-dollar practice like, say, periodontics." And then Keith launched into a conversation about the different types of dentistry, their individual complexities and specialties, how much more lucrative some practices were than others. Conner, to his credit, did not go to sleep.

"And you chose your specialty because?" Conner finally asked.

"I'm good with kids," he said with a smile. "When I did the pediatric rotation I knew that was the best place for me. I actually have to push the kids out of the practice to adult dentists at some point—most of them would stay with me forever. They're not afraid of what's going to happen to them in my office."

Well, at least the boys will probably grow up with good teeth, Conner thought.

And then, thankfully, Katie's voice broke in, calling them all to dinner.

Fifteen

Well, Conner observed, Keith was right—he *was* good with children, just not necessarily at the dining room table. Thankfully, he had Katie to back him up. When they started to squirm, when they picked up their mashed potatoes with their fingers or sloshed their milk because they were totally careless, Keith tried reasoning with them. "Andy, you're going to spill." "Mitch, you'll make a mess if you do that."

Katie, on the other hand, used her soft but firm voice to say, "Stop." And they stopped.

Maybe Katie would cut Keith in on her secret weapon eventually. She knew how to make them behave most of the time because she could separate them. They were identical twins and didn't like time apart. True, sometimes they *wanted* to separate, but that was up to them.

If they got in enough trouble with their mom, she would put them in separate rooms and talk to them one at a time. They would have time-out without being allowed to communicate verbally. Conner still wondered if maybe they did a little telepathic talking because they did seem to read each other's minds.

Conner had never done a lot of disciplining where the boys were concerned, and when he did, his style was very different. His voice was louder, his expression much more fierce, and he was not above grabbing a twin and hauling him physically into time-out. Conner called time-out "the penalty box."

Keith did pretty well for a newcomer. He liked them, that was the important thing. And he was very nice.

Conner learned that Keith had only recently paid off all his school loans and bought himself a larger home. He'd been in a small town house for a long time, paying bills and saving. At least he hadn't been living with the mother and sister he was so close to. Now he had a fairly large four-bedroom home with a big yard in a good school district.

Why he mentioned the school district kind of stumped Conner until he thought about it and realized that Keith might be courting Katie *and* her sons. That's what you did when you were dating a woman with children. Unless… *He's not weird or sick, is he?* Conner had no idea how to check for something like that. He'd never even known a guy who—

He took a deep breath. He'd brave that discussion with Katie after the good dentist left. But despite his not very well-founded worry, he thought Keith was probably a good guy, just a guy with a very different lifestyle than Conner's.

When the evening was beginning to wind down,

when dessert was done and coffee cups were low and talk turned to work the next morning, Conner volunteered to put the boys in the shower and make sure they donned clean pajamas. It was a good forty-five minutes later when he left them in their bedroom and ventured down the hall toward the living room.

The house was so small, he could see Katie and Keith standing at the front door from the bedroom hallway. They faced each other, smiling, and talked softly. Katie looked up at Keith with somewhat adoring eyes; Keith put his hand on her shoulder again and gave that little squeeze. He leaned down, and Conner thought he was going to kiss her, but no. He said something, smiled and left.

Katie turned and saw him. "Well. Are you *watching?*" she asked with a slight, teasing smile.

"Yup. Though I wasn't watching much."

"Like I said, he's being very proper. Want more coffee? Something else?"

He shook his head. "The boys are not quite in bed. They're clean, and if they're not tired, I'll go knock 'em over the head."

"I'll go tell them lights out," she said, heading for their bedroom. And once again, Mommy's word carried weight because the light went off, the door was pulled almost closed, and it got pretty quiet in there. Just a little murmuring.

Katie sat on the couch, tired. She leaned back and pushed her hair away from her face, tucking the long strands behind her ear.

Conner was rooting around in the kitchen. "I'm having a beer. Can you choke down another glass of that fancy wine?"

"Did you like him?" she asked.

"I'm having a beer," he repeated.

She sighed deeply. "Bring me wine."

He popped the top on his beer and poured the wine, taking it into the little living room. He handed it to her. "I didn't not like him."

"Spit it out. What did you find wrong with him?"

"Nothing. Really, nothing," Conner said. "What do you find right with him? He just doesn't seem like your type."

"He's kind. Sensitive. Sweet. Good to the boys. Conscientious. Trustworthy. Dependable."

"He could be all those things and have a little more backbone, I'm thinking," Conner said.

"He has plenty of backbone!" she replied, a little heat in her voice. "He has a successful practice, is respected in the community, is a good family man...."

"Hey, don't get mad. He's not like the other men in your life. Not like Charlie was. Not like me or Dad."

Her chin dropped. "But he's so kind. Sweet."

"Seems to be," Conner said. "But, Katie, what's with that hand on the shoulder? Is that the extent of his physical...you know..."

"He's been up front about that. He doesn't want to get physical with an employee. Even though he really likes me."

"He said that?" Conner asked.

"He said that."

Conner whistled.

"Oh, stop it! I know he's not like other men I've been attracted to, but…" And then, inexplicably, she began to cry. She lowered her face into her hands, and soft, quiet sobs came from her.

Conner moved closer to her, slipping an arm around her shoulders. "Aw, honey. What's the matter?"

"What's taking him so long?" she asked. She lifted her face and peered at her brother. "All I want is a kiss! Well, okay, that's not all I want, but we have to start somewhere." She leaned against Conner and wiped her cheeks.

He stroked her pretty hair. "He's safe, is that it?"

"Partly," she said. "Or maybe mostly."

"Is that the way to go?"

"Well, jeez, Danny…I mean Conner. At least he isn't going off to war!"

"There are lots of guys who aren't quite as…quiet and refined who aren't going off to war."

"There is nothing wrong with quiet and refined!"

"You know what I mean. It just doesn't look like he's going to ring a lot of bells, if you get my drift."

"Yeah, I know. I thought about this a lot. The kind of guys I'm used to, the kind I've always been attracted to, men like my father and brother, are risk takers. Been there, done that. I'm ready to play it a little safe. I don't want to keep losing husbands—I don't want my boys to keep losing fathers."

"But, Katie, honey, I'm not a risk taker," he argued.

She laughed outright. "Yes, you are. An ordinary guy would run for his life after being threatened after seeing a murder, but not you! You're going to take the stand, look him in the eye and convict him! You risk your life to do that!"

"Not exactly," he said. "I'm taking every possible precaution."

"I want a quiet life," she said. Her eyes grew sad; she shook her head in frustration. "I want my kids to have a good education, a safe upbringing, a stable environment...."

"And good teeth," he said with a laugh.

She wiped her tears and laughed, too. "And good teeth."

"He's...like...perfectly normal. Right?"

"Just because he loves kids doesn't make him a pedophile," she said.

"But you don't take that for granted, right? You got your eye on that, right?" Conner asked, because he couldn't not ask.

She lifted her head off his shoulder and with her blue eyes in slits, peered up at him. "Like white on rice."

He let go a big laugh and squeezed her tight. "Katie, Katie." This was what people didn't get about her because she appeared so docile. She was a lioness. A dragon. Because she stepped and talked softly, people sometimes took her for a pushover. Not Katie. No way she was letting her boys near an "iffy" guy.

"You've had your eye on him," Conner said.

"Every second. Every. Second. I swear, I won't stop

watching, but he just plain loves kids. He wants to have some of his own. He feels like he put it off too long, and he hopes it's not too late."

"Don't get into this for the wrong reasons, Katie," Conner said. "I can respect safe, but he also has to ring all your bells." He ran a knuckle down her jawline. "I saw how you were with Charlie. Just try to get lit up by the right guy because, seriously, I'm getting old!"

"Isn't Leslie kind of safe?"

He burst out laughing. "No!" he said. "No-ho-ho!" he emphasized. "She's got some of her own crap. Not quite as dramatic as mine. She has a weird ex who wants to be her best friend even though he's remarried and has a pregnant wife. And her parents, who are actually awesome people, are pretty eccentric. But safe? Oh, man—so not safe. She blows my mind. Falling in love with her is huge." He tilted Katie's face up to his. "If she dumps me or otherwise hurts me, I'm a guaranteed wreck. Leslie is a big risk for me. That make you feel better?"

She looked at him and shook her head. "No. I don't want to do that. I don't feel like taking chances."

"Then tell me, honey. Tell me what he does for you…."

She took a breath. "He makes me feel comfortable. Cherished in an everyday way. Seriously. There are times at the office or over lunch away from the office when he talks about simple things like riding bikes with the boys through the park, and he'll remark on how they will absolutely stop at the end of the sidewalk and wait for me before crossing the street. He'll tell me how much he admires the job I've done with them, a mother alone without a husband. He sees that Mitch and Andy are secure, that they don't act out like a lot of little kids…. He has said, a number of times, that I'm exactly the kind of woman he'd want to raise his children, and he says, 'If you take that to mean hope relationship grows, you're right.' Sometimes he'll ask my opinion about something minor to me but major to him—like whether to seed or sod that new yard of his, like whether to texture and paint walls or look at wallpaper…. I know, that doesn't seem like anything, but it just feels so *normal*. And God, Conner…I just want to feel normal."

Conner patted her arm affectionately. "We've always been able to talk very openly, very honestly, haven't we, Katie?" She nodded. "Then let me say something that's kind of hard to say to my little sister. It sounds like you're choosing a roommate, not a husband. You like him more for what he doesn't do for you than for what he does. He doesn't make you feel too much."

"Oh, you're wrong," she insisted. "I could really tear his clothes off. The big question is—does he want to tear my clothes off? Because if he can be the gentleman in the light of day and a wild man when the lights go out, he's absolutely what I want. I'm not stupid—I'm not going to get hooked up with a guy who doesn't have any passion."

"You have to promise me that," Conner said.

"I promise, of course. But if he has all the traits I

mentioned—the kindness and the gentleness and *also* passion, then he's exactly what I want. Exactly. This isn't the frontier—I don't need some macho man who's going to protect me from the grizzly. I need a dependable, loving, caring man who will come home from work every night."

Conner heard it, but he didn't believe it. That might be what Katie thought she needed—the comfortable old shoe. But it would leave her hungry and a little empty.

His baby sister was afraid to fall in love, love like she'd had with Charlie—hot, irrepressible, sizzling love that left her flushed and breathless. Because when you had that kind of love and lost it, the pain was just terrible.

But he said, "You'll do the right thing, Katie. Just be sure to ask all the right questions of yourself before you get in too deep."

"Of myself?"

"Yes," Conner said. "Questions like, can you be happy with almost everything, or do you have to have it all? Because it's hard to be honest about that."

Leslie found the warm weather and lengthening of the days to be such a comfort, especially as she was missing Conner. When she got home from work, there was still enough daylight for her to enjoy the front porch. And if neighbors happened to walk by, she gave them a wave, sometimes they even stopped to chat for a while. Mrs. Hutchkins was an energetic walker; Mrs. Clemens was slow but earnest.

Nora walked over with her kids, and while Berry played on the grass with her little talking box that made all the animal sounds, Nora sat in the chair beside Leslie to give Fay her bottle.

"Let me," Leslie said, reaching for the baby.

"Sure. She's a cuddle bug, that one is." Then she gave Berry a little nod. "And that one is so independent, sometimes it worries me."

"Why?" Leslie asked. "She seems happy."

"I think she is, at least most of the time. I had such a completely dysfunctional relationship with her father, I wonder if she's scarred for life. Emotionally. At least he wasn't around all that much, but still… I'm working through some of that now. Pastor Kincaid is a wonderful counselor."

"Is he?"

"Truly," Nora said. "I'm not a religious person at all, and when Mel Sheridan suggested I talk to him, I was very reluctant. I wasn't sure I was brave enough to unburden my sorry soul to a minister." Then she laughed a little. "One of the first things I learned about him is that he was a counselor before he was a minister."

"Do you mind if I ask? How old are you, Nora?"

"Twenty-three. Only twenty-three. Going on forty."

"Sounds like you've lived a lot."

"Fast," she said. "You look pretty comfortable with that baby," she said with a smile.

"I wanted children," Leslie confided. "I was married for eight years, divorced at thirty-one, and I wanted children. But my husband wasn't interested in having kids and I let it go." She shook her head and frowned. "I let a lot of things I wanted go. Now I'm trying to figure out why I'd do that."

"What we do for men, huh?" Nora asked.

"Are you divorced, Nora?"

"Never married," she said with a shake of her head. "I met this handsome, badass baseball player when I was nineteen and got pregnant not once but twice. He brought me up here and dumped me—Fay was only a few weeks old when he left. He had this idea he was going to get into the marijuana business, but he was too unreliable for even that and he took off. He left me right before this whole town was buried in the biggest snowstorm and the wind was blowing under my door! He took everything—the truck, even the refrigerator. I was scared to death and had no idea what I was going to do, and now? Now I feel like I should write him a thank-you note or something! Got my girls in a nice little town where I don't have to be afraid of all the things I was afraid of before."

"My God, how did you get by?"

"On the generosity of new friends who didn't owe me a thing. Your boss sent someone over to my house to seal the doors and windows against the cold. Preacher's wife brought over clothes and blankets and even an ice cooler for me to keep my milk and stuff. Adie told Pastor she thought I could use a Christmas food basket. It just spiraled from there. When the snow started to melt, Mel Sheridan gave me a part-time job in the clinic—she said I could bring my kids as long as

I could manage them—that's what she had to do when hers came along." She reached over and gave her baby's fat foot a squeeze. "I owe everything to the people in this town. I really don't know what I would have done!"

"Where are you from?" Leslie asked.

"Berkeley. I lived there from the time I was ten—left three years ago when I was pregnant with Berry. Where are you from?" she asked.

"Grants Pass, Oregon. My boss, Paul Haggerty, worked there with his father and brothers for years, then came down here to open another arm of their construction company. I came down to work for him. Mainly to get away from my ex-husband."

"He's abusive?"

Leslie's brows shot up. "Not at all!" she said too quickly. Then she realized why Nora might have made that assumption. "Let me rephrase that. No, Greg is not abusive in the usual sense of the word. He's self-centered and egotistical and manipulative, but in the nicest possible way. He wants us to be best friends—even though he remarried right away and his new wife is pregnant. I just want him to go away!" She pulled the sweet little bundle closer. "I take it yours was… abusive?"

"He's an addict. He was a minor league ballplayer when I met him. He had big dreams of the major league, but he tinkered with drugs. I tinkered, too—I have to own that. But I got pregnant and stopped the second I suspected. But Chad indulged. He got caught, of course, and was dropped from the league. Then he really bottomed out and pretty much took me down with him."

"Do you know where he is?"

"No idea. Hopefully gone back to the Berkeley or Oakland area where he had all his old drug connections. I just need to never see him again. But you—you have a new man in your life," she said.

"Conner," Leslie confirmed. "He's away—attending to some family business. It's giving him a chance to visit his sister and nephews. He's enjoying that a lot—he's very close to them."

"When will he be back?"

"I'm not exactly sure, but hopefully in a week or so. Maybe two weeks. He hasn't seen his sister in a long time. But I talk to him every day." She snuggled Fay a little closer. "You're right about this one—a real snuggle bug."

"I had no crib for her, so I barely put her down. The three of us sleep together, all cozy."

"That sounds kind of wonderful," Leslie said.

"Isn't it amazing how some of your biggest blunders can end up being the best thing that ever happened to you?" Nora asked. And she gazed lovingly at little Berry, who sat on the grass between the flower beds, picking at the grass and making sounds that seemed to be a two-year-old's version of singing.

"I have an idea," Leslie said. "How would you and the girls like to ride into Fortuna on Saturday? Just wander around, maybe do a little shopping? Go to the big park?"

"That's so sweet, but I don't have car seats. Pastor Kincaid keeps his eye open for some to be donated to the church for one of their rummage sales. He says when and if that happens, he'll snag them for me. Until then…"

"Well then, I think we should see if either Martha or Adie or both of them can babysit for a few hours," Leslie suggested. "It might be good for you to have a break, get out of town for a while."

"Maybe I could leave the girls with one of them during their nap time. I'll ask…if you're sure."

"I'm sure," Leslie said. "Not only would I enjoy the company, it would give you something fun to do. Let me know if you can rope those ladies into sitting for a while!"

Sixteen

Leslie found herself hoping that Nora would be outside with her children when she came home from work. She'd love to wave to her—three doors down the street—and invite her for a glass of tea. She'd offer to hold the baby for her bottle....

Instead, there was a shiny Caddy parked in front of her house, and she groaned.

"Crap," she said aloud. "What *now?*"

She quickly considered her options. She could go to Jack's and wait him out. She could drive out to Paul and Vanni's house and get herself some backup. Fortuna was an option—she could just go to a restaurant, shop, kill time. But she wasn't afraid of Greg—she was simply *sick* of him! So she pulled into her drive and got out of the car.

He wasn't waiting in his car but on the porch, sitting in one of those canvas chairs, the collar of his white dress shirt open and his sleeves rolled up. And she didn't recognize his expression. It was odd. Maybe sad. Possibly contrite. Neither was an expression that was familiar to her.

When she stepped away from her car, he stood. He put his hand up, palm toward her. "Don't shoot me with anything. I just came to talk. Not argue, just talk."

She approached the porch. "You're not coming inside," she said with as much authority as she could muster.

"Fine. Will you sit out here and talk to me for a few minutes?"

"How did you find my house?"

"I've been down here a couple of times before. It's a little town, and I spotted your car in the drive. I also spotted a great big construction worker's truck parked on the street. I finally decided I had to brave the new boyfriend if I wanted to talk to you."

"You didn't think approaching me at work again was a good idea?"

"Paul seemed kind of opposed to that notion the last time I ran into him," Greg said.

"Right. He offered to beat the shit out of you if you didn't just leave me alone."

"I'm not going to hurt you, for God's sake! Can't you give me ten minutes?"

She sighed deeply. "Stay right there. I'm going to pour a glass of wine. Can I get you anything? Merlot? Glass of tea? A little hemlock?"

He winced. "Tea would be nice."

She went up the step and onto the porch. She opened

the door. "You come in this house and I'm going to shoot you. Do you understand?"

"Leslie…"

"I'm serious. I'm so bloody sick of you, I will shoot you if you get in my space."

"Fine. I'll be waiting right here."

She locked the door behind her for good measure. After dropping her purse on the counter and pouring a glass of wine and a glass of tea, she went back outside. She handed him his tea and sat in the other chair. "I came down here to get away from you," she said. "I've told you that a number of times. When are you going to hear me?"

"I'm sorry," he said. "I have heard you. I'm having a hard time letting go."

"No kidding. But since you're the one that ended our marriage and you have what you want, why not just enjoy it?"

"That's the problem." And then he sipped his tea and didn't say more.

"What's the problem now?"

"I hardly know where to begin," he said, and he looked down into his glass. "I've made so many mistakes…."

"There's a mouthful…."

He met her eyes. "Your boyfriend isn't here, is he?"

"He'll be along shortly," she lied. "If I were you, I'd make this quick. What is it you want now?"

"Leslie, I'm sorry. I made a mess of our lives. I'm

not sure what happened. But I'm now a man with many regrets."

She was a little surprised to hear this. "What's the matter, Greg? New marriage not working out so well?"

"It's exactly what I thought I wanted, and now, I'm very embarrassed to say, it's not what I want at all. I was a fool. I made a terrible mistake letting you go. I'm still in love with you."

She was stunned speechless. She struggled to recover. There'd been a time, not very long ago, she would've given the earth to hear that. "I'm afraid that ship has sailed...."

"Has it? Because it's never too late to repair the damage, if we handle ourselves appropriately. It's time to put the cards on the table, Leslie. I'm not sure what happened to me—I was seduced, I guess. I was vulnerable for some reason and seduced and look what a fool I made of myself."

She took a fortifying sip of her Merlot and then leaned forward in her chair. "You've fathered a child! Regrets or not, you have obligations!"

"Absolutely. And I intend to honor them. Allison makes a good living—she doesn't need alimony from me but I will insist on supporting my child, both financially and emotionally. The sad truth is, I can't stay in that marriage. It was a mistake, Leslie. I never really let you go and you're the soul mate I should be with for the rest of my life. I want you to give me another chance."

She actually gasped. "Are you *crazy?*"

"No, sweetheart, I *was* crazy. I was crazy when I

thought an affair with a pretty young woman made sense, but I'm recovered now. I came to my senses. Late, I admit, but I finally see how wrong it was to leave you. I can't tell you how sorry I am or how much I want another chance. We were so happy—"

"No, we weren't," she said, though she said it softly. And to her surprise, he turned his head to meet her eyes. "We weren't. In fact, that's what you told me when you were leaving me—that you weren't happy. That you couldn't live a lie. That you were really in love for the first time! And now that it's in the past and I have some perspective, I can see that I wasn't happy, either. I gave up so much to be your wife." She shook her head. "I'll never be that foolish again."

"What?" he said, scooting forward in his chair. "What did you give up? I gave you everything!"

"No, you gave nothing and I gave up everything. We both worked tirelessly for your success and never discussed what was important to me. I wanted children, Greg. How many times did I tell you I wanted a family? You were so busy talking about yourself and your ambitions, you never listened to a word I said."

"You want children? Fine, then. We'll have children."

She shook her head. "No, Greg. You're much, much too late."

"Don't be hasty, Leslie. Don't make the same mistake I made. We had a good life, you and me. You begged me to stay and I was the idiot who didn't take you seriously when I should have." He tried to reach for her arm.

"No," she said again. "I'm over you. Completely. In fact, I have no respect for you."

"God!" he said. "How can you say that to me?"

"Easily. It's time for you to get over yourself. You didn't honor your vows. You betrayed me and left me and went on your merry way to a new life. Made a mistake there, did you?" She shook her head. "Well, there are consequences, Greg. I guess you're going to have to live with that."

"Leslie!"

She shook her head, though she was *not* completely unmoved. She couldn't imagine what he must be thinking and feeling. She couldn't guess what it might be like to be him right now. Greg wasn't used to being rejected. "I wish you'd leave so I can enjoy my wine."

"Is this about *him?* The man you've been seeing?"

"Did I trade you in for a new man? Absolutely not—I was completely faithful while we were married. I didn't so much as go out for coffee with a man for a year and a half after you left me. Have I found someone worthy now? Oh, yes," she assured him. "In fact, in about thirty seconds I'm going to go inside and phone around to see if I can find him. I'm going to ask him to hurry up and get you off my porch. Seriously. Because if you have regrets, it's your own damn fault and I'm not even slightly interested in giving you another chance to hurt me."

"I would never—"

"Listen to me," she said. "You don't even tempt me. For the past few months I've been trying to remember what I saw in you in the first place."

"I can't believe you're saying this to me," he said. "We were so good together!"

"Go. Please, go. Ask Allison to forgive you for being stupid and take good care of her and your child."

"Leslie, if you think about this—"

She slowly stood and went into the house. She threw the dead bolt and then went around to the back door to be sure it was locked. She took her glass of wine with her to the bedroom and sat on her bed, leaning back on the pillows. Using the cordless phone, she dialed Conner's cell. It was about eight-thirty on the East Coast. When he answered, she said, "I miss you so much."

"Not much longer, baby."

"Are you in the middle of things?"

"I was doing dishes," he said with a laugh. "Katie's getting the boys showered and ready for bed. I was going to call you the minute the house got quiet. What I really want is to roll over and grab you and pull you closer. And make you beg…"

"I want that, too."

"What's wrong, Les? Something's wrong."

"How can you tell?"

"Your voice—it's in your voice. Tell me. Don't make me worry."

"It's just Greg. I found him on my porch when I got home from work. He's sorry—how about that? He'd like another chance. He'd like us to try again."

Conner was quiet for a long beat. "Is that so?" he finally said.

"Have you ever heard anything so absurd?"

"And what do you want, Les?" he asked softly.

"I want to take a shower with you, that's what I want. I want to roll around in the bed with you. I want to feel your prickly mustache against my neck." She sighed. "I want to be with you because I understand you, because I'm understood by you. Because I trust you and love you."

"But he screws up your head," Conner said.

"I can't for my life figure out why," she said. "He has only one agenda. It's all about him. Why does it even distract me? I'm finished with him."

"Maybe not quite," Conner said. "Something is unfinished…."

She thought for a second. "Conner, I'm going to go see my parents this weekend. I'll drive up early Saturday morning and come back here on Sunday. I'll have my cell phone with me. It works just fine on the road to Oregon. I'm not going to see Greg, I promise you that."

"I didn't ask. Les, if you have to see him, I'm not going to try to talk you out of it. Do what you have to do. I've told you before—when we move on together, I don't want you to have any doubts. I want you to be sure."

"I am sure, Conner. I love you."

"But something's eating at you…."

"And I'm not sure what it is. All I'm completely sure about is that I want to be with you. Only you. I just have this baggage…. How do I dump the baggage?"

"I don't know him like you know him. I can tell you what I did. I wrote Samantha a letter."

"I didn't know that."

"I did it right before I left," he said. "I told her I was happy in a way I'd never been happy before and it had nothing to do with her. I wished her well and said I was moving on and hoped she would, too. I didn't give an address for her to respond to—but I said goodbye in the only way I knew how."

"I *keep* saying goodbye to Greg and he just won't go!" she protested.

"You'll figure this out. And I'll be with you soon."

"I need my mother," she said. "I'm going to go home, see my mom and get her to help me with this. My mom never liked him to start with! God, I wish she'd have told me and saved me the time!"

"If not for your marriage and divorce, we'd never have met," he said.

That stopped her. She thought about that for a second. "Isn't it funny," she said, "that our biggest blunders can end up being the best thing that ever happened to us."

When Leslie looked outside again, the shiny Caddy was gone, and she breathed a sigh of relief. Then she walked three doors down to Nora's house and made her apologies—she had to cancel their Saturday trip into Fortuna together. "I have to take a drive up to Grants Pass to see my mother."

"No problem, we'll do it another time," she said. "Is everything all right?"

"I'm not sure. My ex-husband showed up again. He's a complete pest. But I need to talk to my mother about him. My mom is kind of…well…*opinionated* would be a mild description. I think she might have some advice for me. I'll be sure to let you know."

"I saw the car," Nora said. "Wow."

"It's a very pretty car," Leslie confirmed. "It's not making him at all happy right now. But it used to. Things like clothes, cars, country-club memberships, all that stuff used to get him all excited. Not me," she said. "Never me."

Leslie hadn't exactly lied to Conner, but there was a little more to her agenda than a nice visit with her mother. She called her mother on Friday morning and said, "I hope you don't have really big weekend plans because I need you on Saturday—I want to come up to Grants Pass."

"Sure, darling," Candace said. "We have a kickboxing class in the afternoon, but we can miss it, I suppose."

"Kickboxing?"

"You just can't imagine how much fun it is. There's a group of us who go to the community center for the class. And you know what? We're not terrible!"

"I'm not at all surprised. But listen—I'm having issues with Greg. He is still bothering me. He was down here again. Can you do a little detective work for me? Make a phone call or two? I'd like to see Allison. Can you call her and maybe set something up? I'll meet her wherever, but I have to talk to her about Greg, who is driving me crazy. And I'd like to talk to her alone. Tell her it's very personal and important."

"Sweetheart, what is it?" Candace asked.

"It's just that I don't understand myself, Mom. How did I not notice this about him for the eight years of our marriage? Does the whole town think I'm just an idiot? And why didn't I know I was being *used?*"

"Oh, crap, Leslie—you're overthinking the whole thing. The 'town' thinks you were the best thing that every happened to Greg Adams and he was a damn fool to let you get away! As for Allison, I doubt she'll confirm that for you. But I'll call her and try to set up an appointment with her. Maybe you can meet her at the mall or something. Get it all off your chest, then we'll go out for sushi."

"Sushi?" Leslie asked.

"We just started eating sushi. It's wonderful. Don't you think?"

She just shook her head. "Be sure to tell Allison I'm not upset or anything—I'm very happy in my new life. I just want to…check in with her. Tell her I have a baby gift. And it's girl stuff—not for Greg! I won't take much of her time."

But when Leslie got to Grants Pass, what her mother had arranged for her came as quite the surprise. "Well, she wasn't very receptive to this idea, nor was she impressed by the baby gift. Do you actually have one?"

"Not yet, but I can get one on my way to see her."

"I bought you one to give her. I had it gift wrapped. And to be classy, I also bought a gift for the mother—some lotions."

"You are the best," Leslie said.

"What's bothering you?"

"I'm not sure. I'm afraid there's a part of me that still loves Greg. I hate that, but…"

"Phhhttt," Candace said, giving her hand an impatient wave. "I saw that godlike man in your house. And I got to know him a little. Funny, smart, attentive… You can't be pining for Greg!"

"Okay," Leslie said, "this time are you telling the truth? Or in ten years are you going to tell me you never liked Conner in the first place?"

"Absolutely not! At least not unless he screws up and hurts my little girl. Now, hurry and put on some fresh makeup. Look your best. You're meeting Allison at Premier Nails on Nineteenth. She's getting a mani-pedi at noon."

"No way," Leslie said.

"That or nothing, honey. She wasn't exactly easy to persuade. She said she has nothing to say to you. She was rather bitchy."

"What's up with that?" Leslie asked her mother. "She won! How can she be mad at me?"

"I'm sure by the time we get to sushi, we'll have at least some of the answers. Now get going!" Candace looked her over. "Don't you have something nicer than jeans to wear?"

"I have a fresher pair of jeans, but that's it."

"Well," Candace said. "Whatever."

The nail salon was crowded, it being Saturday. The owner immediately asked if he could help her, and she shook her head. She lifted the gift bag. "I'm just here to see someone." And she craned her neck, trying to spot Allison.

Fortunately she was in the back of the room, sitting in a large, leather chair that reclined slightly, soaking her feet in the pedi whirlpool tub. Her eyes were closed—ah, clearly unstressed about this meeting. And her pregnant belly was huge. She wore a red sundress with spaghetti straps and some kind of pattern in blue and green—very bright. Her thick blond hair was pulled back and held with a headband, as though she might be getting a facial today, as well.

Leslie approached warily. "Allison?" she said softly.

Her eyes opened lazily. "Oh. It's you."

"I brought you something," Leslie said, holding out the bag.

"You can put it right there," she said, pointing to the floor. "Right beside my purse and shoes."

Leslie put down the gift bag and looked around uncomfortably. "I was hoping we could talk. Maybe privately."

"Unfortunately I don't have time for a private meeting today, Leslie. You can pull up a chair and state your business or forget about it. This is just about the only time I have for myself all week. This is it. Take it or leave it."

"It's personal," Leslie tried.

"Then speak a bit softly if you like. I assume it has to do with Greg."

Leslie tilted her head. This wasn't like Allison. She

was usually much more pleasant. Not warm, certainly, but at least polite. Leslie looked around for a chair; there were only little ones on rollers, the kind the manicurist used to be seated at the client's feet. She shrugged and pulled one over to the pedi tub, sitting at Allison's feet. Like one of her subjects.

"Well," she began. "I'm tired of telling your husband I don't want to be friends. We've been divorced for two years and—"

"Not my husband much longer," Allison said coolly. "I filed for divorce a month ago."

Leslie's mouth fell open, and she stared at Allison in shock; Allison returned the stare with cold eyes. "But you're having a baby!" Leslie said.

Allison rolled her eyes. Right at that moment a young Vietnamese woman pushed a low chair on wheels over to the pedi tub and pulled on her latex gloves. She gently lifted one of Allison's feet out of the tub and began to remove the polish.

"Please," Allison said, not in the least intimidated by their audience. "I don't need Greg to have a baby. He's pretty useless anyway. What does he do? He does nothing but schmooze and network and try to impress people. Sometimes I wonder if he even has an office—it seems all his work is done on the golf course or at lunch and dinner meetings. It didn't take me too long to get bored with playing on the Greg Adams team."

"But, Allison, you haven't been married all that long!" Leslie said.

"Long enough, in my estimation. I have a very busy practice. I don't have time for more than one baby."

"But, Allison," she said, lowering her voice. "I thought the two of you were madly in love."

Allison just shrugged. "I thought we wanted the same things. When I first met him, he was all about forming a power couple. His ambition was tantalizing. He put a very good face on it. I admit, I got a little hooked."

"When did the two of you meet?" Les asked. "I don't think I ever heard that story...."

Allison sought the answer in the ceiling tiles. "Hmm. I think it was at an investment seminar. He was talking with a couple of my partners about tax shelters and limited partnerships, and I asked him if I could buy him a drink to learn more about it. He was more than willing. And willing and willing. I thought he had a lot of money. I thought we were headed in the same direction. He said you were holding him back."

"Me?"

"Uh-huh. It took me a while to figure out—he wanted me to play second chair. He wasn't really interested in playing Bill and Hillary. He wanted to play George and Laura." She made a little face. "I could go along with that as long as we were perfectly clear—I'm George. Greg just isn't smart enough to take the lead."

"And his money?"

Allison laughed. "Leslie, he doesn't have any money. He *spends* money, he doesn't save or invest, not exactly a big earner, either. Big talker, though. Thank God I kept our finances separate and wrote us a pre-nup."

Leslie started to wonder if she'd ever be able to close her mouth again. "I'm not really hearing this."

"You can have him back," Allison said.

"I don't want him back! But don't you love him?"

"I suppose I did. For a while. He does seem to know how to treat a woman. Most of the time."

Leslie frowned. "Most of the time?"

"He's chivalrous. Amusing. He does things like bring flowers. Loved the engagement ring—I think I'll go ahead and have the stone reset." Then she leaned closer and whispered. "He does have that little bedroom issue."

"Bedroom issue?" Leslie asked.

Allison leaned back again and ran her hand over her big belly. "Not exactly reliable in the erection department. You know what I mean?"

Leslie tilted her head and affected a perplexed expression. "I have no idea what you mean. Of all Greg's shortcomings, that certainly wasn't one of them. At least with me. In any case, it seems to have worked well for you—" she nodded toward Allison's belly "—at least once." She stopped herself just short of claiming Greg was a stallion. Leslie stood up from her little chair. Now she could look down at Allison. "So—what tipped you over the edge?"

"I decided to run for City Council. He informed me, in that extremely polite and superior way of his, that he would run first, and then, if I was still interested, I could file the paperwork for my own campaign. I told him to go to hell. It pretty much deteriorated from there."

"Oh, my. And are you? Running for City Council?"

She nodded. "The baby's due next month. The primary is in the fall."

"Well, then. Best of luck." She nodded to the gift bag. "Do you know if it's a boy or girl?"

"Girl. Thank heavens. I don't imagine Greg will take much interest."

"Best of luck, Allison. I hope it all goes well…the delivery and everything."

"Sure. Right."

Leslie just looked into those icy blue eyes for a second, and without really meaning to, she uttered, "Poor Greg."

"Poor *Greg*?" Allison repeated. "He's a *loser*! Poor *Greg*?"

"He's a lot of things, true. You're right—he's pretty self-centered. He's also kind. There's not an ounce of malice in him. I can't say that about you."

"Hit the road, Leslie. You've wasted enough of my time."

Leslie left feeling as though she'd just had an out-of-body experience. And yet—she suddenly felt she understood everything. First of all—Allison had gone after him. He'd been what she wanted at the time. And while Greg was always looking for someone to promote him, Allison was undoubtedly every bit as inclined. She'd wanted Greg because she'd thought he'd be good arm candy. And she was also cruel. Cold and very, very calculating.

And where did that leave Leslie and what she'd experienced in her marriage and in her divorce? Well, it was pretty simple and awfully sad.

"I think I was a pleaser," she told her parents with a shrug. "As annoyed as I could get with Greg, I never wanted any trouble. I just wanted a happy home. I wanted to laugh and relax and have harmony. I didn't care if Greg wanted to be the mayor, if that made him happy. That Allison," she said with a shake of her head. "Boy, she's cold. I wouldn't want to tangle with her. But if you ever have to go to court—you should hire her. Not a lot of emotion there."

"Seemed like she adored him and he adored her," Candace said.

"Birds of a feather," Robert said. "I almost feel sorry for Greg."

"Well, I do feel sorry for him," Leslie said. "He's always had these grandiose ambitions and this truly inflated image of himself and yet…he's so totally alone. He has no one to believe in him. Even when we were married, I did what he asked me to do—wrote letters for him, took messages, kept his calendar. But I did all that to keep the peace, make him happy and show support, not because I really believed he was going to be a big political hero. I didn't believe in him, either."

"But he has a shiny Caddy and a very nice wardrobe," Candace said.

"The poor slob," Robert said. "He's so shallow. You must have been so lonely while you were married to him!"

And she smiled. "Nah. I had you, I had a really fun

job with a bunch of great guys, sometimes girlfriends. I was actually pretty happy. And yet..." She thought for a second and remembered what Conner had said to his ex-wife. *I'm happy now in a way I was never happy before and it has nothing to do with you.*

"I'm going to skip sushi and just drive back to Virgin River," she told her parents. "I want to spend some quality time on my flowers tomorrow so that when Conner comes back from visiting his sister, the yard looks perfect."

Seventeen

It took Leslie almost four hours to drive back to Virgin River, and during that time she thought a lot about her years with Greg. He'd wanted so much more than she had since the day she met him. Then he'd traded her in for a prom queen, but boy did he get a tiger by the tail. Not only had Allison dumped him, Leslie had no doubt the word was out—he'd been cast aside. Chucked. Humiliated.

Greg would never be a mayor. He might not even be elected to City Council. But she wasn't worried about him—he would land on his feet. He'd find another woman because he wasn't good at being alone—he needed reinforcements, needed an audience. Now this whole business of wanting to be friends with her—it didn't matter anymore. She could afford to be charitable. She wasn't angry. In fact, she was grateful. If Greg and Allison hadn't driven her out of Grants Pass, she might've never found Conner.

She asked herself if she should have doubts about

whether Conner would turn out to be a bad choice, but she just couldn't summon any. In fact, while she wasn't a religious person, she found herself uttering a little prayer. *Please, please keep him safe!*

And her cell phone rang.

"Are you out to dinner with the fun couple?" he asked.

"I was just thinking about you! No, I'm driving home. I did what I went to Grants Pass to do, felt much better about everything and decided to go home. Tomorrow is my day off and I want to spend it in the yard. If there's time, I might drive my neighbor, Nora, into Fortuna just for fun."

"And what did you go to Grants Pass to do?" he asked.

"Well, it was a very interesting day, now that you ask." And she told him all about her visit with Allison and the conclusions she had come to. At the end of her story she said, "I feel a kind of peace about my divorce that I just didn't feel before."

"I understand," he said. "I totally understand."

"If I could just have your trial over and you back here, there wouldn't be a tight nerve in my whole body."

He laughed deep in his throat. "I really enjoy the job of loosening up those tight nerves of yours."

"You're very good at it, too. What's on the agenda for you tonight?"

"We're taking the boys to a pizza joint that will be crazy with loud kids and games and life-size singing puppets. We're having a party because I'm headed for

Sacramento in the morning. If there's a God, it won't take too long and I can do what I have to do and come home."

"Aw. You think of this place as home...."

"I think of you as home, baby. You."

His words wrapped around her like his arms had, and she knew she was more in love than she'd ever been. Her feelings had been quite real when she'd met and married Greg, even though she'd been so young, but with Conner, love had taken on a new dimension. It was grown-up love, steady and deep. Leslie didn't have to worry about holding on to Conner by meeting his expectations. This love she felt for him, that she felt from him, was bigger than the biggest love she had ever imagined.

She embraced his pillow while she was falling asleep, inhaling his special scent, that woodsy musk with just a dash of his sandalwood cologne. They had talked for almost an hour as she drove, talked until his nephews were pulling at him and telling him to *come on, come on, come on....* He had talked about how he not only wanted a life with her but a different kind of life than the one he had before, that life that had been drenched in hard labor and only punctuated by short breaks of leisure time with his family. Until this visit he had never spent more than a day with them. He'd rarely taken a weekend or evening off away from the store —they had been open almost 24/7. After the trial was over, he was in search of more balance. And that balance included her in a major role.

When he gave in to his nephews' urging to hurry up, he said, "All right, all right. I love you, baby. I'll call later." And in the background Leslie heard a small boy's voice say, "What baby do you love, Uncle Danny?" followed by Conner's deep, sexy laugh.

She was dreaming about him when somewhere deep in the night she was awakened by a noise. At first she thought it was a cat, then she realized it was crying. A baby was crying and crying. There was the sound of a door slamming, more crying from at least one baby or small child, then a shout. And another shout.

She sat straight up in bed. Another slam, but she wasn't sure where it was coming from. And then there was a pounding at her front door and she hoisted herself out of bed and she ran. Without thinking, she threw the door open. There stood Mrs. Clemens, looking tinier than ever, wrapped in a very old, faded blue chenille robe, her white hair all springy and misshapen from sleep.

"He's back," she said with a small cry. "That man is back and I think he's hurting her!"

"Who?" Leslie asked.

And before Mrs. Clemens could answer, Mrs. Hutchkins came sprinting down the street. She was wearing a gray sweat suit with a hoodie, and flip-flops on her feet. "Adie," she yelled. "Go get someone right now! Go get Preacher or Nick Fitch or Ron from the Corner Store. Hurry!"

And with that, Martha Hutchkins ran right up to Leslie's house, through the flowers that bordered the yard and grabbed the rake from the side of the porch where it had been leaning. "Hurry up, Adie!" Martha headed back through the flowers, the rake in hand.

"It's Nora," Adie said. "That man's hurting her!" And then she shuffled at her fastest speed down the street and away in search of help.

Leslie shook the cobwebs out of her head. She heard another scream—these houses must be made of paper! The baby was crying her lungs out. She ran back inside and grabbed her broom and thought, *I need a baseball bat!* She put some power in her stride to catch up with Mrs. Hutchkins. "Did you call anyone?"

"I called Mike V, our town cop, but he's at least ten minutes out of town. I'm not waiting for him, but he's our closest law enforcement." And with that, she moved quickly up the walk to Nora's front door, which stood open. Mrs. Hutchkins pushed her way right inside, Leslie close on her heels.

What Leslie saw next was terrifying. The baby was on the couch, crying and wildly kicking her little legs. Berry was nowhere in sight, and some tall, skinny ugly guy held Nora up against the wall. Her hands were locked on his forearms, trying to push him away, and her legs were in motion as if she was running in the air.

While Leslie took in the scene frozen in shock, Mrs. Hutchkins wasted no time. She turned the rake around in her hands, holding on to the edge with the prongs, walked right up to the man and, with all her might, whacked him in the head with the handle of the rake. He dropped Nora to grab his head.

Nora slid to the floor, gasping in fear, while the man whirled around and, with eyes blazing, snarled at Leslie and Mrs. Hutchkins.

Leslie, feeling a little late to the party, pointed the handle of the broom at him, hanging on to the business end. "All right, back away from Nora!" she commanded. "The police are on the way!"

He laughed, and when he did, Leslie caught sight of rotting teeth. Who was this? Not the good-looking, badass baseball player, surely? This looked like a vagrant! His holey jeans hung low on his hips, the sleeves were torn off his T-shirt, his curly hair was long and dirty, and he didn't exactly have a beard so much as hadn't shaved in quite a while. And he had very scary-looking sores on both arms.

He reached right out and grabbed both the rake handle and the broom handle and shoved them away. In an act of fantastic cowardice, he settled his attention next on his small, white-haired attacker, advancing on Mrs. Hutchkins, giving her a slap and a hard shove that sent her tumbling backward and to the floor. And then he turned on Leslie.

Baseball player, was he? She assumed the batting position, broom handle over her shoulder, rocking back and forth. Behind him, Mrs. Hutchkins was slowly getting to her feet, and Nora was crawling away from the action, still looking terrified. She appeared to have a nosebleed and she wasn't yet standing.

The man approached Leslie, and she took her swing. He intercepted the broom handle easily and gave it a hard tug to either wrest the broom from her or bring her close enough to hit.

Mrs. Hutchkins whacked him on the back of the head with her rake again. Leslie marveled. Martha was fearless! He whirled on her, and Leslie whacked him in turn with the broom handle. And now the growl that came out of him was enraged and a little crazed. He was done fooling around. He whirled on Leslie, grabbed the broom out of her hands and flung it aside with very little effort. He advanced on her fast, and she did the only thing she could think of—she kicked him in the balls. He never saw it coming; he dropped to his knees, grabbing himself in the crotch. He looked up at her with watering eyes that made it clear he was going to kill her.

He rose slowly. Slowly and as menacingly as possible while still clutching himself. Behind him Mrs. Hutchkins was scrambling around, looking for something else to hit him with. Leslie braced herself; she'd never get off another kick. With one big, meaty, dirty hand he circled her throat, hit her in the jaw with the other hand in a hard fist and lifted her clear off the ground.

And then he was gone. An arm appeared around his neck and pulled, and she fell from his grasp.

She shook herself, trying to clear away the stars, as she watched Pastor Noah Kincaid wrestle the man out the door of the house.

Leslie ran to the front door in time to see the good

pastor rolling around on the front lawn, a lawn that was more dirt than grass, trying his best to stay ahead of the bad guy. She watched the pastor take a slug to the jaw, then return one. Nora was suddenly beside her, pressing the baby close. "He's high," she rasped out. "He's going to be hard to subdue."

"What's he high on?" Leslie asked.

"Meth. Look at the sores on his arms. Meth sores. Oh, *no!*" she said suddenly. "Adie! Leslie, intercept her and take her to your house or something!" And sure enough, there was Adie, walking up the street in her old chenille robe, headed right for the fistfight on Nora's front lawn.

Leslie turned around and scanned the little living room. "Where's Mrs. Hutchkins?"

"She's kneeling on the other side of the couch, trying to talk Berry out. Berry has been hiding behind the couch. Did someone call the sheriff or something?"

"Mrs. Hutchkins called Mike Somebody." She looked back outside and saw Adie taking up a position behind a big tree. This was turning into an old lady military campaign.

A big, jacked-up truck came screaming down the street and screeched to a halt. Jack and Mike Valenzuela jumped out and ran to assist Noah. And then, just as Nora had predicted, it took all three of them to subdue him. He was so wired on meth, he had the strength of five men.

Adie came quickly to the doorway of Nora's house. The three of them—Nora, Adie and Mrs. Hutchkins—

all worked at comforting the children while Leslie couldn't pull herself away from the front door. For the first time she noticed there were other neighbors with lights on in their houses, a couple of them looking out windows and opening their doors.

Eventually, Mike and Jack trussed Chad up like a roped calf. He was laid on his belly, his hands tied behind his back with a rope strung to his bound ankles. And he was still yelling and rolling around, trying to get loose.

Dr. Cameron Michaels showed up by the time the suspect was tied up and administered first aid in the form of ice packs and bandages to those who needed it. The sheriff's deputy had been called, but, as the folks in this town had grown accustomed, he wouldn't get there real fast. He had a lot of territory to cover.

"Nora, did you open the door for him?" Noah asked her.

She nodded and held both Berry and the baby close. Tears welled up in her eyes as she fought the feeling of being completely responsible for so much damage. "He said he'd break it down. I told Berry to hide behind the couch, put the baby on the couch and prayed he wouldn't hurt anyone but me. Pastor, he could've gotten in anyway. I didn't know what else to do. He wanted money. I gave him what I had, but it was only sixteen dollars. And it made him so mad!"

"It's not your fault, sweetheart. It's his fault. I'll come over tomorrow afternoon with better locks. We'll get the doors and windows reinforced. And it's time for a phone, Nora. I know you've been avoiding it because of the expense, but you can't put it off now. You need to be able to call for help from the inside of your locked house."

She nodded and buried her face in Berry's curls.

"How'd you get into this, Reverend Kincaid?" Leslie asked.

"Bad sermon," he said with a shrug. "I was hoping for inspiration. It was keeping me awake and I didn't want to bother Ellie. If I get up in the night, she gets up, too, so I decided to try the church office. Sometimes the church, in the middle of the night, is a wonderful place." He ran a finger over his cut lip. "Ellie's going to yell. She doesn't even know I slipped out of the house."

Jack put a hand on Noah's shoulder. "I didn't know you were so scrappy, Noah. Next time we have trouble, I'll give you a call."

Noah looked at his bruised knuckles. "I might've had a slightly wayward youth on the Seattle docks before I tried the seminary. He is going to jail, isn't he?"

"He's going to jail," Mike said. "With any luck, he's got meth in his pockets or his vehicle so we can double up the charges."

This was when Leslie had a chance to look around Nora's house. It was sparsely furnished, just a sofa and chair with quilts covering them, a small table with two chairs, a rug that didn't cover enough of the floor, some toys for Berry, the stroller by the door, and it was *spotless*. Shining clean.

The men stood in the living room, Mrs. Hutchkins

and Mrs. Clemens occupied chairs at the table while Leslie sat on the couch with Nora. Berry wasn't even crying; she was clinging to her mother with wide eyes. Leslie reached for the baby. "Let me, Nora. Want me to fix her a bottle?"

"I'll do that in a minute," she said. "Leslie, I'm so sorry you were dragged into this."

"Don't start," she said. "I'm a woman alone, too, as are Mrs. Clemens and Mrs. Hutchkins. If we don't back each other up, we're sunk. As it is, I think that maniac was held off by me, a preacher and two little old ladies."

"Who are you calling little?" Mrs. Clemens said.

It was another half hour before the sheriff's deputy arrived. Henry Depardeau stepped out of his car and approached the men in the front yard. "Well, Sheridan, this has the look of your work. I think the county would save time and paperwork if we'd just deputize you."

"We can't do that, Henry," Jack said. "We look forward to your visits. You getting a little backup out here?"

"Am I going to need it?"

"Possibly," Jack said with a shrug. "Took three men to hog-tie him. And that was after two women weakened him with blows to the head."

"Crap," Henry said. "I hate long reports."

It was midmorning when the phone beside the bed woke Leslie. She answered tiredly.

"What's up, sleepyhead?" Conner said. "I thought you'd be working in the yard!"

"Hmm," she hummed. "I'm sleeping in. Where are you?"

"Changing planes in New York. Then I change planes in Denver. Then I drive straight to Sacramento from Redding so I can get there by morning."

"Oh, Conner, sleep on the plane if you can! You'll be so tired!"

"Are you sick?" he asked. "You don't sound right."

"Not sick, just tired. I was up late last night. We had excitement in the neighborhood and I didn't fall asleep until five this morning."

"Block party?" he asked.

"Not the usual kind," she told him. "Nora had an intruder. Her ex…ex-boyfriend, I guess. He brought her up here six months ago and just dumped her here, leaving her with the babies. He came back looking for money and got real mean and physical and the sheriff had to be called."

"Is she all right?" he asked.

"No one required stitches or anything…just ice packs and… Well, Noah had to have a butterfly bandage to close his lip. And Mrs. Hutchkins has a sore tush from being shoved and falling on the floor. But Jack and Mike V only have bruised knuckles."

"What?" he said as if he hadn't heard right. "What?"

"Mrs. Hutchkins and I were able to hold him off for a while with a rake and a broom. That Mrs. Hutchkins—don't mess with her!" She laughed a little. "She grabbed my rake and walked right in that house and clobbered him on the back of the head. Then it was game on!"

"Leslie, were you really in a fight?" he asked.

"A short one. Then Noah, Jack and Mike saved the day and the sheriff's deputy came, eventually, and took him away. Thank goodness! The ex, he was high as a kite and really strong."

"Wait a second, wait a second...." She heard a beeping sound in the background.

"What was that?" she asked.

"I'm boarding. That was the boarding pass being scanned. Are you all right?"

"Oh, sure, just a little bump on the jaw. It doesn't hurt. But I got one off on him, let me tell you. Kicked him right where it hurts most and brought him to his knees. Amazing what you can do when you have to."

"Leslie, listen to me—I want you to get the crowbar out of your car and keep it handy, just in case—"

He was cut off by the sound of her laughter. "Conner, if I ever see that lunatic again, I'm not going after him with anything stronger than a broom! He'd take a crowbar away from me and kill me with it! He was out of his mind!"

"Then I want you to go stay with Paul or Dan until I get back there!"

"Conner, I'm fine. He's in jail. I'll check with Jack to make sure he's staying in jail for a while, but seriously, he was taken away by three deputies. And besides, only a fool would go up against me, two little old ladies and a minister again." And then she laughed.

"Stop laughing," he said. "You have me scared to death! Now listen, they're closing the door, but I'll try to call you from Denver when I change planes again. Are you sure you're all right?"

"Conner, I'm fine. I think I'll take another nap, though. It was a long night."

"I'll call you when I can."

"Just have a safe flight and don't worry. I never should have told you!"

"Be careful," he said. "I love you."

Leslie had no idea when to expect a call from Conner from the Denver airport, but she knew one thing she had to do for sure. She took a walk down her street to check on Mrs. Clemens, Mrs. Hutchkins and Nora and her family. The elderly ladies were still a little riled up and excited from the earlier events. Nora, on the other hand, was so embarrassed and filled with regret, Leslie spent almost an hour trying to comfort her and get her back to her old self.

"I feel like I shouldn't even be here," Nora said. "I don't want to be found by him again and I don't want to bring trouble to my neighborhood. Not after everyone has been so good to us."

"Your neighbors will hunt you down and try to protect you if you do anything crazy, like try to leave. You don't even have a car. I don't know how you manage!"

She shook her head. "Every couple of weeks, Jack or Noah will add my shopping list to theirs when I need groceries, or Mrs. Hutchkins takes me with her into Fortuna while Mrs. Clemens sits with the girls during their nap. And until now, I was never afraid or worried."

"Once you get a little rest and a few quiet days, you won't feel that panic anymore. I'm going down to Jack's to ask him what he knows about your ex's jail visit. I'll let you know what he says. I'm sure he won't mind checking in with the deputy—they seem to be friends."

"Les, Berry hasn't talked all day," she said in a whisper. "She was talking so well for her age."

Leslie patted her hand. "She's probably still scared. Try not to panic yet. Ask Mel and the doctor about it. Ask Noah."

"Right," Nora said.

That information did seem to bring some peace of mind to everyone. The suspect was still in jail and in fact had quite a few warrants outstanding from other cities, so it looked as though he wouldn't make bail. The sheriff's department was planning to let Oakland, California, have him back—a more positive outcome for Leslie and her neighbors than the idea of him being released.

But of course, she must have missed a call from Conner while she was out, taking the pulse of the neighborhood. She just hoped he would have time to call before he began the five-hour drive from Redding to Sacramento.

It was ten at night, and when she still hadn't heard from him, she started to imagine flight delays or even canceled flights. Then there was a knock at her locked door, and her first thoughts returned to the night before. She didn't have a peephole; the kinds of precautions a

person would take even in a city the size of Grants Pass
had never crossed her mind since being in Virgin River.

"Who is it?" she asked the locked door.

"It's me, Les," Conner said.

Stunned, she threw open the door and was instantly
in his arms.

He just held her close and in great relief for a minute,
then slowly pulled away to look at her. He ran a knuckle
across her bruised jaw.

"What are you doing here?" she asked him.

"I couldn't go to Sacramento without seeing you,
without making sure you're all right. You made the injuries sound like nothing. This is something."

"We're very proud of our bruises," she said. "They're
badges of honor. How long are you staying here?"

"Till early morning."

"Aren't you supposed to be there by morning?" she
asked.

"I think they'll wait for me." And then he pressed
his lips gently against the corner of her mouth, opposite
the bruise. "Goddamn, Les. It's killing me that you got
hurt."

She smiled at him. "You have a lot of people you try
to take care of, don't you? I told you, I'm fine. We're all
fine. What about Katie? Is she all right?"

"I think so. As of right now, she wants to stay there.
She thinks she's cultivating something with the dentist,
but I don't know about that. I don't know how long she'll
last. He seems kind of…" He shrugged. "He's very nice.
He likes Katie and the boys. But something's missing."

He bent his head to gently kiss her again, careful not to be rough. "Nothing is missing for me, though. Let me lay down with you, let me just hold you."

She smiled at him. "I don't think I really got it until now. You were responsible for your sister from such an early age—it's natural for you to be a caretaker. I'm not used to that."

She took his hand and led him to the bedroom; she pulled him down beside her. He sat to take off his boots and then pulled her into his arms. It felt so good, so safe to be with him like this.

When she was young, her parents had looked out for her. When she married and left their house, she became the caretaker. For a long time, she was the protector, the supporter. It was a brand-new experience to have a man like Conner, so responsible and protective that he'd drive hours out of his way to be sure she was all right.

Eighteen

Conner woke Leslie with a gentle nudge at about four-thirty in the morning. "I have to start driving," he whispered.

"The sooner you just get it behind you, the sooner you're done with it. And when you come back here after the trial is over, are you going back to that little cabin? Or will you stay with me?"

He gave a nod and nuzzled her neck. "You're going to have a hard time getting rid of me."

"Do you think that someday we'll actually be able to lay down on a bed together and not make love?"

"Maybe someday. Not soon."

"Get in the shower, Conner," she said. "I'll get a pot of coffee going. You need to get on your way. And thank you. Even if it's just a few hours with you, it means everything to me."

Almost an hour later, he reluctantly left her at her front door and began his drive to Sacramento. Once he reached Clear Lake he phoned Max at the D.A.'s office and told them he was running a little late, but en route.

By ten he was walking into the district attorney's complex. Max came out of his office to meet him in the reception area and escort him in.

Even though Max—Ray Maxwell, officially—had caused him a lot of personal complications by relying on him to testify in this trial, Conner liked the guy. He was young for a D.A.—under fifty—and no question about it, he was decent and honest. Judging the pictures in his office, he was also a happily married father of two. Conner could sense a certain commanding nature in Max, accentuated by his dark hair barely touched by silver at the temples, but today there was obvious warmth, as well. And he never for a second doubted Max's gratitude.

"Good to see you, Conner. You won't be Conner on the stand, by the way. However, there's no legal trouble with your name change. Once you've testified, there's a judge who will sign off on the petition immediately. Thanks for coming so quickly. I take it your family is doing well?"

"Katie and the boys seem fine and she's decided to stay in Vermont, at least for now," Conner said. "How long is this going to take?"

"The prosecution presents first," he said. "We'll prep you over the next couple of days and run your testimony by Friday at the latest. With any luck, sooner. Then you're free to go, but understand you can be recalled by the defense, in which case you'll have to return. Which brings us to the next item—you've had some more time to think about it now. Have you thought of anything they might bring up to discredit you?"

He frowned and shook his head. "I think we went over all this. I had a traffic ticket—speeding. Seven years ago. I paid my taxes on time, took my sister and nephews to church once in a while, never got arrested. No mental illness in the family that I know of and I don't take any drugs, prescription or otherwise."

"And never visited a massage parlor or strip joint?"

"Never had the time. I'm not saying I'm above that sort of thing," Conner said with a grin. "I just never had the time. I had a business and a family."

"You're sure?"

"Trust me, I'd remember."

"Because your ex-wife was an occasional visitor to The Blue Door, one of Dickie's more notorious clubs. One in which Regis Mathis was a silent partner."

"Yeah," Conner said. "Not a big surprise. I told you about her. What does that have to do with me?"

"While you were still married, it turns out," Max said.

He was shocked into silence, but then an immediate huff of laughter escaped him. "I take that back. Consider me surprised. Of course I didn't know that. Still, what's that got to do with me?"

"No telling," Max said. "They haven't listed her as a witness, but the information that our only witness's wife frequented the victim's club—that turned up. Whether they'll use it, we don't know."

"How could they use it?"

"Oh, let's use our imagination on that," Max said. "How about—you're a very jealous man and you had a motive for killing the owner of one of the clubs your wife frequented for extramarital sex."

"Wow," Conner said. "No offense, but I'm glad I don't have to think like a prosecutor. That would never have occurred to me. I never hurt my ex, never hurt the kid I caught her with, never knew she went to clubs. I'm not all that surprised, but I didn't know."

"If there's anything…"

"Max, I'm such a straight arrow I've missed half my life, working and taking care of my sister and her kids. In fact, if I hadn't been taking out the trash after closing the store, this wouldn't be happening to me."

Max showed him a half smile. "Every prosecutor knows he's telling the jury a story—'Here's what happened.' Then the defense takes over and tells a different story—'Here's what *really* happened.' In some ways this is predictable—I usually try to run the police testimony first because they're well-trained witnesses. Then the eyewitnesses and finally, the forensic experts. Even though we have powerful forensics, the defense will undoubtedly cite cases in which evidence was mishandled or misinterpreted, trying to discredit the science." He gave a shrug. "Even though an eyewitness account is often the least reliable, you're our ace. Exactly why we've gone to some trouble to keep you out of harm's way. This isn't going to be a long trial—five to seven days, then deliberation."

"It can't be over soon enough," Conner said.

"Hang in there. I need to sit you down with the A.D.A. for a few hours today and tomorrow, throw you a few possible curves and prepare you for the kind of questions they might ask if they decide to cross-examine or recall you. You up to that?"

"I guess it's what I'm here for."

"We have you booked at the Hilton. I have a couple of off-duty cops who can stay with you if…"

"You think I'm in danger right this minute?"

"Honestly? I don't know. We suppose you *could be* at risk. We only go to these lengths when there's been a direct threat, and there *was* a direct threat. But—"

"Look, if you could put someone in a room across the hall or something, I wouldn't argue with that. But there haven't been any other threats that I'm aware of. Have you heard of any?"

"Nothing," Max said, shaking his head.

"Then let's do the prep. I have a couple of favors to ask."

"Name them."

"Katie and I have done some thinking and talking about this—we're going to sell the Sacramento properties. After the trial, we'd like both houses—mine and hers—emptied and furnishings and belongings put in crated storage. Then we'd like to sell the houses. The lot the hardware store was built on has been listed, but it's a bad time for real estate. We'll be patient, but we're starting over after this. We'll take possession of our household goods when we've settled permanently and split the proceeds from the land sale and insurance money from the fire. We're going to do it all in the name of Conner Danson—I'm the executor anyway and our dad died a long time ago. Katie knows I'll always see she's taken care of. Can you help me do that?"

"No problem. You want to go through the houses and make sure you've taken everything you don't want in storage?"

"Katie took her late husband's mementos but yes, I'll take a run through both houses. My folks left behind a lot of stuff I'll just be pitching in the end, but for now, let's crate it up. I'll contract a cleaning crew and painters to get the houses ready for sale. Let's just get it done. I'm for moving on."

Max smiled. "Brie said she thought you were settling in up north."

"It's a whole new life, Max. Much as it kills me to say this, I might not have discovered how much I needed a change if this whole fiasco hadn't happened, from Samantha to the killing in my alley. So, let's get our business taken care of so I can get back to it."

Max put a hand on his shoulder. "We'll do it, buddy. No one deserves it more."

A couple of consultants and an assistant district attorney spent a few hours on Monday morning and again on Tuesday morning firing questions at Conner that might never be asked by the defense, but they were offensive enough to make him angry and eventually wring an outburst from him.

"Isn't it true that you knew your wife was a frequent visitor at The Blue Door, a bar thinly disguised as a strip club that was, in reality, an adult sex club?"

"No."

"How many times did you go to that club?"

"Never heard of it before I became a witness."

"How many times?"

"Never heard of it, never went there."

"And if I could produce a charge receipt from your credit card showing you had been there with your wife before the murder…?"

"It wouldn't be mine," Conner said.

"Are you aware of the consequences of perjury?"

"I said I didn't even know about it much less go there!"

"Yet your wife went there while you were still married?"

"So I hear!"

"Are you alleging that your wife went *alone* to this couples sex club prior to your divorce and you had no knowledge of it?"

"I have no idea if she went alone! She didn't go with me!"

"Then what would you suggest as the reason for your divorce?"

"A nineteen-year-old college kid who delivered bottled water!" Conner stormed.

"Back to the night in question. Was there a light behind the store, in the alley where you allegedly witnessed the crime?"

"His headlights were on," Conner said.

"Answer the question, please."

"No! No light behind the store. There was one, but it wasn't on. His headlights were on!"

"And you say he walked in front of the car?"

"Yes."

"So the headlights hit him where? Right about the level of his thighs?"

"The police found blood in his car!"

"Okay, okay, this is the reason for these questions, Conner," the A.D.A. said. "We don't know what will be asked, but if it's going to set you off, let's let the anger out here, during the prep, not on the stand. Just try to hold it together and answer the question without elaborating. Yes or no, whenever possible."

It went like that on and off for two long mornings.

When he was finished on Tuesday afternoon, he drove to the house in which he grew up, a police officer in an unmarked car following him. Conner seriously doubted that Regis Mathis had anyone sitting surveillance on his empty house a couple of days before the trial, but he used caution. Conner wanted to look around the property and pick up a couple of things. He was cautious and observant.

His folks had bought this house the year he was born—thirty-five years ago. It had been a small three-bedroom on a large lot—the size of the lot remained a value to this day. When Katie came along, his dad had remodeled and built an addition, doubling the size of the kitchen and living room, adding a bedroom and bathroom. It was a process that Conner barely remembered but his dad had reminded him frequently that it had taken about three years to complete since he'd done it mostly alone.

After their parents had died, Katie lived there with him until she got married. Then she came back to live with him in that house again when Charlie deployed. When Charlie was killed, Katie stayed with him, like it was a foregone conclusion.

Eventually, she'd found a small three-bedroom not that far from Conner and together they'd bought it. It was in both their names. And even though Conner had been somewhat relieved not to be awakened in the night by a teething baby, he had been very lonely when she left. He'd been happy for her—she'd seemed to be getting on with life. But it had been a little too quiet.

Now she would be three thousand miles away. That was going to be a *real* adjustment, even with Leslie.

He looked around the house he had lived in for thirty-five years. Given his business, he'd been good about keeping things updated—like cabinetry, paint, woodwork, fixtures, et cetera. But the furniture? It should be given away. It was old and worn. Even the mattress had belonged to his parents, and he wasn't sure how outdated it was. The TV was a large-screen, but not high-definition or flat-screen or anything that had been marketed in the past ten years.

Samantha had wanted to renovate the house, but he'd told her to go to work on Katie's house; that house had needed it more, and he wasn't ready to make any big changes in his. He probably should have let her—it seemed so old and shabby now.

There were two things he wanted to take from the house. His desktop computer with portable backup hard drive and his guns. He was making do fine with his laptop, but he should have the computer with the larger memory and the store records from the past few years. Of course, the store computer had been destroyed in the fire.

In his gun safe he kept a rifle and two handguns. He unloaded the guns, stowed the bullets and put them in a duffel, wrapped up in a winter parka. Then he placed the computer and duffel in the backseat of the extended cab. He covered the computer with a tarp he found in the garage. Even though the guns had been secure in the safe at the house—with a gun safe so heavy and hard to move, it would take a very determined thief to steal it—he had already decided he wanted them with him in the hotel. Not because he was necessarily worried about anything, but because why wouldn't a man whose life had been threatened make an effort to defend himself?

Then he drove a few blocks away and called Katie.

"I'm sitting in front of your house," he said. "I talked to the D.A. about helping us just move this property under my new name and he said it wouldn't be a problem. So I went through the old house. Katie, has the furniture always been that terrible?"

She laughed. "I agree, it's seen better days, but it was still functional. Nothing was torn or sagging. There were scratches on tables—we call that 'distressed.'"

"It's all very distressed," he said.

"Why are you sitting in front of my house?" she asked.

"I wondered if there was anything you missed when you left that you want me to grab, to keep out of storage?"

"I got the important things—Charlie's pictures and medals. My wedding pictures and the baby pictures. I packed a few boxes like the place might be burned down..."

"Aw, Katie, what a lot I've put you through...."

"Stop! I came home to you with two babies and you've always taken such good care of us."

"It's going to be hard to take good care of you when you're in Vermont and I'm in California," he said.

"Maybe it's time I learned to take care of myself, Conner. It's strange—I'm finally knowing the new you. I think maybe you've grown into the name."

"As much as I resisted the change, it's what I want now. Not such a big change, really. More of a reversal. So—when I order the household goods packed, where should I have yours shipped? Vermont?"

She was quiet for a moment. "Hold off on that, can you?"

"Changing your mind?" he asked hopefully. "Second thoughts?"

"Not so much changing my mind as putting off making a decision. Can you have my stuff stored in Sacramento until I make a final decision?"

"What's happening, Katie?" he asked. "Are things cooling with the dentist?"

"Not so much cooling as not heating up, but then you knew that. No, it's more about you, I'm afraid. While you were here with us, it felt so right. So comfortable. Since you left, I've been asking myself if I can really be this far away. I don't want to move in with you again, to be that kind of burden. But I might just have to make the hard choice. I might have to decide who I'm willing to give up—you or Keith."

He took a deep breath. "A lot of that is going to depend on Keith," he said. "And, Katie, if I could, you know I'd consider Vermont. I'm not real big on shoveling snow, but…"

"No! You've found where you want to be. And who you want to be with. Unless I misunderstood—you have no doubts. And you so deserve this. You've waited long enough."

But so had Katie waited, he found himself thinking. She'd had such a hot young love with Charlie, that whenever they'd been in the same room, there'd been steam. No surprise he not only got her pregnant on the honeymoon, but with twins. In losing him, Katie had lost her taste for passion, apparently. In thinking over the past five years, the few dates she had had were with men who failed to bring that flush to her cheeks the way her young husband had.

He wanted that for her. But he wasn't about to say any more about her losses.

What a team, he thought. As brother and sister they

had held each other up through all sorts of strain. And he, for one, had had about enough of that!

"Don't do anything hasty, Katie," he lectured. "Make sure Keith is completely right for you before you take that next step."

"I will. Of course I will."

They talked a little bit about the upcoming trial, although Conner wasn't at liberty to discuss the prep. He did tell her he hoped to be back in Virgin River on the weekend. Worst case, he might be driving back to the city the following week. And when the conversation was done, he made a couple of phone calls—one to a cleaning service and one to a painter he knew and trusted. Then he called the D.A.'s office and asked Max's trusted assistant to arrange for the packing and storage of household goods to commence immediately. The cleaners and painters would follow the movers, leaving the homes ready for sale.

Jack Sheridan was puttering behind the bar in the afternoon, making his supply lists and balancing his cash drawer. When no one was in the bar, like now, he had the national news on the TV. He wasn't a news fanatic and didn't have anyone close in the wars right now, but he checked in from time to time. He got a little news about the economy—hardly ever good these days—some major national stories from kidnappings to shootings. Nothing big from Humboldt County, usually, unless they had an earthquake or something. Or maybe that occasional giant pot bust.

He was crouched behind the bar, counting bottles, when he heard the news anchor talking about a big murder trial in Sacramento. He went on to say that the arresting officers and forensic experts had testified for the prosecution, but there was only one eyewitness to the crime.

It was pure coincidence that he happened to stand up at that time and see, on the screen, the face of someone he knew. Conner Danson. He didn't catch the name, but the face was unmistakable—except for the absence of the neatly, tightly trimmed and sculptured mustache and goatee. And he caught the last of the broadcast.

...will testify for the prosecution tomorrow. The trial is not televised but our reporters will be on the scene for any breaking news....

What the hell, he thought. That was the breaking news.

He went to the kitchen and picked up the phone. He called Paul's office in the trailer even though he knew catching him there was iffy. Leslie answered, and he said, "Hey, Leslie, it's Jack. Did you know your boyfriend is testifying in a murder trial in Sacramento?"

There was a moment of silence before she laughed just a little and said, "Really, Jack, you're totally full of it. Very funny."

"Yeah, I'm just a real card. Is Paul around?"

"Sure. Hang on."

A second later Paul came on the line with a, "What's up, Jack?"

"Your man, Conner," he said. "I just saw his picture

on CNN. They do a break from national news for local stuff. What did he say was his reason for needing time off?"

"Family emergency," Paul said. "Unspecified."

"I think I can specify it. He's the only witness in a murder trial in Sacramento. His picture was on TV. He's going to testify tomorrow."

Paul was completely quiet for a long, still moment. Then he yelled, "Lessssleeee!" And next he said, "I gotta go. I'll get back to you." And he hung up.

Jack turned to where Preacher was chopping something on the work island in the kitchen and said, "Can you get on the computer and look something up for me?"

"I guess so. If you'll pay me for it."

"I'm not paying you for it! Do it for the cause! Take one for the team!"

"Fine," Preacher said, putting down his knife and wiping his hands. "Murder trial in the capitol, Conner Danson. Got it. Don't get your panties in a twist."

"Don't say panties to me," Jack nearly roared. "Don't ever call what I wear panties!"

And Preacher said, "Sheesh. Take it easy. You weren't murdered."

Leslie stood in Paul's doorway, her eyes as round as beach balls. She twisted her hands.

"Are you going to tell me what's going on with Conner?" Paul asked from behind his desk.

Without uttering a word, she shook her head.

"His picture was on TV," Paul told her. "That's how Jack knows. That's how anyone who watches the news is going to know. Did you realize he's going to testify tomorrow?"

She shook her head and clutched her hands tighter so they wouldn't shake. Tears gathered in her eyes.

Paul stood up from behind his desk. "Les, don't go through this alone."

"I'm not alone," she said in a very soft voice. But she *was* alone. And so needed some support.

The phone on Paul's desk rang, and he picked it up. "Haggerty Construction. Yeah? Yeah? I'll be damned. Well, I guess I'm not at all surprised. I'll see you in a couple hours, then. And I'll bring Les." Then he hung up.

"Bring Les where?" she asked.

"Apparently it took Preacher about two minutes on the computer to find out that Danson Conner, the owner of a hardware store in Sacramento, witnessed a murder in the alley behind his store and is going to testify against a very powerful man in the murder trial. And guess what? He's been here for a few months. Did you know that Jack's little sister was a Sacramento County prosecutor? He says this has Brie's fingerprints all over it, so he called her and offered to buy her a beer at around four today. We're going to join them."

"We are?"

"Yes, we are. I can see you're scared. Brie knows how much of this she can let out, and that's bound to reassure you a little bit. So you can talk!" He sat back down. "Go on—get things wrapped up and we'll go have a beer."

Nineteen

Conner had skipped the opening remarks at the trial, but decided to go to court for the testimony of the police officers who answered his call. He was escorted by an officer in an unmarked car, his truck safely stowed in a very large, crowded mall parking lot where it would not be linked to him and not tampered with.

There were a lot of cops testifying, not to mention a coroner. The coroner's report would come later, but the photos and examination of the deceased at the scene were entered as evidence and testimony.

For the first time since this whole ordeal had begun, he had a very uneasy, unsure feeling. Regis Mathis didn't look like a murderer in this setting. Conner already knew he didn't sound like a murderer, this pillar of the community. There was nothing slick about him. He didn't look like the kind of man who would be friends with Dickie Randolph. And the D.A.'s allegation that they were even in business together seemed impossible.

Mathis was a tall, regal man with expensive tastes. This wasn't something Conner would have known, had his off-duty cop protector and escort not said to him, "Man, that's at least a ten-thousand-dollar suit." And as Conner watched Mathis from the back of the courtroom, the man was very clearly comfortable, confident, very much at ease with these proceedings, as if he didn't have a care in the world. And he had four attorneys up front, more assistants in the gallery along with his distinguished-looking family and two priests.

On the other side of the courtroom, divvied up like the bride's side and the groom's side, sat a couple of cheap-looking young women with men who had a disreputable look about them—Randolph's associates, perhaps?

At one point Mathis looked straight at Conner and gave him a half smile and nod, almost a welcoming gesture. *Welcome to the party, son!* It was impossible to picture him in an orange jumpsuit. If he hadn't seen it with his own eyes, he couldn't imagine him doing what he'd done. It was, in a word, incomprehensible.

And Regis Mathis did not expect to be convicted.

Conner wondered if he'd been too optimistic. If he were a seated jury member it would be hard for him to imagine this stately, polite and reserved man as the kind of cold-blooded killer who could put a bullet in a man's head, drag his body out of a car and heft it into a Dumpster. Harder still, if a meticulous man such as Regis Mathis, a man who constantly pulled at his crisp white shirt cuffs, wanted someone dead, why didn't he hire it out? Why get his own hands dirty? He was, after all, richer than God.

Conner didn't expect him to be convicted, either. While the story was completely true, it was unbelievable. If it had been any other kind of murder, maybe. But this kind? In a dingy alley, bullet to the head, tossed in a Dumpster? A victim with duct tape over his mouth and binding his wrists and ankles? Not this man, this very classy man who endowed charities and endorsed politicians.

He was required to be in court the next day, or at least in the building, available. He had a brief temptation to buy an equally expensive suit, though he knew it wouldn't look the same on him as it looked on Mathis.

While he paid attention to the testimony of cops, homicide detectives and other officials who had been on the scene, all he could think about was that he couldn't wait until the day was done and he could call Leslie and Katie. And he was afraid to call them. He wasn't sure how he could keep from saying, *It's hopeless. I'm going to be in hiding for the rest of my life. And anyone who throws their lot in with me will be hiding, too.*

When court was dismissed for the day, Conner exited with his cop and waited in the hallway for the room to empty. Then he doubled back to the courtroom and said, "Give me a second with the D.A." Then he reentered the courtroom. At the front table, Max was speaking quietly with one of his associates as they both shuffled papers into their briefcases. Conner came up behind them and cleared his throat.

Max turned. "Yes, Conner?"

Conner looked around to be sure they weren't overheard by any bystanders. Then he looked back at Max. "You're never going to get him, are you?"

"I am going to," Max said confidently.

"He doesn't look like a killer," Conner said. "If I were a juror—"

"I have a lot of faith in the system," Max said. "What we're going to do now is deliver the evidence we've prepared, solid evidence, irrefutable evidence, and win the day. That's what we're going to do."

"And you're counting on *me?*"

"You're the only eyewitness to the crime, but you're not the only thing we've got. We have a motive."

"Care to share?" he asked with a tinge of sarcasm.

"Your wife wasn't the only person hanging around that drug-infested shit hole. There was another person of interest there. A person Dickie Randolph took great joy in messing up and filling with drugs and alcohol and probably dirty sex. Mathis's twenty-one-year-old daughter. The light of his life."

Conner's eyes grew large. "Are you going to be able to present that?"

Max lifted his chin. "If it's not suppressed. It is his daughter…."

Conner looked at him for a long, still moment. He finally understood why a man like Mathis would take it upon himself to deal out revenge rather than outsource the job. But could it be proven? And would the jury ever hear it? If they heard it, would they believe it of this good, classy, God-fearing man?

He gave a nod—what were his choices? And then he said, "We're fucked."

Conner and his cop left the courthouse from the side door and walked around the block to the parking lot because Regis Mathis was playing to the press. Conner didn't have that kind of savvy, and, while he couldn't avoid the questions forever, he was bound to come off sounding unsure and vulnerable. Or angry, because as time went by, this whole thing just made him angrier. As they were entering the parking lot, he heard his name, the name that still made him turn.

"Danny?"

Samantha!

Well, she could find a way to get a letter to him, why wouldn't she be able to find him leaving the courthouse? "What are you doing here?" he asked her.

"I had hoped to talk to you," Samantha said.

He just shook his head and laughed. "I've tried to be very clear and very kind at the same time— we don't have anything to talk about."

"But, Danny, we do," she said, taking another step toward him. "I was contacted by some lawyers and they're thinking of calling me as a witness for the defense. I wanted you to know."

RoboCop stepped up. "Ma'am, that's a discussion we can't be having with you. You'll have to move along now."

Conner put his hand on his cop's arm. "What can you possibly have to say to defend that man?"

"Don't!" his escort said. "Don't discuss it!"

Samantha put her hands up, palms toward Conner and his escort. "All right, all right, we won't discuss it. But can't we have a short conversation? About what's happened in the past two years?"

Conner looked at her. In fact, he looked her up and down and shook his head. She was beautiful with her small, buxom but trim frame, dark hair, pale skin and red lips. That was the first thing that had attracted him. The second thing was that she was so focused on him, flirting and entertaining. Sexy, she was very sexy, and she had liked him. Why wouldn't a man go for that? And she was smart. Manipulative, but very clever—any man would be willing to be manipulated by a dish like Sam. Until they knew, of course.

"Why me?" he finally said.

"Why you?" she repeated. "Because we were married!"

"No, no. Samantha…Sam. I mean, why do you keep bothering me? Look at you. You don't need me for anything. We were married for a very short time, then divorced. You can have any man you want. In fact, you probably have. All I want now is for you to leave me alone."

"What if I say you were with me at that club? The one the dead man owned?"

His lips curved in a slight smile. "What? You think

that threat will make me want to take you out? Buy you a drink?"

"Ma'am," the cop said.

"Hey, knock yourself out," Conner said. "I'm sure my protective friend here will be in touch with the D.A. who will be in touch with the judge who will be sure you get a day off from court. Enjoy. Get your hair done or something."

And he turned and walked with his escort into the parking lot.

"Danny!"

Please, God, please make her go away! He got in the car and his escort started the engine.

"We're going to have to report that."

"Come on," Conner said. "She just wants to…" What? Get laid? Get back with him? Get what? Control? "Yeah," he finally said. "You want to call Max or should I?"

"I'll call him," the cop said. "When I get you back to the hotel, you can also call him. We'll get you some room service tonight, and I'm handing you off to another officer. I'm going home to dinner."

"Wish I was going home to dinner," Conner mumbled.

"You will be in a couple of days, pal. Um, that lady—I assume by what she said she was your ex-wife? She might have a little jail time and a big fine. What she was doing, for whatever reason, that's against the law. It's called witness tampering."

"Well, if it makes any difference, I'm not looking to punish her for anything. I just want to get on with my life, that's all."

"This has to stay in this tight little group," Brie said, holding on to a longneck beer. "Just between the five of us. Jack?" she asked.

"What?" he returned, insulted.

Her gaze connected with Paul, Leslie, Preacher and finally her brother. "You're the only one I worry about. You know—you like to talk."

"Not if I *know* it's a secret!" he said.

"Until this trial is over, it's a secret. Until the trial is *completely* over, it's a secret, get that? Because being the only witness is a pretty tenuous position."

"Got it!" Jack said, not happily.

"So, he's the only witness. He left town to spend a little time with his family, location confidential, and then to Sacramento to appear. Another week or so, depending on how long the jury takes, it should be behind us. Then, with luck, he's no longer a threat to the defendant and we can all relax."

"Have you talked to him?" Leslie asked.

"I haven't. I'm keeping up with the trial and it seems to be going all right for the prosecution so far. They've called police, detectives and the coroner—there were so many on the scene, it took the first days," Brie said.

"Hold on," Preacher said, reaching for the remote.

The volume on the TV had been turned way down, and he turned it up as a face appeared. A very confident and distinguished man was speaking into a lot of handheld microphones. "Blood?" he asked. "I don't know that there was blood in the car. There certainly wasn't any blood anyone could see. I hear claims that there had been blood at one time, revealed by some old lab test. One of my sons wondered if it could be his— apparently he had a severe bloody nose after a round of golf. I was unaware of that because he was fine and it was cleaned up."

"The defendant," Brie said.

"Didn't the prosecution allege it was the victim's blood?"

"From some C.S.I. kind of magic lab test?" he returned with a chuckle. "We know those DNA tests are never wrong, don't we?" he asked facetiously. "That's why so many wrongly accused felons have been released from prison lately, right?"

"How would you explain the presence of blood in your car?" someone asked.

"No further comment," another man, presumably his lawyer, interjected.

"Mr. Mathis, it's been speculated that you invested in Mr. Randolph's businesses...."

"Look, I have a lot of employees, a few of them responsible for accounting and investments, and I assure you, if it is discovered they invested in shady businesses like those of Mr. Randolph, they'll be looking for work. We're investigating that now. But I had never met the man."

"Wasn't your car seen at the scene?" a reporter asked.

"Cherry," he said, smiling, "my family owns fourteen cars."

"Clever," Brie said. "He knows the reporters by name…."

"No further comment," the lawyer said again. "We'll let this play out in court and I have no doubt, it will have a satisfactory end."

While the reporters continued to fire questions at the men, a confident and smiling Regis Mathis walked away from the cameras, giving friendly waves as he got into the backseat of an expensive town car with a couple of his lawyers. A group that appeared to be his family, two younger men, a mature woman and a very young woman, entered the town car behind Mathis's.

Preacher turned down the volume. Leslie sank onto a bar stool, looking pale.

"You all right?" Jack asked.

She turned dark liquid eyes up to his face. "He doesn't look very worried."

"Mr. Mathis has been to court before," Brie said. "He knows how to act. Try not to worry. I know the district attorney. He's a brilliant man."

"Why isn't there some kind of gag on him?" Leslie asked. "How can he be allowed to talk to the reporters about evidence that's going to come up?"

"There's more than one way to play that hand, Leslie. I don't have any idea what the D.A.'s strategy is, but you can believe if he didn't want to hear what Mathis has to say to the press, he'd find a way to gag him. You probably just heard part of his defense—old blood, forensic errors, maybe it was someone else driving his car, et cetera. That's not to say there won't be surprises, but…" The color wasn't coming into her cheeks, so Brie said, "Jack, give her a drink."

"Coming up."

"Don't panic yet," Brie said.

Leslie took a sip of her wine. "When can I go ahead and panic?"

"I'll give you a call when it's time," Brie said.

"Paul," Leslie said. "I think I might have to take tomorrow off. Hang around the TV."

"Want to watch at my house?" Brie asked. "I have good satellite reception."

"I'd rather be home, near the phone, but my TV reception is iffy."

"Call him tonight," Brie said. "Tell him where you'll be. Court doesn't convene until 9:00 a.m., so don't rush. Come when you can."

"I'll be there by nine."

"Understandable," Brie said.

Several hours later, when it was late, Leslie called Conner's cell phone. He answered, "Hey, baby."

"Conner, I can't get you off my mind. And you didn't call."

He sighed. "I thought maybe I shouldn't tonight. I'm testifying tomorrow morning."

"Oh, Conner, why couldn't you call? Did they ask you not to?"

"No, but I didn't want to drag you into this drama. Les, I'm not coming back this weekend. I'm not going anyplace I can be followed until it's all over. Until there's no chance I'll be recalled."

"I understand. Conner, I saw him on TV. The man you're testifying against. Talking to reporters."

"I saw it, too," he said. "Apparently I'm testifying against a sainted soul whom the police have been trying to trap for one reason or another for years...."

"Oh, Conner..."

"He's convincing before he even opens his mouth," Conner said. "And then he's even more convincing. Max says we have to trust the system. He says there's good, solid evidence. But they're going to claim I couldn't have seen his face."

"But you did...."

"I did. He looked rumpled and messed up that night. He didn't have that classy, sophisticated, starched look to him. He looked like a furious guy who didn't have an ounce of guilt about what he'd done. He was covered with blood from moving the body. I'll never forget it. And when he was walking back to his car...he moved slowly. Leisurely. Like the whole thing had been just another chore, like he was completely justified."

"Conner..."

"He's got a good game face," Conner said. "I'm working on mine."

"I hate that you're going through this alone," she said.

"Alone is the only way I want to get it done. I don't want anyone I love even close to this mess. And it is a mess."

"I'm staying home from work tomorrow, watching

the news from Brie's house because she has better reception than I do. So if you're looking for me, that's
where I'll be. And, well, if it means anything, I'm really
proud of you."

"It means everything, Les." He paused. "I want you
to get some sleep. We'll talk tomorrow after it's over."

After Conner called Max and told him about Samantha's veiled threat, the D.A. said that he'd already
heard from the police officer escort, and, unfortunately,
she was going to be taken into custody. "I just want to
make it clear, Max, I'm sure she wasn't acting on the
behalf of the defense team. I'm sure that was meant to
manipulate me. She's been trying to reconcile with me
for two years and I've been ignoring her."

"Sadly for her, her motive isn't an issue," Max said.

Conner was told exactly what to wear to court—a
light blue oxford button-down without a tie, and tan
pants, pressed with a sharp crease. Brown shoes. Ordinary clothes on an ordinary guy. The irony was—he
already had those clothes, and it was exactly what he
would've chosen. Max, who was very well turned out,
wanted him to look like a blue-collar kind of guy whom
the jury would believe and empathize with.

Conner *was* a blue-collar guy. Since the crime and
the fire, he'd had occasion to look over his net worth,
trying to figure out what to do next, and while he had
quite the nice nest egg to start over with, it wasn't as
though he had brilliantly built a fortune. He'd worked
a business he'd inherited and had a pot of money from

insurance—not his first choice of how to become financially sound. The sale of the lot and two houses would put him in a higher category, even after splitting it with Katie—but he couldn't claim much of that came from his business prowess.

He did have some business savvy, however. He was giving more and more thought to a small hardware store in the area between Virgin River and the coast. He could get Paul and his subs anything they needed; he could provide building and repair items for the town and outlying areas. He might buy a motorcycle to take Leslie for long rides in spring and summer.

He hoped to God he'd get to the point of making some of those decisions soon. This hiatus for the sake of a testimony was getting old.

Today's cop was Scott, a homicide detective getting a little overtime. They had room-service breakfast together in Conner's room and made small talk. Scott was a sports nut, never missed a televised ball game. When breakfast was done, and it was time to head for the courthouse, Scott asked, "You doing okay, buddy?"

"Ready for this to be over," Conner said. And then, for no particular reason, he said, "You know, I've been laying low in this small town, working construction, and after a lot of years of putting in too many hours, life slowed down a little. And I met someone. You married, Scott?"

"Eleven years," he said. "Two kids."

"I'm thirty-five," Conner said. "I'd like to be able to say that someday."

Scott clamped a hand on his shoulder. "It'll be over soon. Let's get going."

"Today I don't feel like sneaking in the back door," Conner said.

"Anything you want, bud. Just don't get caught by the reporters. I don't know what Mathis's game is, but you're not to talk to anyone."

"I know. I understand. I don't want to talk to them. Ever. But Mathis had me threatened and my store burned down. I'm tired of letting him think he worries me. He walks in the front door, head up, no problem looking me in the eye. Fine. Game on."

Scott gave him a little smile. "Good for you, bud."

It didn't take them long to arrive at the courthouse and park the car. They walked around the block and headed for the glut of people and cars out front. Conner marveled at how quickly he'd come to recognize some of the featured players. It was barely eight-thirty, and there were lots of people showing up for many court cases in addition to this big trial, but still he managed to spot the lawyers—prosecution and defense—hurrying into the building with briefcases. People he remembered from the gallery were either hanging around outside or quickly going inside—the brassy-looking women, the priests, men in expensive suits. There were the reporters, of course, easy to spot by their cameramen and camcorders and microphones. And of course there were a lot of uniformed and plainclothes police around, but as Conner had already learned, cops testified every day.

The courthouse and area surrounding was full of them, coming and going.

Then the car service pulled up. Of course Regis Mathis and his high-priced attorneys and family couldn't be expected to drive themselves to court—they arrived in three Lincolns driven by uniformed drivers. In case anyone had forgotten these people were rich and influential. The doors opened on the first two in the line, emitting Mathis and lawyers from the first, and behind them, the family.

Conner stopped on the sidewalk with Scott beside him. "No scene," Scott said into his ear.

"Of course not," Conner said. "Just watching the parade."

"Stay out of the way of the reporters," Scott said.

Conner vaguely noticed a white SUV blocking the street on the other side of the Lincolns, letting someone out.

Mathis stepped out of the car like arriving royalty, lifting his hand in a wave to the press. He and one of his lawyers waited for the family to meet them before they all made a grand entrance into the courthouse.

But they didn't make it that far. One of the women Conner recognized from the day before was suddenly standing in front of them. Her back being to Conner and Scott, he didn't know anything was happening. In one split second he wondered if the woman wanted to talk to Mathis.

And then there was the sound of gunfire. *Pop. Pop.*

Pop. Pop. Mathis crumbled. His lawyer crumbled. One of his sons fell.

Scott pushed Conner to the ground and covered his body with his own, but Conner lifted his head to look out, to see what was happening. There was more gunfire and Conner wasn't sure where it was coming from. Then next thing Conner knew, Scott moved enough for him to see the young woman was tackled by two very large, uniformed police officers, and immediately following that, there was a rush of people swarming the area. A couple of men ran to the SUV, but an officer, with gun extended toward the driver, blocked it from moving. That's when he noticed that even though Scott was lying on top of him, he had his gun out, too, leveled in the direction of the shooting.

"Holy shit," Scott muttered, pulling Conner roughly to his feet. While Conner instinctively started in the direction of the melee, Scott strong-armed him in the direction of the courthouse doors, wrestling him inside.

"What the hell?" Conner asked.

"Shooting," he said. Scott pulled out his cell phone and plunked in some numbers. "415A in progress in front of the courthouse. Wounded. Looks like they might have one in custody. It's a mess of people out there." He leveled a steely gaze at Conner. "Do. Not. Move."

Scott stepped out of the building, but only for a second. Then he was back. The sound of sirens seemed to accompany him.

"Did you get help?" Conner asked him.

He gave a nod. "There's more help than we need out there. Every person with a cell phone on the courthouse steps or on the sidewalk called it in. Looks like they have the woman with the gun on the ground, disarmed. And there are a couple of guys who decided to get away, too, who are detained, but I have no idea if they're part of this."

Conner poked a finger in his chest. "You wearing a vest?"

"Not today. Not to court."

"You covered me with your body!"

"Yeah, you lucky devil. It was instinct, that's all. Let's get you inside." He pulled out his ID and escorted Conner through the metal detector. Scott showed his ID and badge and set off the alarms with his gun; the guards and marshals gave him a lot of attention before they passed him through. And then he took Conner not to the courtroom, but to the room where the A.D.A. met witnesses.

And there they sat.

Conner was in a state of shock for a good fifteen minutes before he finally said, "I thought if anyone got shot going up the courthouse steps, it would be me."

Twenty

It was an hour before Scott was informed that court was canceled, and he relayed this message to Conner. "I'll take you back to the hotel."

"What happened?" Conner demanded.

"Details are fuzzy, but our defendant has been injured and is being treated. His injuries are serious. There were two other injuries, as well."

"Can't you get more information?"

"Eventually you'll get information, but for right now court is canceled. Come on," he said. "This time, the back door."

"Yeah, you bet," Conner said. "I've never seen anything like that."

"Me, either," Scott said. "And I've seen stuff. The homicide unit usually shows up after, not during."

"You going to wear a vest from now on?"

"I wear a vest when I'm on a case, but this is court. I go to court all the time. I usually wear a *tie!*"

They took the elevator down to the ground level,

through a bunch of corridors to an exit manned by marshals and out into the sunlight. They drove back to the hotel without talking, and Scott left Conner in his hotel room.

"I'm sure you'll hear from the D.A.," he said. "Just lock up and don't open for anyone but me or the D.A."

"Sure," Conner said. "Thanks. Really."

"Anytime, Conner," he said. Then he grinned. "All in a day's work."

Alone in the hotel room, Conner looked at his watch. Almost ten and about an hour and a half of excitement under his belt. He turned on the TV, and unsurprisingly, the shooting at the courthouse was all the news. He watched for a half hour. Details were still sketchy, but two of the shooting victims were in surgery, one of them being Regis Mathis, both in critical condition. The third victim, his son, was treated and released. The woman in custody was a former girlfriend and employee of Dickie Randolph. The two men trying to get away appeared to be former employees of Randolph who didn't want to be caught up in the drama.

The whole thing was captured on film, which the networks played over and over again. Conner strained to catch himself on film, but he didn't seem to be there.

He sat there for an hour, waiting for the phone to ring, waiting for someone to tell him what the disposition of the trial was now that the defendant was shot. It occurred to him that, obviously, someone took their pound of flesh from Regis Mathis. The woman with the gun—young. Pretty, if you put her in classier clothing and scraped a few layers of makeup off her face. Maybe she knew about the young Mathis woman? Maybe she knew what Mathis had done to avenge his daughter?

Maybe a lot of things. But Conner was done with this, at least for now. He called the front desk and asked for a bellman with a cart and a cab. And he moved out of his hotel room. He took a cab to the mall parking lot where the truck sat, unloaded his duffels into the backseat and the bed and began to drive. He would have cell service most of the way, until he got into the mountains.

He didn't call anyone. He was waiting for his cell to ring and for Max to tell him to get right back to Sacramento. But until that happened, he drove north.

Leslie had driven all the way to Fortuna to pick up sticky buns and coffee to take to Brie's house. She didn't get there until about ten after nine and by that time when Brie answered the door, she had a shocked look on her face. "Les," she said solemnly.

"What?"

"Conner's okay, but there's been a shooting at the courthouse."

Leslie dropped the coffees, and they splattered all over the front walk and her feet. "Oh, God," she said, not even bending to wipe the hot coffee off her feet.

"Conner is okay," Brie repeated. "Come in, just leave that mess and come in." Brie grabbed her hand and pulled her inside. "Someone shot the defendant and a couple of the people with him. Three were wounded and two are in surgery."

"What did your lawyer friend say?"

"He's waiting for information himself. He said to sit tight. Obviously Conner won't be in court today. I'm sure you'll hear from him when he has more details. Come in and sit down—there's news coverage."

Leslie walked in on shaky legs, sitting in the great room in front of Brie's big screen, clutching her paper bag of sticky buns. "Are you sure it's not Conner?"

"Absolutely sure. Max said he told the police escort to take him back to his hotel and he's waiting for more information. When a shooting victim goes into surgery, it could be something easily treated or it could be serious. Max has no idea at this point. Max said when he knows where they stand with the continuation of the trial, he'll call. Obviously, he has a lot on his plate right now."

"Can I try Conner's phone?"

"I tried calling him, Les. It went straight to voice mail, but I didn't leave a message. I'm not sure if he just has nothing to say or if he has the phone turned off from when he was going to the courthouse. Let's try to stay cool. He's not hurt. He wasn't involved. Someone went after the bad guy."

They watched the same coverage over and over for two hours with no new information. Finally, at noon, Leslie had had enough. "I'm going to shop for some groceries and go home," she said. "If I can stay busy making soup or something I might not lose my mind. My TV reception is spotty, but I have a phone. If there's any new development, will you call me?"

"Of course. Will you be all right?"

"I have to be all right," she said. "He'll call me the second he has something to tell me. I know he will."

Leslie went to Fortuna, bought beef, barley, fresh vegetables, flour, yeast, apples, butter, a few other things and headed home. She got a soup going, a bread rising, an apple pie in the works. She didn't cook and bake to eat but to keep her hands busy and her mind free and her body in the house where the phone was.

She knew she'd hear from him.

Conner drove around Clear Lake and up the highway toward Humboldt County. He'd been on the road for four hours. Before he headed into the mountains, he pulled off the road and placed a call to Max.

"Did you notice I'm missing?" he asked.

"Frankly, I've been too busy for that," Max said. "Where are you?"

"Just about back in Virgin River," Conner said. "Any new developments?"

"A significant one. It hasn't been released to the press yet, so please give it a few hours before you throw your freedom party. Mathis didn't make it out of surgery. The bullet went through his heart—impossible to repair. His lawyer will recover, his son is fine and the shooter is in custody. Randolph's girlfriend. Or whatever. Apparently you weren't the only one to worry he wouldn't be convicted. And Randolph did in fact dope up Mathis's daughter."

"God," Conner said, shock and relief flooding through him.

"That's right, my man. No more trial."

"You don't sound that happy."

"No, I am. There's at least one bad guy off the streets. He looked real upstanding, but he was a bad guy, you can trust me. But what the hell," Max said. "I wanted to get him!"

Conner actually chuckled. "You'll get the next one."

"Wanna bet I'll never have a witness with a conscience and balls like yours?" Max asked.

"Nope. Don't want to take that bet. Been fun, buddy. Good luck." And he clicked off and got back on the road.

He might've driven a little fast on the road up the mountain to Virgin River. The clock on the truck console said almost five o'clock, but there was plenty of sunshine left on this day and he was so damn glad he'd made a decision to just *drive*. He was done with this nightmare. Right after he reassured Leslie, he'd call Katie and tell her.

When he pulled into town, it was with an entirely new appreciation for the way the sunlight sifted through the tall trees and cast late-afternoon shadows along the street. There were a few cars at Jack's, but no throbbing music—folks would be having a quiet, friendly beer or early dinner. The streets were still; dinner was being fixed in these houses. Tomorrow was Saturday—kids would be anticipating soccer and softball.

He turned down Leslie's street. She'd been such a rock through this. It reminded him yet again how like his sister she was—she was brave. Stalwart, a word he hadn't heard or used since his long-past military days.

He pulled up to her house and saw her on the porch. The second she saw his truck, she stood up from her chair, and he jumped out of the truck, coming around to her side. For a moment, he just looked at her. She was so beautiful with a soft smile for him.

Then he said it. "He's dead, Les. Mathis didn't survive a gunshot wound."

Her hand came up to her open mouth, and a little squeak escaped her. Then she ran down the porch steps and flung herself into his arms.

For a while all he could do was kiss her and kiss her, changing the angle of his mouth to get a deeper kiss. Finally he broke away enough to ask, "Did you know what was going on down there? That he was shot on the courthouse steps? I didn't call you on purpose—there wasn't any solid information and I kind of made a run for it."

She nodded. "Brie called about fifteen minutes ago. But why, Conner? Who would shoot him?"

"The victim's girlfriend, or a reasonable facsimile. I talked to the D.A. less than an hour ago—he's dead. No more trial. No more villain."

"God, Conner. The one thing I never dared imagine."

"It's over, Les," he whispered. "Over."

She shook her head. "No, Conner. This is just the beginning."

"Right," he said, giving her a kiss, longer, deeper than before. "*Our* beginning."

* * * * *

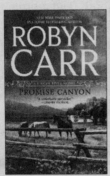 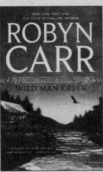 

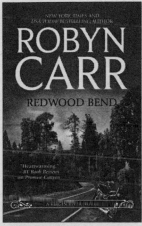

REQUEST YOUR
FREE BOOKS!

2 FREE NOVELS
FROM THE ROMANCE COLLECTION
PLUS 2 FREE GIFTS!

YES! Please send me 2 FREE novels from the Romance Collection and my 2 FREE gifts (gifts are worth about $10). After receiving them, if I don't wish to receive any more books, I can return the shipping statement marked "cancel." If I don't cancel, I will receive 4 brand-new novels every month and be billed just $5.99 per book in the U.S. or $6.49 per book in Canada. That's a saving of at least 25% off the cover price. It's quite a bargain! Shipping and handling is just 50¢ per book in the U.S. and 75¢ per book in Canada.* I understand that accepting the 2 free books and gifts places me under no obligation to buy anything. I can always return a shipment and cancel at any time. Even if I never buy another book, the two free books and gifts are mine to keep forever.

194/394 MDN FELQ

Name	(PLEASE PRINT)
Address	Apt. #
City	State/Prov.	Zip/Postal Code

Signature (if under 18, a parent or guardian must sign)

Mail to the **Reader Service:**
IN U.S.A.: P.O. Box 1867, Buffalo, NY 14240-1867
IN CANADA: P.O. Box 609, Fort Erie, Ontario L2A 5X3

Not valid for current subscribers to the Romance Collection
or the Romance/Suspense Collection.

Want to try two free books from another line?
Call 1-800-873-8635 or visit www.ReaderService.com.

* Terms and prices subject to change without notice. Prices do not include applicable taxes. Sales tax applicable in N.Y. Canadian residents will be charged applicable taxes. Offer not valid in Quebec. This offer is limited to one order per household. All orders subject to credit approval. Credit or debit balances in a customer's account(s) may be offset by any other outstanding balance owed by or to the customer. Please allow 4 to 6 weeks for delivery. Offer available while quantities last.

Your Privacy—The Reader Service is committed to protecting your privacy. Our Privacy Policy is available online at www.ReaderService.com or upon request from the Reader Service.

We make a portion of our mailing list available to reputable third parties that offer products we believe may interest you. If you prefer that we not exchange your name with third parties, or if you wish to clarify or modify your communication preferences, please visit us at www.ReaderService.com/consumerchoice or write to us at Reader Service Preference Service, P.O. Box 9062, Buffalo, NY 14269. Include your complete name and address.

New York Times and *USA TODAY*
bestselling author

SHERRYL WOODS

proves once more that home is always
where the heart is.

Continue to discover Chesapeake Shores with

The Summer Garden

Available February 2012, wherever books are sold!

ROBYN CARR

32974	SHELTER MOUNTAIN	___ $7.99 U.S.	___ $9.99 CAN.
32942	HARVEST MOON	___ $7.99 U.S.	___ $9.99 CAN.
32931	WILD MAN CREEK	___ $7.99 U.S.	___ $9.99 CAN.
32921	PROMISE CANYON	___ $7.99 U.S.	___ $9.99 CAN.
32917	SECOND CHANCE PASS	___ $7.99 U.S.	___ $9.99 CAN.
32899	JUST OVER THE MOUNTAIN	___ $7.99 U.S.	___ $9.99 CAN.
32898	DOWN BY THE RIVER	___ $7.99 U.S.	___ $9.99 CAN.
32897	DEEP IN THE VALLEY	___ $7.99 U.S.	___ $9.99 CAN.
32896	A VIRGIN RIVER CHRISTMAS	___ $7.99 U.S.	___ $9.99 CAN.
32870	A SUMMER IN SONOMA	___ $7.99 U.S.	___ $9.99 CAN.
32868	THE HOUSE ON OLIVE STREET	___ $7.99 U.S.	___ $9.99 CAN.
32768	MOONLIGHT ROAD	___ $7.99 U.S.	___ $9.99 CAN.
32761	ANGEL'S PEAK	___ $7.99 U.S.	___ $9.99 CAN.
32749	FORBIDDEN FALLS	___ $7.99 U.S.	___ $9.99 CAN.
31294	PARADISE VALLEY	___ $7.99 U.S.	___ $9.99 CAN.
31290	TEMPTATION RIDGE	___ $7.99 U.S.	___ $9.99 CAN.
31286	WHISPERING ROCK	___ $7.99 U.S.	___ $9.99 CAN.
31271	BRING ME HOME FOR CHRISTMAS	___ $7.99 U.S.	___ $9.99 CAN.

(limited quantities available)

TOTAL AMOUNT	$ _____
POSTAGE & HANDLING	$ _____
($1.00 for 1 book, 50¢ for each additional)	
APPLICABLE TAXES*	$ _____
TOTAL PAYABLE	$ _____

(check or money order—please do not send cash)

To order, complete this form and send it, along with a check or money order for the total above, payable to MIRA Books, to: **In the U.S.:** 3010 Walden Avenue, P.O. Box 9077, Buffalo, NY 14269-9077; **In Canada:** P.O. Box 636, Fort Erie, Ontario, L2A 5X3.

Name: _____
Address: _____ City: _____
State/Prov.: _____ Zip/Postal Code: _____
Account Number (if applicable): _____
075 CSAS

*New York residents remit applicable sales taxes.
*Canadian residents remit applicable GST and provincial taxes.

www.Harlequin.com

MRC1111BL